2 FOR 1

By David Farrell

Also By David Farrell

The Last Resort

The Glove

You Can't Get Rid of Me That Easily

Twelve

Dropping the Belt

Twelve More

Portals

Printed in Australia

First Printing 2020

ISBN: 978-1-64516-130-1

For Ted

Welcome to the family.

<u>CHAPTER ONE</u>

September 2003

Bree Fielding was on the verge of doing something that she'd only heard about in sex education classes and only seen in movies. She'd waited longer than most of the girls in Year 12, which was important to her. Bree didn't want to be one of the first to cross this threshold, but she definitely didn't want to be the last. She composed herself, catching her reflection in the mirror. The girl staring back at her looked poised for the next step.

The evening air in Canberra was changing from impossibly cold to tolerable. Winter was finally over. Bree's current view through the windscreen of Ryan's car was of a non-descript wall, which wasn't the most romantic facade. It would have to do. They'd chosen this car park because it was isolated and they were unlikely to be disturbed at this late hour. Even though Bree was approaching the age of seventeen she still lived at home with her parents. Her male companion had the same restrictions and neither could suggest a better place for the rendezvous.

She'd met Ryan while working at the mall, where they were both labouring to stock the shelves at Toys R Us. The job itself was a tedious one and Bree was happy for the distraction. Ryan had a sweet nature about him and boyish good looks. Fate had placed them in adjoining aisles on Bree's first night. During the shifts that had followed they'd exchanged loaded glances constantly. A surge of adrenaline had struck Bree whenever he'd smiled in her direction. Ryan had always restocked the board games quickly, so he'd had an excuse to lend Bree a hand. She'd liked how direct he was. Guys had never expressed any real interest in her before and it was a refreshing change from the boys at school. They seemed more captivated with throwing scrunched up garbage at one another like savages than having a real conversation, or finding an honest human connection. Ryan was only a year older than her, but he seemed mature and Bree felt drawn to that.

Their first kiss had taken place in a service corridor. Ryan and Bree had accumulated a large stack of cardboard boxes and had needed to dispose of them. Together they'd manoeuvred the waste via trolley to a compactor that was isolated in the rear of the store. Standing side by side they'd fed the machine's opening, one box at a time. Each look from Ryan and every smile that Bree returned had verified the electricity flowing between them. On their way back Ryan had taken a chance and pressed a willing Bree against the brick wall of the corridor. Her heartbeat intensified as their mouths collided. In her shocked state Bree had released the empty trolley that she'd been pushing and it had rolled ahead on its own, its odd wheels giving it unusual momentum. While the trolley came to a natural stop, the young pair continued.

A spell had been cast. From then on Ryan was all that she could think about. She'd patiently linger out of sight of the other employees and on occasion their lips would find each other again. Suddenly it wasn't enough to just steal kisses anymore. Bree wanted to take things to the next level. Tonight was the night.

Bree nervously played with the radio between them. Delta Goodrem's *Innocent Eyes* was halfway through and she quickly changed the channel. She exhaled. Bree glanced over to the driver's side of the car as *Where is the Love?* by the Black Eyed Peas started on FM 104.7.

'You okay?' asked Ryan, sensing her trepidation.

'Uhuh.'

She'd instigated this vehicular get together but things had now stalled. Bree wasn't sure how to proceed but luckily Ryan took the lead. He removed a metal flask from his glove box and took a swig.

'Do you want some bourbon?' he asked, sloshing the liquid back and forth hypnotically.

'Yeah… sure,' she replied as confidently as she could.

Alcohol was yet another new frontier for Bree. Taking a sip she discovered that she didn't mind the taste, but disliked the burning sensation in her throat that accompanied it.

'Are you sure you want to do this?'

'Yeah, I do. Are you? I mean… do you want this?' asked Bree.

'Well, yeah. I've done this before though… so…' Ryan let his voice trail off.

'Okay,' said Bree, 'but like… do you want to do this with *me*?'

'Yeah.'

Ryan climbed gingerly over to her side of the car, taking care not to nudge the gear stick with his knee. The whole world tilted when he lowered the passenger seat that Bree was occupying into its horizontal position. Her view had vastly improved.

'What's that cologne?' asked Bree.

'Cool Water.'

Ryan's smile put her at ease. Clothes were hastily removed in between bursts of adolescent kisses, some missing the mark.

'Wait…' said Bree.

'What is it?'

She placed one hand on each of Ryan's cheeks and looked into his eyes. He stared back like an eager puppy.

'What's up?' repeated Ryan.

'I just want to remember this moment, you know?' Bree offered a hopeful little half-smile. Ryan nodded hastily in agreement.

'Yeah,' he said, exhaling out of the side of his mouth.

Ryan kissed her once more before moving ahead. While the experience was brief it was still special to Bree. She'd found this guy and this moment on her own, and it had unfolded organically. Nobody from College knew about Ryan. This was her secret.

'You won't tell anyone about this… will you?' she asked as they shared the surface of the reclined car seat.

'No. This is just for us,' replied Ryan.

'Can you drop me off at home? It's starting to get late and I don't want my parents to worry.'

'Actually your place is kind of out of the way. Can I just drop you back at work?' Ryan's words were more dismissive, less tender now.

'Yeah... I guess that would be fine. I could get a taxi or something.'

'Great. Thanks.'

Ryan shifted and pulled his pants up quickly. Bree thought he looked angelic in the moonlight. She felt compelled to speak.

'I love you,' blurted Bree.

'Oh yeah?' He looked up momentarily from the task of redressing.

'Yeah.'

'That's cool,' said Ryan.

'It really is,' replied Bree.

In the coming weeks Ryan shied away considerably. He wouldn't search for her in the service corridor anymore or linger behind to kiss her in the staff room. He wasn't racing to pack his shelves so they could flirt. Bree suddenly found herself walking trolleys of cardboard to the compactor on her own. Ryan wasn't glancing her way and she didn't know why. The relationship was different now and Bree didn't have anyone to talk to about it. It remained her little secret. Sometimes Bree would have to remind herself that her night with Ryan had actually happened, and that it wasn't just a wonderful dream.

CHAPTER TWO

Bree could smell it, but she always waited for the announcement from her mother. It was a tradition, and she liked the familiar routine and predictability of it all.

'Dinner's ready!' called Carol proudly as she placed a thick ceramic baking dish onto the table. It was a Thursday, which meant tuna pasta bake with vegetables. Bree arrived at the dining table first and eyed the food hungrily.

'So? You had the interview?' asked Carol.

'Yeah. I got it! They gave me the job!' Bree's face lit up enthusiastically.

'That's amazing! Oh, I knew you would honey.' Carol breathed a sigh of relief.

'They want me to start this weekend,' continued Bree. 'Apparently it takes a while to learn everything.'

'Of course. Working at a cinema is probably a lot like any other retail job at the end of the day... and I'm sure you'll be great at it.'

Bree knew that her mother had been a seasoned retail employee at the very same mall. She'd heard the stories. In her youth Carol had worked at clothing shops primarily. It was never any of the high-end stores, and besides a tale about burning herself with an iron she'd always said that the work had been pleasant enough.

'I would have enjoyed working at a cinema,' mused Carol. 'Did I ever tell you that my parents met at the Theatre?'

'Yeah. The Regent Theatre in Melbourne, right?'

'That's the one. So *opulent*... you'd love it. More stage productions than movies though I think. Oh, I'm just glad you got the job. I was sick of you complaining about Toys R Us.'

'It started off alright…'

'But this one will be better hours,' said Carol with a smile.

'Right,' said Bree. 'Well… sometimes I'll still finish at midnight.'

'And soon you'll be able to drive *yourself* home.'

'Yeah, that's true,' grinned Bree.

'And then maybe you'll meet some new people… and you can close the textbooks once in a while.'

'What are you saying Mum? That I study too much?'

'It's not that. I'm just worried that you're going to look back on this time in your life and wish you'd taken more chances,' said Carol.

In that moment Bree considered telling her mother about Ryan. It would be hard to argue that she wasn't being rebellious in the face of that bombshell.

'I take plenty of chances,' offered Bree.

'Do you? So, when you get your licence, where are you going to drive?'

'I'll drive to CIT next year… and to work…'

'*Whoa,*' her mother exclaimed sarcastically.

'Whatever…'

'I just don't want to see you retreat from the world, okay? You can break the rules every now and then… a little bit.'

'The next time I get the chance Mum, I promise. Oh… so, the manager at Central told me I get free tickets now. I'll have to take you and Dad. You guys haven't been out in ages.'

'I wanted to watch that Pirates movie. The one with Johnny Depp?'

'The Pirates of the Caribbean?'

'Yeah. I read that it's supposed to be good.'

'It's based on a *ride*,' stated Bree as she raised one eyebrow.

'Well, whatever we watch… that all sounds lovely,' replied Carol as she eyed the doorway. 'Where is your father?'

'I haven't seen him. Can I start eating anyway? I'm starving,' stated Bree as she scooped a serving of baked vegetables into her shallow bowl. 'Look Mum! I'm breaking the rules!'

'Ha ha… very amusing.'

After serving herself Bree pulled her brown hair into a ponytail and expertly tied it. Carol smiled and sat down opposite her.

'I remember having long hair like that. Don't you just want to cut it all off sometimes?'

'No, I love it,' replied Bree. Her mother Carol had always had a bob of light auburn hair. She had a rounded face that was starting to wrinkle, but it was only visible when she smiled.

'I sure don't miss it! Long hair does make *you* look grown up though.'

'I *am* grown up,' declared Bree.

'You're sixteen,' replied Carol.

'Almost seventeen. And I'm taller than you.'

'Ha! Because being tall makes you a grown up. HENRY?' called Carol in no particular direction.

'WHAT?' Bree's father's voice sounded like it was coming from the upstairs study, a rarely used space that was cluttered with the overflow from the rest of the house; the items that had never quite found a permanent place in their lives.

'DINNER!'

Henry didn't reply. Bree watched as Carol started placing her own portion into a matching shallow bowl. They had purchased this set of kitchenware recently and Bree was still not used to the shape of them.

'Do you think Dad could drop me off for my first shift?' asked Bree. 'I want to get in early and make a good first impression.'

'I'm sure he'd be happy to.'

'Cool.'

'Do you need anything before you start?' asked Carol. 'We could go shopping together if you'd like.'

'No thanks Mum. I've got black pants... and they gave me the uniform.'

'I'll have to get a picture of you in it!' teased Carol. This was something of a ritual for the two. Her mother always wanted to take photos of her, especially when she completed some arbitrary milestone. Bree was quietly afraid of the amount of moments that were being compiled and recorded for posterity. She imagined having to sit through an embarrassingly endless slideshow when she eventually turned eighteen.

'We *don't* need a picture!' she shot back.

'Now Bree... I'm sure it's a lovely uniform. And one day you'll be glad you have a photo in it. You'll be able to show your kids.'

'And maybe I'll meet *my* husband at the theatre... the same way *your* parents met there...' said Bree sarcastically.

'I think you're still too young for that.'

The comment made Bree sit up straighter. Carol picked up her fork, only to change her mind and place it back down again.

'It's *not* a lovely uniform. And who says I want kids?' replied Bree, screwing up her face.

'Don't you?'

'Not really.'

'That's because you're still a kid yourself,' stated Carol. 'When you're older you'll feel differently.'

'When I'm *older*?'

'Yes, when you're older you'll know what you want.'

'I'm not a child Mum… I'm almost seventeen. And kids are a hassle. I want to have a career and become a CEO. I don't want to have to take a year off to have a family.' Suddenly Bree realised what she'd said and quickly added, 'No offence Mum.'

'None taken.'

Bree's mother had worked at a law firm with three male partners. She'd described it as a boy's club that she had slowly infiltrated over time. Unfortunately her career had stalled after the birth of her only daughter. Legal opportunities were in short supply at her age, which meant that Carol had settled for a lesser position as a researcher and legal aide. In Bree's eyes it seemed like her mother had lost her ambition in the process.

'Do you ever wish you'd done things differently?' asked Bree.

'No. You're the best thing that's ever happened to me,' said Carol with a wrinkled smile, 'and when you're running your own company you can hire me and we'll have lunch every day.'

The two grinned at the notion.

'It's going to happen,' said Bree, manifesting her destiny out loud.

'If anyone can do it, it's you,' replied her mother. 'Love you Bree.'

'Love you Mum.'

Bree's father stepped slowly into the doorway of the dining room. He slumped slightly against the wooden frame. While they'd both noticed his demeanour, Carol was the first to comment on it.

'Are you… *drunk*?'

'No,' Henry replied. There was no emotion in his voice. He ran a hand up past his face and wiped his brow several times.

'Dad?' Bree placed her palms on the table, a million worrisome thoughts announcing themselves. Her father rarely drank to excess these days, which meant if he was inebriated now something was very wrong. He looked as if he might collapse at any moment. Bree wondered how much alcohol he'd consumed.

'How *could* you…' he started, before tears welled in his eyes.

Bree felt nervous energy swelling up around her. *Did her father know about her night with Ryan somehow?*

'What's wrong?' asked Carol as she rose up and moved towards her husband. Henry waved her away with a single swipe, as if trying to deter an irritating fly. Carol stopped short, just a few paces in front of him.

'Is this what I think it is?'

Henry thrust a piece of paper towards her and Carol took it with both hands. Bree noted that her mother's eyes were now wide, an expression that seemed unnatural on her. *What is she hiding?*

Carol looked at the paper and covered her mouth. Bree held her breath anxiously as she watched the scene unfold.

'I…'

'So, it's *true*?' asked Henry, his posture worsening.

'Y-yes…' she stammered in confirmation.

'Mum?'

There was no immediate response from either one of the adults. The atmosphere of the room had undergone a tense shift and Bree's heart was now pounding out of her chest.

'Will someone *please* tell me what's going on? What's on that paper?' she demanded.

'Go to your room Bree,' said her father without making eye contact.

'No! Just tell me wh-'

'Goddamn it Bree, NOW!' he shouted, this time staring directly at her, fire in his normally kind eyes. Bree looked to her mother for support. Carol was stationary, the only movement coming from two tears that were racing their way down the curves of her cheeks. She was still clutching the mysterious paper.

Bree abandoned the scene as requested but didn't go directly to her room. She loitered at the top of the steps to eavesdrop, as she had sometimes done as a child.

'When did this happen?' demanded Henry.

'I didn't want you to find out like this…' replied Carol.

'You didn't want me to find out at all!'

'Please… just stop yelling.'

'You and Adrian must have laughed and laughed about it behind my back, didn't you?'

Bree could hear the pain in her father's voice. *Adrian*. She vaguely remembered an Adrian, who'd worked with her mother.

'It wasn't about you. I've been… *unhappy* lately,' said Carol with a sob.

'Lately?' You've been miserable company for years.'

'I suppose so.' Her mother sounded so defeated.

'So, you slept with someone else? Unbelievable!'

Bree hoped it wasn't true, internally pleading for her to deny it.

'It just… *we*… just happened.'

'You're a *we* now?'

'I don't love you anymore Henry. I know you feel the same way.'

'*Seriously?*'

There was another ominous silence. Bree thought about heading back downstairs into the warzone. She wanted to scream at her mother, to challenge her. *Why was this happening?* The air at the top of the steps felt thinner now and Bree's body wouldn't obey her. She wished that someone would say something. Eventually her father did.

'If you want to be with Adrian then I think you'd better go.'

'I didn't want it to end like this. Can we talk about things… about Bree? Please…'

'She's not coming with you. Bree's staying here with me,' said Henry.

'I know you're upset, but you can't keep us from talking. She's my daughter too,' said Carol.

'You should have thought about that before you threw away our marriage. Why did it have to be *Adrian*?' There was venom in her father's words now.

'I don't know… I don't…'

'I want you to leave now Carol.'

'Can I just go and talk to Bree?'

'NO!'

Another painful silence. Bree edged upwards, distancing herself from the battle below. If her mother walked to the front door and looked back, Bree would still be visible in the space where the stairs hooked around on their way to the second floor. Her mind raced. Her mother wasn't a liar, or a cheater. *Or was she?*

'I need some things,' her mother said.

'I'm so MAD at you right now! I'm trying so hard not to…'

Suddenly there was a crash. It sounded to Bree like her father had just thrown the tuna pasta bake against the kitchen tiles.

'Aaaarrrgh!' her father yelled, seemingly out of frustration. Bree hugged her knees to her chest.

'Henry, I'm so sorry. I know I've hurt you.'

'You've *destroyed* me. You can't fix this! Oh, that's right, you don't WANT to fix this! You can run away with Adrian then. I don't ever want to see you again.'

'Bree still needs me.'

'She'll be fine without you… and your lies.'

Bree heard her mother weeping. It triggered an instant reaction, something primal that connected them, and she found herself crying as well. Through the tears she saw a flicker of movement and watched as her mother, handbag in hand, moved gracefully towards the front door. Henry was not pursuing her, and Bree contemplated calling out. The fifteen feet of space between them was expanding by the second. She wanted to know what had changed between her parents. Bree wanted to go back to one hour earlier and burn that piece of paper before her father had brought it downstairs. But she felt like a helpless child, and so she said nothing.

Carol moved in slow motion as she unlocked and opened the door to the family home. She fled into the liquorice coloured night without looking back towards her offspring. As Bree shivered at the top of the stairs she felt an overwhelming sense of shame. She went into her bedroom and lay in the dark weeping. When her phone buzzed, the word *MUM* on the screen, Bree rejected the call. Carol was a liar and she'd ruined everything.

CHAPTER THREE

As Bree stood waiting in the foyer that morning she couldn't help but notice the ugly multi-coloured carpet beneath her feet. It was a mixture of pink and blue with ridiculous, and unexplainable, splashes of green. Bree wondered why someone would commission such an unpleasant blend of colours for Central Cinemas.

She straightened herself up as she heard footsteps approaching from the service corridor. Bree hoped she looked presentable. She'd taken great pains that morning to straighten her hair before locking it into a ponytail with hairspray. She needed to make a good first impression.

The double doors in front of her splayed open and another employee stepped into the foyer. He had headphones over his ears and was dressed entirely in black. Bree wondered why he didn't have to wear the same striped orange ensemble that she did. As if by muscle memory he started punching a code into the silver eight-digit combination lock and opened the door that led into the back of house area. Halfway through the door, he looked left and spotted her.

'Oh, hi there,' he said taking his headphones off and letting them rest around his neck. He smiled at Bree and propped the door open in a state of limbo. Whenever she met new people Bree had a habit of comparing them to the first celebrity that came to her mind. This guy reminded her of Josh Hartnett, who she'd swooned over in *Pearl Harbour*. Bree was reasonably pleased with the comparison; the exception being his brown, spiked up hair and what appeared to be a shark-tooth necklace. She suspected he was about eighteen or nineteen years old.

'Hello,' Bree managed to say, as she shifted from one foot to the other nervously.

'Are you one of the new staff members?' he called out across the foyer.

'Yeah, it's my first day.'

The two cinema employees sized one another up for a moment. Neither moved from their position and there seemed to be an ocean of distance between them due to the vast depth of the cinema foyer.

'I'm Matt.'

'I'm Bree. Nice to meet you.'

'Did you want to come in?' asked Matt, indicating towards the half-opened door with a tilt of his head.

'I'd better not,' she replied. 'I'm supposed to meet my trainer here in the foyer.'

'Okay. Good luck!'

'Thanks.'

Matt went inside and the door closed itself slowly behind him. Bree checked her watch and found she was still ten minutes early. She wondered how many other new staff members were starting today.

The cinema ceiling was very high above Bree's head and decorated with small lights that twinkled like stars. She counted eight light bulbs that required changing. The wide room housed both the Box Office and Candy Bar, the latter cloaked in darkness before her. The colourful carpet spread throughout the complex, the only exception being a tiled area in front of the Candy Bar. She let her eyes wander from poster to poster. *Kill Bill: Volume 1*, *The League of Extraordinary Gentlemen*, *Intolerable Cruelty*, *Gigli*. She couldn't wait to watch them all. Bree wondered where she would be training today. Both the Box Office and the Candy Bar required cash handling and customer service skills, neither of which had been a feature of her former workplace.

At Toys R Us Bree had been hired under the pretence that it was a front-of-house role at the registers, but was disappointed to learn that she would only be re-filling the shelves with toys. Every shift had started late at night, after the doors had closed, and without fail the manager would leave the store's jingle playing over the loudspeakers on repeat.

It had felt like a fluorescent nightmare that she couldn't wake up from. The only memorable part of being there had been her interactions with Ryan, but they hadn't endured for long. Bree had felt completely drained stocking shelves in the lead up to Christmas the year before. She'd worked four or five nights a week as requested. Bree then had her shifts reduced in the New Year despite management promising the opposite. An irregular shift here or there had been demoralising, leading her to apply elsewhere. Central Cinemas would be a fresh start for Bree. She would finally get some real work experience in a place she actually enjoyed frequenting.

Working at Central Cinemas was one of the more social jobs for a girl on the cusp of seventeen. From the outside it didn't appear to have any manual labour or undesirable working conditions, and the perks appealed to her. She was looking forward to being surrounded by like-minded teenagers, making some friends and watching movies for free.

Bree wandered to the far side of the foyer. She sat down on an oval-shaped leather seat. Her Nokia 3310 buzzed in her pocket and she declined the call before switching it off entirely. Her mother had been ringing consistently since the night she'd left but Bree had refused to talk to her or return her messages. Today was the day that movers were coming to the house and collecting Carol's things. Her father would be there to supervise. In a way it was a blessing to have something else to occupy her mind during such a weird day.

The double doors creaked open and two young men laughed their way into the foyer. The taller of the two introduced himself to Bree as Andy. She decided that Andy most closely resembled Jude Law, even though the eyes were duller.

'I'm one of the staff trainers here at Central,' he explained.

'Great to meet you,' she replied shaking his hand briefly. Bree forced a smile, knowing that Andy might be her trainer.

'And this is Liam,' he continued, 'he's starting today as well.'

Blonde Christian Bale she thought to herself, satisfied with the assessment. Bree had seen Bale's performance in *American Psycho*, which she'd watched on VHS late one Saturday night after her parents had fallen asleep. Her father had rented it without knowing what it was.

Bree shook hands with Liam and detected a confidence about him that she found a little unnerving. She wondered what they had been laughing at on the way in and wished she could have been in on the joke. Liam unzipped his dark jacket. At least he was being forced to sport the same uncomfortably bright orange shirt as she was.

'Orange suits you,' Andy said to Liam as he playfully messed up his hair.

'Cut it out,' grumbled Liam as he started meticulously re-parting his light blonde hair, even though the styling gel had ensured it retained its shape. Bree was unsure of the nature of their relationship but certainly felt like a third wheel.

Andy revealed the entry code at a door marked with the words *Staff Only*. He told them both that it was changed regularly before correcting himself.

'In truth the combination code is changed when the more *troublesome* staff members are let go and management fear some… *retaliation*,' said Andy. It all sounded very sinister to Bree.

They were taken through to the manager's office where Bree was pleased to see a familiar face. Paul was the manager who had interviewed her for the job. He was a thin man who wore a vest and resembled an accountant. During the interview she'd mentally likened him to a shy Elijah Wood from *The Lord of the Rings*. They'd had an easy rapport when they'd first met, but today Paul was busy on the phone. He offered only a friendly wave, indicating he couldn't get off the line. Andy grabbed some keys, a sheet of paper and black two-way radios before leading Bree and Liam back out into the foyer.

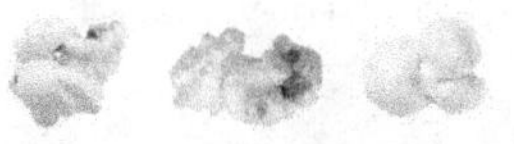

'I'm actually only supposed to be training Liam today. You're meant to be with Lizzy but she's running late.' Andy shrugged indifferently to himself.

'Oh.'

The news annoyed Bree. She'd wanted to make a good impression and hated that her trainer was late. Lizzy would be oblivious to the fact that she had arrived early, and Bree was feeling invisible walking around with Andy and Liam. They seemed to delight in being a step ahead of her.

The three employees looked at the staff room first, which was located upstairs. It consisted of a worn red sofa, cheap table, ironing board and a small microwave placed on top of a fridge. There were two side-by-side doors that led into smaller rooms filled with lockers. Naturally one change room had been assigned to each gender. Andy demonstrated that the doors swung open easily with a push. There was nothing to prevent people from walking in on each other while they were changing. Bree made a mental note to arrive fully dressed for work, to avoid any embarrassment.

As they travelled around the complex on their tour Andy kept praising Liam. He took every opportunity to pat him on the back or offer him a compliment. As they continued to ignore her, Bree decided that neither of these two were particularly nice people. Then she immediately felt bad for being so judgemental.

Twenty-five minutes later Lizzy caught up to them as they were looking at stock levels in the storeroom.

'I'm *so* sorry,' she said looking flustered. 'Yesterday was my birthday and we went out for drinks and I overslept. I'm Lizzy.'

'Bree. Nice to meet you.' They shared a courteous nod.

Lizzy had thrown her hair up in a messy bun and might have been wearing some make-up from the night before. Bree wasted no time in continuing her private game. *Perhaps Australian Actress Rose Byrne from Two Hands* she thought to herself, even though Lizzy seemed to have fuller cheeks and longer hair.

Andy pivoted up a ramp towards the Projection room and Lizzy, looking somewhat frazzled, decided that she and Bree would follow. After Andy opened the first of two doors a faint metallic churning could be heard in the distance. The staff trainer covered his hand while he punched in the security code and opened a second door, allowing them all to step inside.

The Projection room was a deep corridor with five impressively large 35mm film projectors on either side. The machines were staggered evenly throughout the space, facing outwards towards the ten individual cinema screens. Next to each projector was a set of three large freestanding metal platters where the film prints were at rest. Bree identified several movies by handwritten identification tags: *Bad Boys 2, Finding Nemo* and *Hollywood Homicide*. From where the group now stood Bree could gauge that the film had been wound from one platter, via a series of plastic green rollers, through the projector and then back down and around to one of the empty platters. It looked complicated. The room was mostly in darkness except for a handful of spotlights that were positioned above the individual machines. Bree could see Matt in the distance strolling between the projectors.

'This is the Projection room,' Andy said, spreading his hands out widely. 'Whenever there is a problem with one of the sessions downstairs you'll call through to the projectionist... today it's Matt... and let him know what's going on.'

Andy unclipped the two-way radio from his belt and brought it to his mouth.

'Hello Projection.' There was a staticy echo as Andy's words reverberated out of Matt's two-way radio in the distance. Bree and Liam watched as Matt poked his head out from behind a projector and looked towards them.

'Go ahead,' he said, staring intently.

'Just showing the trainees how the two-ways work,' Andy stated before holstering the radio to the back pocket of his pants.

Matt gave a quick thumbs up and went back to his work. They were soon steered towards the exit. On the way out Bree noticed that there was a concrete staircase between the two Projection doors, but was feeling too shy to enquire about what was up there.

Andy ushered them from Projection by way of a sloped path, before taking the new staff members down a red metal staircase into a storeroom behind the Candy Bar.

'This is back of house Candy Bar,' announced Andy. 'A lot of cleaning supplies, ice machine over there... that's our walk-in freezer...'

Lizzy followed at the back of the group, licking her fingers and attempting to wipe the nightclub stamps from her wrists as discreetly as possible. Bree was pretty sure that her trainer was still in the process of waking up.

'People make choc tops back here... sometimes we store excess popcorn there...' continued Andy, casually pointing around the area.

They were packed tightly into the space and Bree found herself wedged partly behind a door. She took a moment to check her appearance in the mirror beside her. Bree's brown hair was still tied tightly in a ponytail. The hairspray had been effective and she was pleased with how professional she still looked. The orange shirt was even starting to grow on her. A brief chuckle stole her attention. Liam had noticed her vanity and Bree blushed almost automatically.

'Something funny?' asked Andy.

'No, sorry. Just clearing my throat,' replied Liam.

'Ok then. If we could head that way we can start talking about front of house... aka *selling stuff*,' said Andy. Bree politely held the door open and the group started to file through one by one. Liam lingered at the end of the line but Bree refused to make eye contact with him, her cheeks still coloured by her embarrassment. Bree had to pay attention. She was finally going to learn how to use a register and serve a customer, an experience that had been denied to her at Toys R Us. Bree was becoming excited at the idea when Lizzy interrupted her reverie with a disappointing announcement.

'Andy and Liam are going to work in Candy Bar today. We're rostered on Floor.'

'Floor?' Bree's eyes darted from Andy to Lizzy in search of answers.

'Floor is what we call the zone where the cinemas are. You know? Ripping tickets and doing torch checks?' Lizzy asked as though Bree should have already been told all of this.

Lizzy led a solemn Bree away from Candy Bar and around the corner. At the top of a set of stairs stood a dark blue podium with the Central Cinemas logo on the front. Bree knew it well. She'd had her ticket torn here before as a patron, but it felt odd being on the other side of it now.

'This is called *Point*. One of us has to stand here at all times and rip tickets as people arrive. If you have to leave Point you should have someone else cover it for you. Standing here stops people from sneaking in, got it?'

'Yes.' Bree's voice was timid.

'Good. You'll also need to learn where all the cinemas are so that you can direct people to the right session. One person cleans and the other takes point.' Lizzy indicated down the corridor towards the various cinema doors. 'Cinema Ten, that's first on your right. Cinema Six, straight down the end. And so on.'

'No worries,' Bree said as she scanned the doors ahead of her, trying to memorise the location of each one.

They walked the length of the tunnel and Lizzy propped open each cinema door that they passed. It was nine-thirty in the morning, so they travelled to the locked front door. Lizzy and Bree paused at the entrance to Central Cinemas, the Candy Bar and Box Office now illuminated behind them and populated with staff. Lizzy revealed a panel, hidden away to the side, and showed Bree how to open the oversized roller door using a small key. The first session was at ten and there weren't any patrons waiting. Bree looked out towards the food court and wondered what time she would get a lunch break. She was already tiring of Lizzy's overbearing attitude.

'So, you have to check the toilets about every hour but when we're busy or you're by yourself don't stress about it. If someone complains though you should probably take a look ASAP. Things can get pretty gross in there.'

'In the men's toilet you mean?'

'No. Women are just as gross as men. Don't get me started. We'll get one of the guys to check the men's toilet today.'

On their way back to Floor, Bree observed Liam enviously at Candy Bar.

'Now you have to check the slides, trailers and feature film of every session on this sheet,' Lizzy said as she pulled a folded piece of paper from her pocket and handed it to Bree. 'You can have this one. I'll get another one from the office later.'

Bree studied the printed grid. It seemed simple enough, with a column for each cinema. The sessions began promptly and Bree found herself repeating the same familiar phrases into the two-way.

'Slides are fine in Cinema Two.'

'Trailers are fine in Cinema Five.'

'Feature is fine in Cinema Ten.'

Each time she spoke she heard Matt's voice thanking her and the whirring of the projectors in the background.

Lizzy was a competent enough trainer but she didn't go out of her way to befriend Bree or get to know her. It was frustrating, so as they tore tickets Bree tried to pry some information from Lizzy.

'So, is Lizzy short for Elizabeth?' asked Bree.

'Yeah.'

'Happy birthday by the way.'

'Thanks,' replied Lizzy without looking up.

'Did you have a good night out?'

'It was fine. I don't usually celebrate my birthday but I was talked into it.'

Lizzy had made no effort to fix her appearance during the shift despite leaving Floor for long periods of time. Bree decided to take initiative and carried her long-handled broom and dustpan, a 'pooper-scooper' as Lizzy had dubbed it, to the foyer to sweep up popcorn. It was a manageable task that broke up the intermittent bursts of customers and the routine of ticket tearing. Liam and Andy appeared to be having a good time behind the Candy Bar. *How have they bonded so quickly?* Bree wondered to herself.

'How's it going?'

Bree turned to find Matt leaning against a nearby pillar. He took a slurp of frozen Coke from a large plastic *2 Fast 2 Furious* novelty cup that must have been part of a recent Candy Bar combo.

'Oh hey. It's going… okay,' Bree said trying to hold her pooper-scooper as elegantly as possible.

'In the foyer again…' said Matt. 'We've got to stop meeting like this…'

'It's kind of *our* spot,' flirted Bree.

Matt smiled. 'I've heard you on the two-way,' he said tapping the radio on his belt. 'Sounds like you're getting the hang of things.'

'You've made it easy so far. Nothing's gone wrong! Speaking of which, if we're both here... then who's keeping an eye on things now?'

'They're actually very automated machines,' Matt said, 'one day soon they won't need a projectionist at all.'

'That's no good for you,' said Bree as she swept a popcorn kernel out from underneath one of the yellow seats.

'I actually moved up through the ranks. So, if it all falls apart I guess I'll have to come back here and sweep with you.'

Bree appreciated that Matt was treating her more pleasantly in the last two minutes than Lizzy had in the last two hours.

'It would cost a lot of money to upgrade the projectors anyway. My job is safe so long as Central Cinemas are cheapskates. Although apparently they are talking about upgrading some of the projectors at Southern Cinemas across town... so if that works out then maybe we're next.'

'That's menacing,' said Bree. '*Maybe we're next.*'

'Well it's out of our control. Hey, what kind of music do you like?' asked Matt.

'Any kind really. Why do you ask?'

'The sound system for the whole cinema is in the Projection room. Do you have any requests? I have a bunch of CD's up there.'

'Oh... I don't know...' Bree's mind went blank.

Matt smiled and took another sip of his drink. 'No requests then?'

'I don't mind. Anything is fine really,' said Bree with a shrug.

'Ok. Well if you think of something you want to hear... just ask.'

'I will. Thanks Matt.'

Bree knew that she wouldn't be requesting a song any time soon. If she asked Matt to change the music she would have to do so over the two-way and everyone working would hear it. She had no idea how the other staff members would respond to her musical tastes, which mostly consisted of pop songs. Bree had only interacted with a few people so far. She wanted everyone to like her, which her mother had informed her was one of her worst character flaws. It had stopped her from making strong friendships, resulting in a plethora of acquaintances.

Matt gave her a wave and went up the stairs behind Candy Bar towards Projection. As soon as Bree was alone an older Asian woman with short grey hair tugged on the sleeve of her orange shirt. She turned and saw the tiny woman waving her hand in front of her nose.

'Toilet ... very *stinky*,' she said in broken English.

'Alright, thank you for letting me know.'

The woman lumbered away slowly in the direction of the food court. Bree found Lizzy and updated her on the situation.

'Well you'd better go clean it up then,' her trainer said matter-of-factly.

What inspiring words Bree thought as she headed into the women's bathroom to investigate. The toilets were situated directly between the Candy Bar and Box Office. The location and easy access of the bathrooms meant that they were frequented by all manner of food court employees and patrons, whether they were planning on seeing a movie or not. As a result, even though it was a quiet day at the cinema, the female toilets looked like they had housed hundreds of unruly women. There was a line of eight cubicles, each one surrounded by discarded toilet paper and rubbish. Bree was surprised. *How could people treat a public space so poorly?* She cleaned up the smatterings of loose toilet paper first before restocking the dispensers. The off-putting smell was emanating from the cubicle at the end. To Bree's disgust she found someone had filled the toilet bowl with a soup of paper and excrement. They had attempted a flush to no avail and the toilet was now supremely clogged.

Bree was out the back of Candy Bar searching frantically when Liam approached her. He checked his reflection in the mirror, adjusting nothing.

'What are you doing back here?' he asked in a cocky voice.

'Trying to find a plunger. Have you seen one?'

'Nope. Enjoying your day with Lizzy?'

Bree straightened up and looked at Liam. She was shocked to find him staring at her chest and even more surprised that he made no effort to hide it. Bree was thrown and evaded his question. She ignored him and continued to search behind a stack of cardboard boxes.

'Hey, maybe we should go out sometime,' continued Liam. 'What do you think?'

Bree could see he was being sincere. 'No thanks.'

'Do you have a boyfriend or something?' Liam asked quickly.

'It's not that... I just don't know you,' replied Bree politely, even though she felt sure that she knew him well enough to know she didn't want to go out with him.

Liam, no worse for wear, shrugged and went back out the front of Candy Bar to serve customers. Bree furrowed her brow. She didn't want to return to Lizzy at Point without having solved the toilet problem. Without a plunger she wasn't sure how to proceed. Bree was contemplating using the stick end of the broom as an alternative, but quickly realised how silly that idea seemed. Matt came clanging down the metal stairs behind Candy Bar two at a time, startling Bree.

'Oh sorry!' Matt said holding out an open palm. 'I was just coming down to fill up my drink before the next session starts.'

The two-way radio on Bree's belt crackled to life.

'Bree from Lizzy.'

Bree felt flustered. If she could just find a plunger she knew she could get back on track. Taking the two-way in her hand Bree tried to reply, only to hear the sound of high-pitched feedback coming from Matt's radio.

'It's because we're too close together,' he said turning off his two-way at the top. 'It happens sometimes. Try again…'

'Go ahead Lizzy,' Bree stated, happy the radio was now working effectively. She was quite pleased with her current proximity to Matt. She didn't know what scent he was wearing but it had provoked her attention.

'Some cinemas are coming out now. I could use your help cleaning if you're done with the bathrooms?' Lizzy sounded impatient, which made Bree feel overwhelmed.

'Tell her you're just finishing up and you'll be there in a few minutes,' prompted Matt. Bree did as she was instructed.

He took the dustpan and long-handled brush from Bree. They walked across the tiles in front of Candy Bar. As they scurried past, Bree could feel Liam's eyes on her. Again she refused to acknowledge him, as he'd been less than helpful during her futile search for the plunger. Matt stopped in front of the women's bathroom.

'Check if there are any patrons in there for me, would you?' asked Matt, indicating towards the closed door.

Bree checked and found that the toilets were unoccupied. When she came back out Matt had restricted public access, roping off the toilet door like an exclusive nightclub. He'd stuck up an *Out of Order* sign to drive home the message. Matt went into the bathroom with Bree and looked at the offending toilet.

'Yep. That's gross,' he said and screwed up his face.

'Obviously. What do we do now?' Bree asked.

Matt shut the lid of the toilet and went into the adjacent stall. He stepped up onto the closed toilet and reached Bree's broom over and down towards the door of the disgusting cubicle. He looked a little ridiculous to Bree as he dangled across the partition.

'Could you close the door for me?' he asked.

Bree sealed the cubicle from the outside and held it in place. Matt swung the broom proficiently and with a few well-placed taps he was able to lock the stall door. He hopped down proudly.

'Now I'll pass on to the night projectionist that he needs to unlock this before the cleaners come. Not your problem anymore.'

Bree was relieved although she felt bad for the cleaners and told Matt so.

'Why? That's their job. As far as they know the toilet got clogged during the last session of the night. Now you'd better head up and clean the cinemas before Lizzy calls you again.'

'Thanks Matt.'

'You're welcome.'

The two employees left the bathroom together and Matt plucked the sign from the door. A woman that had wandered over from the food court marched straight in, giving Matt a sideways glance as she passed by. He scoffed at her hostility and handed Bree back her broom.

'These toilets are always a mess. Don't feel bad. They get used by everyone in the mall all day long.'

'Thanks for your help. There's a lot to learn and I...' Bree trailed off.

'Anytime.'

CHAPTER FOUR

A week of College passed uneventfully and the following Friday night Bree found herself cleaning cinemas with a short bespectacled boy around her age. His name was Warren and he seemed content to hum instead of talk. His undeveloped frame reminded Bree of Frankie Muniz from *Malcolm in the Middle*. Warren had a nervous tick and adjusted his glasses regularly. Lizzy was commanding them both from Point instructing them which cinema to clean next. As the night wore on the mess seemed to intensify.

'Do you like working here?' she asked Warren, as they wandered into Cinema Four.

'Yeah.' Warren smiled politely and started to put the bulkier garbage into a large black bag. Bree decided that if Warren preferred silence, that was fine with her.

It was manageable work and later, while standing at Point, Bree decided she enjoyed seeing the faces of people on dates. There was something therapeutic about it. The idea of cinema, of love and happy endings, was in polar opposition to the reality of her parent's relationship. Her mother had moved out to be with Adrian. Bree had been dodging her calls; unable to process the disappointment she was feeling. Her father had decided that the house held too many bad memories and had hastily found them an apartment. It was hard for Bree to argue. Their family home was to be sold as soon as possible, the assets divided. Bree hated the unspoken resentment in the air. While their lives were changing quickly, she'd hardly been there to bear witness. Bree had enthusiastically been picking up shifts after school, her Year 12 workload now easing as the year wound down. Central Cinemas had become a source of joy and distraction. Bree liked walking up and down the aisles with a torch and confidently reporting that each film was fine. With the exception of some minor out of focus issues everything had been on time and as expected from the Projection room, although Bree didn't recognise the voice on the other end of the two-way. She crossed off each session against her printed grid as it commenced. There was simplistic repetition to her job that made her feel like she was in control.

While they were cleaning Cinema One Bree found a brown men's wallet on the floor near a pile of popcorn. She tucked it under her arm and carried it out towards Lizzy, who had been tearing tickets and texting friends. Bree bit her tongue, not wanting to attract contempt from her trainer.

'I need you to take Point for a while Bree, they're getting busy at Candy Bar,' Lizzy announced as she started to walk down the stairs.

Bree placed the lost wallet inside the podium, which had a small compartment for storage. Lizzy departed and Bree stood dutifully at Point. A couple who looked like they might have been on a first date approached Bree.

'*Alex and Emma* is in Cinema Nine, enjoy the movie.'

They smiled, thanked her and wandered along, arm in arm. Warren moved to and fro announcing the sessions as they started. He was extremely timid on the two-way as well, cautiously declaring the trailers were fine in such a way that Bree wondered whether they actually were. She liked tearing tickets at Point. It was the best part of working on Floor, which wasn't a contest considering the alternative tasks included cleaning the cinemas, foyer or toilets. In retrospect she kept comparing her current situation to her old one at Toys R Us. She had despised the fluorescent lighting and still cringed when she thought of the jingle playing on a loop. This was definitely an improvement.

A tall man with a goatee came striding up the stairs in a panic.

'I was just watching *Freddy vs. Jason*. I've left my wallet in there!' he announced as he started to walk past Bree.

'What did it look like?' she asked, stopping him in his tracks.

'It's brown. Leather?'

Bree opened the podium compartment where she had deposited the misplaced item. She flipped it open and noted the picture of the man with the goatee on the driver's license inside. His relief was palpable and he happily took the wallet from Bree.

'Thank you so much!' he said as he checked its contents.

Bree was shocked to see the wallet was full of money. She hadn't even though to look inside. The man took a fifty-dollar note out and offered it to Bree as a reward.

'Oh no… I couldn't,' she said stepping back behind the podium.

'I insist. Please,' he said as he tried to force the money towards her.

'Thank you but I was just doing my job,' replied Bree.

'Okay… well thanks again.'

The man walked away and Bree beamed with pride. Her sense of achievement was interrupted by Lizzy's voice over the two-way.

'Warren, can you head to Point? We need Bree at Candy Bar.'

'Sure,' stated Warren. He truly was a boy of few words.

Bree watched him walking back through the tunnel and was filled with dread. *Why did she have to go?* Bree hadn't received any training on Candy Bar yet and hoped she would be a fast study. When Warren arrived she made her way down the stairs as quickly as she could, trying to shake her anxiety. As Bree turned the corner, she was flabbergasted to see a crowd loitering impatiently. She hadn't heard them from Point at all, which was hidden around a small bend. Bree caught several disapproving looks from customers, who must have been afraid that they would miss the start of their movies. She wanted to reassure them but she couldn't. All the films would start on time, with or without the patrons in their seats. She hopped behind the counter as quickly as she could and looked to Lizzy for guidance.

'Grab a large box and fill it with popcorn.'

Bree obeyed.

'Now get me a small.'

Bree filled box after box for the staff in front of her that were serving the crowd. She observed Lizzy filling up several drinks and took over without being asked. The rotund Indian employee next to her was too busy to introduce himself. Bree noticed him wiping away sweat from his brow on two occasions. It was understandable. Their close proximity to the popcorn machine coupled with their frantic movements in such close quarters was starting to have the same effect on her. Bree was also learning that here, at the source of its creation, the smell of popcorn was the most pungent of all. After some effort all of the patrons were on their way to their seats and it was quiet once again.

'Thanks Bree. You did well,' Lizzy said wiping her forehead with her sleeve.

'No problem.'

Using a small metal container Lizzy scooped popcorn kernels into the rounded popper at the top of the machine. She threw in a tablespoon of salt and then pressed a button, which proceeded to drown the seasoned kernels in a generous soup of oil.

'Sometimes when all the cinemas are clean we have to come down here and help. Otherwise people will be late into their movies and that's when the managers have to hand out comp tickets,' Lizzy said as she restocked the packets of chips.

Bree picked up a broom that had been placed next to the wall and started to sweep up loose popcorn from the tiles.

'There's no point starting with the floor, the counters are covered in popcorn. Once we knock it all down then you can sweep.'

'Oh,' replied Bree, feeling a little deflated.

'Why don't you stay down here with Victor and learn the ropes? I'll head back up and help Warren out for the last sessions of the night.'

'Ok, that would be great.'

The Candy Bar team that night had consisted of Andy and Victor; the former having taken an ill-timed break during the recent rush. Liam had called in sick, which was annoying as it meant they were short staffed on a demanding night. Victor seemed very jovial and comfortable with customer service. He reminded Bree of Jack Black, with only a hint of a facial hair. He offered a kind smile to each potential sale and they seemed to appreciate the effort. After Victor had demonstrated the basic functions of the register he started to explain upselling and suggestive selling. Bree recognised it, having fallen victim to it many times during her visits to the cinema.

'You see, if a customer wants some popcorn, you can suggest a drink. And if they go for the drink you can explain it's cheaper to buy both in a combo that incorporates the drink *and* popcorn.' Victor showed her the promotional material for the current combo. It was ten dollars for a large popcorn and large soft drink.

'That's pretty expensive,' stated Bree.

'Actually it's a pretty cheap combo for a cinema. It's hard to believe, I know! But if they're here at the Candy Bar they're already prepared to part with their money. People that don't want hot buttery popcorn will get their snacks from the supermarket downstairs.'

'I for one *love* hot buttery popcorn,' declared Bree.

'It's the best!' replied Victor. 'Also, on a Friday or Saturday night people are here on dates. That's when we can really get their business. They want to impress so they upgrade and buy large.'

Bree thought of the piles upon piles of popcorn she'd been cleaning up after each session. This item that had been so hot just two hours earlier was discarded as cold garbage, having lost all of its value in the dark. A whistling noise came from the popcorn machine, followed by the familiar bubbling of kernels completing their transformation. The batch that Lizzy had started was overflowing now. With one hand Victor pulled a lever and tipped the fresh cluster of popcorn down. It landed on top of an existing pile, that sat on display beneath some heat lamps inside the machine. In a rehearsed gesture Victor mingled the old and the new together with a plastic scoop.

'The smell is important too,' he added.

Bree nodded enthusiastically. She liked how much Victor seemed to care about his environment.

'Would you feel comfortable serving some customers?' he asked.

'I might be a bit slow,' Bree responded, 'but I'd be happy to try.'

After the Candy Bar was cleaned, crowds of patrons funnelled out of the cinemas and into the foyer. Some loitered while others rushed for the toilets. The noise dissipated and soon Bree was eagerly preparing to serve the early arrivals for the next sessions. Victor had sourced her a badge that said *Trainee*.

'This will help,' he said with a smile. 'It lowers expectations.'

The first couple to approach her were easily into their fifties. They had arrived early and moved buoyantly up to the Candy Bar. Bree imagined they had been married for years and that going to the movies was a long-standing tradition between them. For a fleeting moment she thought about her parents and found herself silently hoping for a miraculous reconciliation. Before Bree could say anything, Victor intercepted.

'Good evening to you both. I'm Victor and this is my trainee Bree. You're her first customers *ever*.'

'Oh, isn't that nice. Hi Bree,' said the kind-looking woman.

'Hi. What can I get you tonight?' Bree asked, attempting her best and brightest smile.

'We're just after a large popcorn,' said the man as he removed his money clip from his breast pocket.

Bree shot a knowing look to Victor.

'Would you like any drinks tonight?' Bree asked, utilising the art of suggestive selling. She held up an empty cup as a means of demonstration. 'The large popcorn is already five dollars sixty but for ten dollars you can get our combo.'

The couple looked at each other and shrugged indifferently.

'Alright,' said the man.

'What are you guys watching tonight?' asked Bree as she gave them their change. Victor had encouraged her to try some small talk.

'Legally Blonde 2,' the woman replied.

'I saw it last week. I think you'll like it,' offered Bree.

Victor nodded in approval and filled up the large box of popcorn for her.

Bree served about thirty more customers during the course of the evening. Victor was engaging and fun which was a wonderful change of pace from the training she'd been receiving on Floor with Lizzy. He even introduced her to a game of his own invention that he called the Central Cinema Olympics. Victor nominated a word such as 'sparkling' and the two would try to incorporate it into their next sale. The first person to use the word in a successful transaction would win the hypothetical gold medal. The words increased in difficulty as the night went on. Victor was far superior to Bree, but she held her own during their game and felt thankful that she could bond with another member of staff.

'So, are you studying next year?' Victor asked.

'Yeah, I'm going to do Hotel Management at CIT,' Bree replied.

'That sounds cool. I'm starting my second year of Web Design.' Victor told her about the course and how working nights at the cinema balanced well with his upcoming study schedule.

'I like it here so far,' Bree stated. 'I did want to ask if there are going to be enough shifts over Christmas. At the last place I worked they didn't need us after the holidays.'

'Where were you before this?' asked Victor.

'Toys R Us.'

Thinking back on her time stocking shelves was bittersweet for Bree. Working late into the night had been boring and monotonous at first but then she'd connected with Ryan, and things had escalated. If Ryan didn't have a car they might never have gone further than kissing. But he drove a sedan, and things had progressed within it.

'Oh, they'll need you here. People go away for the holidays so if you're around you'll get shifts.'

'Good.'

'Has anyone told you about the Christmas party?' Victor asked as he started to bag leftover popcorn.

'No.'

'They set aside money all year so it's a pretty big deal. And there is alcohol and they give out awards, which is nice.'

Bree blushed. She wasn't sure that she would be allowed to drink at an official work event, being underage and all. The memory of drinking with Ryan was still fresh in her mind. Bree didn't know if her father would even let her attend. He'd been quite overbearing lately in the light of her mother's misdemeanours.

'Everyone working here is aged about sixteen to twenty-five so there is always some new relationship forming,' added Victor.

'Are you dating someone that works here?' Bree asked innocently.

'No... I'm actually going to partake in an arranged marriage.'

'Wow. That's... great. Are you excited?'

'I will be when I know who I'm marrying! My parents are working out all of the details and I will meet her on the morning of our wedding.'

'That's amazing,' replied Bree. 'I hope they find her for you.'

'Me too. Maybe someday soon.'

Bree couldn't imagine committing to someone sight unseen but commended Victor all the same. It was a brave and romantic act. Victor explained that it had been that way in his family for generations and he'd always known it was in his future.

'Are you a staff trainer here?' Bree asked. She'd heard about the hierarchy within Central Cinemas and was still trying to work out where on the ladder everyone stood.

'Not yet.'

Victor was very knowledgeable and seemed great with customers. In her opinion he would make an excellent staff trainer. Bree had heard another employee say that the position didn't come with a pay rise and that some people saw it as a scam. If there was any prestige to being a staff trainer it wasn't clear to her what it was. It seemed to be an excuse to make some staff work harder than others.

Paul was the night manager on duty as Bree counted up her till in the office. In an effort to make-up for being on the phone during her orientation he'd been peppering her with questions. It was increasingly difficult to keep count as he hovered beside her.

'So, did you like Candy Bar? First time right?'

'Yeah it was alright,' said Bree without making eye contact.

'Did Victor tell you about his little Olympics game?'

'He sure did.'

'That's a bit of fun, isn't it?'

'Uhuh.'

'We're all about fun here. It's a great place to work. Did he tell you about the Christmas party? That's coming up soon.'

'Uhuh.'

Bree finished her addition and announced her total to Paul.

'Two hundred and forty dollars and forty cents.'

Paul checked the report in front of him and furrowed his brow.

'Do you want to double check?' he offered.

Bree re-counted and came up with the same figure.

'Hmmm…' Paul fell silent, which she found worrisome.

'How much was I supposed to have?' Bree asked.

'Two hundred and *ninety* dollars and forty cents. Fifty dollars short. This happens from time to time. Just head back to Candy Bar and check the drawer. Sometimes money will just get folded up and stuck in there. Victor can show you.'

Bree wandered back to the Candy Bar in a daze. She'd started to question herself and wondered if she had accidently given out the wrong change. It was possible that she had, of course. It was the first time she'd ever handled money professionally and perhaps she'd been distracted. Bree had started on Candy Bar halfway through her shift and inherited the register from Victor. *Was it possible that he'd miscounted before she'd even taken over?*

Bree checked the till drawer and the surrounding areas thoroughly. There was no forgotten or misplaced money that she could see. She thought about asking Andy or Victor whether they had seen any money but didn't want to come off as accusatory. Beneath her orange work shirt she'd started to sweat. In her mind Bree formed the belief that this was a fireable offense. She didn't want to lose this job or be suspected of theft.

'Everything okay?' Victor asked looking up from the industrial-sized popcorn machine that he was scrubbing.

'Everything's fine,' she said and ambled away. She didn't like the way the lie sounded coming out of her mouth.

Bree slipped out of the foyer and into the food court. Nobody noticed as she snuck away. She went to a nearby ATM and withdrew fifty dollars from her savings account.

While she was standing there, feeling out of place, her phone vibrated. Bree hadn't even realised it was in her pocket. It was her mother, and in a moment of frustration she answered it.

'What?'

'Bree? Honey, it's Mum...'

'Stop calling me. I don't want to talk to you.' Before she knew it Bree had terminated the call. She was shaking. Her mother's desire for forgiveness and understanding was like a leech that she couldn't detach, draining her. Bree just wanted to shut Carol out of her life.

When she returned to the office she smiled at Paul and held up the fifty-dollar note.

'Found it.'

CHAPTER FIVE

The family dynamic was strange now that it was just Bree and her father. Neither was used to the degree in which their lives had changed recently. Bree hadn't complained when he'd announced his desire to relocate, but now she wished she'd stipulated some rules. The Walker Court Apartments were a short drive from the mall, and seemed to mostly house single parents and retirees. Henry had found them a two-bedroom place and they'd settled into their new residence easily. Nobody was lining up for the accommodation. Their new home was on the ground floor, with neighbours on all sides. It felt bland and unexciting to Bree. The walls were cracked and there was water damage, but it was liveable. Bree had decided that a positive attitude was needed and told her father it was great.

'Thanks Bree,' he'd beamed.

'And Dad?'

'Yeah?'

'I'd like to contribute towards the rent.'

Her father had protested at first but when Bree insisted he crumbled under the pressure.

'Fine. You can give me money but I'll just set it aside for you.'

'We'll be housemates!' joked Bree. 'Just like on *Big Brother*.'

At night she thought about her mother. Even though Bree missed her voice sometimes, her infidelity still felt unforgivable. She knew that her father was still harbouring a lot of resentment towards Carol and had noticed he'd increased his drinking during his downtime. Bree hoped that this was a phase and that it would get easier for them both. There was no discussion of divorce and Bree was pleased about that. If her parents weren't talking then they weren't fighting. Carol had been calling them less often, which had also helped to put the affair into the background. Bree wasn't interested in hearing her side of things, but she knew that Canberra was a small place where people bumped into one another. She couldn't avoid seeing her mother forever.

Central Cinemas calling her in for an evening shift was a welcome distraction. Her father had jumped at the chance to drive her. In the past Bree had struggled to find common ground with him. Work had bridged the gap and given them something neutral to talk about besides the Canberra Raiders.

'So, are you finishing at ten again tonight?' Henry asked as he looked at himself in the car's rear-view mirror. He had started balding last year and he was constantly checking to see how much of his grey-brown hair remained. Bree often caught him looking at his reflection but never mentioned it. It had only receded a little, after all.

'Yeah, ten o'clock. I'll text you when I'm done?'

'I'll be up.'

'Maybe we can have another driving lesson this week.'

Henry nodded and promised she could take the wheel again soon. 'I'm pretty confident you'll get your licence as soon as you turn seventeen. Are you still going to do a one-off test?'

'That's the plan,' said Bree with a smile.

'Well I hope that works out,' he replied. There was sadness behind his eyes. Driving lessons had been her mother's idea. Carol was still swimming in their heads, causing hurt and quiet reflection. Bree wondered whether Adrian would want to marry her mother. She imagined how painful that dynamic would be for her father, to be cast aside, dismissed and replaced with another. That was one reason Bree had declined her calls: she was afraid of what her mother would say about the future.

When they arrived at the mall Bree collected her small silver bag and said goodbye to her father. She'd been informed by Victor that many staff used the fire escape near the bins as a back door to the Central Cinemas complex. This felt like confidential information, and she appreciated being trusted with it. As she advanced to the covert entrance Bree saw a teenage girl sitting alone on the concrete. She wore the orange employee uniform, although Bree had never seen her before. The teenager had a deliberate and striking mop of short black hair and in her left hand she held a burning cigarette. The smoke trail was hovering upwards in one unbroken line.

'Hi,' said Bree as she approached, not wanting to startle her.

The girl looked up with a vacant expression. Bree noticed that she was wearing purple eye shadow. The girl spotted the matching uniform on Bree and with a look of recognition her face softened.

'Oh… hey.'

'I'm Bree.'

'Mallory,' she replied and stubbed her cigarette out on the concrete wall next to her. 'You new?'

'Yeah it's been a few weeks.'

Mallory looked malnourished as though she might be on the verge of anorexia. Bree thought she might be a model. She was certainly attractive enough to be one. Mallory was the first person she'd met that could actually pull off the hideous shade of orange that they were all required to wear. She had a detached edginess that Bree was drawn to right away. The girl in front of her was hard to define. *A young Angelina Jolie maybe…*

Mallory played with a black lighter with the image of a flame on it. As she spoke she clicked the igniter at the top, lighting a fire momentarily, as if to punctuate her words.

'Were you hired with Liam?' Mallory asked as she tucked her short black hair behind her ear. It rebelled, coming loose again almost immediately.

'Yes.'

'He's a tool,' said Mallory matter-of-factly.

Bree burst out laughing. She couldn't help herself. She was so pleased that another person shared her opinion.

'He *is* a tool, isn't he?' said Bree confidently.

'He's strutting around like he owns the place. He has this unearned confidence about him,' Mallory continued.

'Totally!'

'Welcome to the party Bree. Nice to have you on board.'

The two workers headed inside and checked the crew sheet for the night. It was printed inside the manager's office where a bookish woman named Rita sat. There were four managers on a rotating roster, and this was the first time Bree had met Rita. She seemed to be on the quieter side and Bree silently decided she resembled a short Uma Thurman, fringed, with sternness beyond her years.

Bree was continuing her training on Candy Bar and Mallory was rostered in the Box Office. Apparently that was where she usually worked, which explained why they hadn't crossed paths yet.

'It's still early,' announced Mallory. 'Do you want to hang out in the staff room for a few minutes before we start?'

'Sure,' said Bree, a little too quickly. She hoped Mallory didn't notice her eagerness as they climbed the stairs and sat down together on the sofa. Someone had left the microwave door open, which bothered her.

'How long have you been at Central?' asked Bree.

'Too long probably. Just over two years.'

'Everyone keeps saying it's a great place to work.' Bree wanted to see what Mallory thought. For some reason she valued her opinion. After all she'd had great instincts about Liam.

'It's *fine*... I guess,' replied Mallory apathetically. 'I mean you get to go to the movies for free if that's your thing. You get free soft drink on the Candy Bar as long as you use their crappy little plastic cups.'

Nobody had told Bree about the free soft drink. She thought of Matt using the novelty combo cup to get a drink. Perhaps he had a rebellious side.

'If you're going to work somewhere in the mall this is probably the best place to be. It's open every day of the year except Christmas and besides the occasional bad patron it's easy enough.'

'Have you worked anywhere else in the mall?' asked Bree.

'Yeah... I've been around. Before this I worked in some clothes shops and a few of the fast food places. This is better,' declared Mallory.

'I was at Toys R Us on Level Three. I didn't like it in the end,' added Bree.

Mallory nodded without asking Bree to elaborate in any way. She stood up and balled her short dark hair into a tiny ponytail.

'You have a boyfriend?' asked Mallory with a raised eyebrow.

'No.'

'Girlfriend then?'

'No... I used to have a boyfriend but I don't anymore,' replied Bree. She'd been trying not to think about Ryan and the way things ended between them, but he still featured in her thoughts on a regular basis. Bree hadn't talked about the experience with anyone and Ryan had promised he'd keep it a secret too, back when they were speaking at least.

'Have you seen anyone here at work that you like?'

'Um... I've only met a few of the guys,' Bree said quickly.

'There are some good ones here. It's pretty incestuous really. Almost everyone here has dated *somebody*.'

Bree considered this. It made sense that if you bundled together a group of age appropriate boys and girls, forcing them to socialise in close proximity, that some would have chemistry. It was like a petri dish of hormones. The cinema was a staple of dating culture and some of the movie magic was bound to rub off.

'Have you dated anyone here?' Bree asked cautiously. She didn't want to offend Mallory by assuming but the way she'd said *everyone* implied that she'd also dipped her toe in the Central Cinemas pool.

'Oh yeah. I've dated a couple of the guys. At the moment I'm kind of seeing one of the projectionists.'

'Oh?' Bree hoped it wasn't Matt. She suddenly had butterflies in her stomach while she waited for Mallory to continue.

'His name is George. He used to work down on Floor and Candy Bar up until about four months ago. We've only been on two real dates, but I like him,' Mallory said sitting down on the edge of the table.

Bree let out a sigh of relief.

'That sounds nice.'

'He lets me hang out in the Projection room with him sometimes.'

'Only sometimes?' Bree asked.

'I can be a bit too... *distracting*.' Mallory had a wicked look in her eyes.

'Right.'

'George has to run ten projectors at a time but once all the sessions have started he always has time for me again,' stated Mallory with a coy smile.

Bree wondered what it would be like to date someone at work again. When she'd had her short-lived relationship with Ryan they'd had to hide it from everyone. There had been clauses about dating co-workers at Toys R Us. Even though they could have declared they were an item without getting into too much trouble, Bree was concerned it would somehow filter back to her parents. Central Cinemas seemed like the polar opposite. Dating was encouraged, at least the way Mallory spoke about it.

'Liam asked me out on my first day,' Bree blurted out. In that moment she felt like she had to share something. Mallory had trusted her by divulging details about George and she knew they could safely bond over their mutual dislike of Liam.

'Did he?' asked Mallory, her mouth open in shock.

'Yeah.'

'And you said no?'

'Yeah… I don't like him,' Bree replied. 'Not like that anyway.'

'Do you know who his mother is?'

'Who?'

'Maxine.'

Bree had no idea who Maxine was and so she said nothing.

'The Location Manager? Maxine White?'

Paul had hired Bree and so far she'd only worked at times when he, Rita or another manager named Carl were rostered on. She'd barely had any interactions with the management team at all. Bree had noticed that there was a separate office for the Location Manager within the main office, but the door had always been closed. If she'd heard the name Maxine White she'd failed to register its significance until now.

'Don't get me wrong,' Mallory said with a grin, 'I *love* that you rejected him but I'm wondering if it will get back to her. People love a bit of a gossip around here.'

'Would that be a bad thing?' Bree asked. 'If it got back to Maxine, I mean?'

'Well, she basically got him the job here. She's going to groom him up quickly and make sure he's on the fast track to management. Everybody knows he's her favourite. Liam has been getting free movie tickets for years. He's always had the special treatment from his Mum. Liam only works on nights when he doesn't have footy training. He's got a customised roster.'

Bree didn't want to cause any drama. She thought back to her first shift at Central Cinemas. That must have been why Andy had been so chummy with Liam. He might have been praising him because of Maxine and her influence. Bree considered that perhaps the Location Manager was a figure that she should fear.

'And you think if I get on *his* bad side I'll get on *her* bad side too?'

'Don't worry about it,' said Mallory, who was watching Bree process all of this new information. 'He'll probably be too embarrassed to say anything to anyone. And I'll look out for you. We have to stick together.' Mallory punctuated the statement with a casual wink.

'I'm sure it will be fine,' said Bree, hoping she was right.

The two headed downstairs to the office together. Mallory and Bree were each handed a cash float before heading to their respective stations. While for Mallory the Box Office was right next door, Bree had to walk her till upstairs alone, past the locked storerooms and around to the back of Candy Bar. It was a security precaution to prevent anyone from stealing a whole drawer of money in one swift movement.

Bree was pleased that she wasn't on Floor tonight, as she needed more practice making sales. Bree had been haunted by the idea that she had lost fifty dollars somehow. She worried that she'd been conned by a customer and accidently given them too much change. Bree wanted another chance, and she was determined to get it right tonight.

Bree set herself up next to Shannon, choosing the same position she'd had with Victor. Shannon reminded Bree of *Shallow Hal*, where actress Gwyneth Paltrow wore a padded suit. She had long blonde hair that was tied up in a plait behind her back like a modern Viking. It stretched down all the way to her hips. Shannon seemed jovial enough and suggested to every patron she served that they might like to buy a choctop. Some customers really responded to her talkative nature.

'They're fresh,' she'd always say, holding the wrapped ice cream by the cone.

Shannon was one of the few employees who regularly asked for 'choctop shifts', which meant four-hours making the cinema delicacies from scratch. During the break between sessions she proudly showed off the industrial-sized ice cream tubs, chocolate and cones. Bree had no idea that the ingredients could be purchased in such large quantities. They ventured into the walk-in freezer and Shannon demonstrated how they were made. She took a metal scoop, dipped it in hot water, and carved out several perfectly shaped orbs of ice cream. As they stood inside the cold room Shannon plonked them onto waffle cones one by one. The clear plastic tray that held her creations had sixteen holes. When Shannon had filled the tray with product she placed it on one of the many shelves that dominated the walls of the huge freezer.

'Next I'd melt some of that chocolate and dunk them,' said Shannon proudly. 'But they need some time to set so I'll do it later on.'

'Don't you get cold spending so much time in the freezer?' Bree asked, watching her breath swirl out in front of her. She had suffered enough during the tutorial and couldn't imagine spending four hours in such an icy environment.

'I like it,' Shannon said with a smile. 'It's my favourite part of the job. Choc tops sell pretty well so I get asked to come in and make them all the time. I put together about two hundred cones per shift so they get their money's worth out of me too!'

During the course of the night Bree was extremely careful with her change. She would announce how much money she'd been handed by a customer out loud and then, ensuring she had hit the correct value button on the register, state their change. She couldn't afford to imbalance her till again.

When Shannon went for dinner Bree found herself working with Victor again. He was covering all of the breaks that night on a floater shift. The two played a couple of rounds of the Central Cinema Olympics before a familiar face appeared on the other side of the counter.

'Lizzy?' Bree was surprised to see her trainer standing opposite her. Lizzy wore a frilly blue skirt that went down to her knees, coupled with a black crop top and a black leather jacket. Bree had never seen her so dressed up or composed before, and thought she looked stunning, despite the exposed midriff that revealed a belly button ring.

'Hi Bree. How's it going?' asked Lizzy, with a small, polite smile.

'Good thanks. Can I get you something?'

'Yeah…'

While she was considering her options a man walked up and put his arm around Lizzy's waist. He was in his mid-twenties and had a shaved head. He looked a little bit like Sam Worthington, who Bree had seen in *Bootmen*. He casually held up two tickets.

'Got the tickets,' he said and gave Lizzy a quick peck on the cheek. She flinched slightly, as if the display of public affection was unwarranted.

'Can we just get a large Coke?'

Bree considered suggesting popcorn but decided against it. Lizzy looked intimidating, and if she wanted a combo she knew how to get it.

'Enjoy the movie,' Bree said, when the transaction was over.

Lizzy let her date walk ahead with the drink as she lingered behind. She beckoned Bree to move towards her, as though she had a secret to share. Bree cautiously looked to Victor, who was out of earshot, and then leaned in.

'Listen, Shannon got called in to cover *my* shift tonight. I told them I was sick, okay?'

'Okay...'

'So don't tell her you saw me. I'm not here,' Lizzy said quickly. Bree nodded without hesitation and Lizzy headed up to the cinema.

This threatening exchange was simply another confirmation to Bree that Lizzy was not someone to emulate. She probably shouldn't be a staff trainer either. Bree wondered whether there was a support group of employees that had received her slapdash instruction. She didn't know who to whinge to about it and so when Shannon returned from her break Bree kept it to herself. She had no desire to make waves and risk a catty comment getting back to her trainer. Bree would be working with Lizzy again soon enough and didn't want to taste her retribution. There was plenty of gossip in the air at Central Cinemas. She'd already heard some random rumours floating around.

'What's up with that new girl?'

'Bree? I don't know.'

'I saw her talking to Liam. I think they might be dating.'

'She's cute. I'd hit that too.'

Bree wouldn't address their speculation. She didn't want to add fuel to the fire of conjecture. It wasn't her style.

At the end of the night Bree was thrilled when her till balanced to the cent. She resisted squealing openly with delight. To add to her joy, while she was mopping up a spilt soft drink a teenager that worked at the Donut King in the food court approached her. He had several bags of donuts, which he happily presented to her.

'We're just going to throw them out otherwise,' he said.

'Thank you so much,' Bree replied as she graciously accepted the bags.

'You're welcome. Have a nice night.'

She showed the donuts to Shannon who was very pleased with the haul.

'Oooh bear claws! These aren't cheap either,' Shannon said taking a bite. 'Nice one Bree.'

They split the donuts up between them. Bree walked over to the Box Office where Mallory was counting out coupons from her till.

'Donut?' she offered and held the bag open at the gap in the glass above the counter.

'No thanks,' replied Mallory.

Bree scrunched up the pink bag.

'Are you off at ten?' asked Mallory as she threw a rubber band around a stack of twenty-dollar notes.

'Yes.'

'Do you live around here?'

'Yeah. I live at the Walker Court Apartments. Do you know them?' Bree was getting used to her new address now.

'Yeah. I know them. I used to date someone that lived there. Do you want a lift home?'

Bree's father was waiting for her call but she wanted to hang out with Mallory. There was something intoxicating about her. The promise of friendship was beckoning. Her father would have to understand.

'I'd love one.'

Bree and Mallory went upstairs to the staff room together. She noticed that as they ascended the staircase they were in perfect step with one another. Their matching movements created a brief but satisfying beat. Once in the change room Bree grabbed her silver bag from her locker. She hadn't brought anything else with her. Mallory unbuttoned her orange shirt and peeled it away as though it was burning her skin.

'I hate this uniform, don't you?'

Bree concurred. 'It's such an ugly colour.'

Now dressed in a black bra, Mallory turned herself towards Bree, who had no idea where to look. *Should I have left the change room?* she wondered. Bree pretended to fiddle with the buckle on her bag, and hoped Mallory couldn't detect the nervous blush of red that was filling her cheeks.

'Do you think I'm too thin?' Mallory asked with her hands on her hips.

Bree turned and studied Mallory's body now that she felt she had permission to do so. She saw thin arms and a small waist but was surprised at how buxom Mallory actually was. While overall she still seemed petite to Bree, from this new vantage point she decided perhaps Mallory wasn't in danger after all.

'No, you look great,' replied Bree, hoping to sound convincing.

'The last guy I dated would always comment on my weight.'

'That sucks.'

Mallory put a grey hoodie on over her bra and zipped it up. She picked up her orange shirt and then started opening lockers one by one.

'What are you doing?' Bree asked.

'Looking for spare shirts.'

Bree was puzzled. Mallory finished searching the area and then pivoted out towards the male change room. She didn't knock at all as she swung the door open, her brazen approach startling Bree.

'Mallory!' Bree exclaimed.

'Relax, there's no one in here,' replied Mallory half-heartedly.

'But there *could* have been!'

'Maybe we'll get lucky next time!'

Mallory had a devilish way about her. Bree nervously looked back over her shoulder as she held the door like a guilty accomplice. The men's change room smelled like feet, and the wooden bench was littered with apparel. Mallory spotted an orange shirt on the floor next to some black shoes. She snatched it up.

'Jackpot.'

'Why do you need a dirty old shirt?' enquired Bree with interest.

Mallory smiled and tossed the Central Cinemas shirt into her bag.

'If you hang out with me on Saturday I'll show you.'

CHAPTER SIX

Bree was supposed to meet Mallory at the parking lot by the far side of the mall. She was nervous, as it was their first time hanging outside of work. She'd dressed and re-dressed a few times before realising that she was being ridiculous. Bree reminded herself that Mallory had initiated this. *She wants to hang out with you.* Her father had been fine with Bree getting a lift home with her in the end. Henry had only wished she'd told him earlier so he could have indulged a few extra beers.

Bree was staring out at the cars, thinking about how annoying it would be to hunt for a vacant space on this insanely busy Saturday, when her phone rang. It was a private number. *Maybe Mallory was running late.*

'Hello?'

'Hi Bree, it's Mum.'

'Oh... hi.'

Bree was dumbstruck. Had she known her mother was calling she might not have answered it. She could hear a deep sigh on the other end of the phone, as Carol collected her thoughts.

'How are you?' she asked her daughter. Carol seemed equally surprised that the call had been answered.

'Fine.'

'How's the new place? Your apartment?'

'It's okay.'

Bree wondered how much she knew. Perhaps her father had told her out of courtesy. Maybe her parents were speaking more regularly than she'd realised.

'Bree… I know this is hard. I just want you to know I'm really sorry about all of this. I didn't want things to happen the way they did.' Her mother sounded distant, like the phone line had a faulty connection.

'Are you…' Bree struggled to complete her question.

'What is it honey?' asked Carol.

'Are you and Dad getting back together?'

'Oh… no… we're… we're not… I can't do that anymore.'

Bree spotted Mallory's car approaching. The headlights flashed to get her attention.

'I've got to go now Mum,' she said sharply.

'Okay… I understand. I love you…'

Bree hung up the phone, terminating the fragile connection just as Mallory drove up in her blue Ford Cortina. Bree hadn't had a good look at the vehicle when Mallory had dropped her home the night before. In the hard light of day Bree could see that the paint was either faded or peeling away in most places. The Cortina was definitely showing its twenty years of age, defying expectations. It was an interesting juxtaposition to see such a young vivacious girl driving such a decrepit car. Most girls their age were driving sporty hatchbacks or Volkswagen Beetles.

'Hop in,' Mallory called as she manually cranked down a window.

Frustrated drivers honked at them almost immediately, but Mallory seemed unfazed. Bree gave an apologetic wave as she hurried around the car and settled into the passenger seat. She tried to put the phone call with her mother out of her mind, vowing to enjoy herself today.

'How's it going?' asked Mallory as she pulled away from the kerb. Bree hastily buckled her seatbelt while the car was in motion.

'Fine… yeah… I'm okay,' she replied. If Bree was showing any signs of distress, she was glad that Mallory hadn't noticed them.

'George has been texting me from the Projection room. Apparently they're having power failures in the mall and the projectors keep stopping. They've had to refund a few sessions.'

'Is that what happens? They just refund all the tickets?'

'Not exactly,' Mallory continued as she turned abruptly away from the mall. 'The managers hand out comp tickets. Complimentary tickets? Have you seen them?'

'No... I haven't worked in the Box Office yet.'

'Oh, that's right. Well... you will. It's pretty easy and you get to sit on your bum all night.'

'That sounds cool,' said Bree happily.

'And if they stick you in there with me we'll just chat. If you're working with someone good it's always a pretty decent shift.'

Bree beamed. She was pleased that Mallory considered her with such high regard already.

'So, they hand out these comp tickets instead of giving people refunds,' continued Mallory. 'It's basically a free ticket they can use the next time they come in. There are always empty seats so it's win-win for the cinema. They keep the money and probably get them at the Candy Bar both times.'

'That's pretty smart.'

Mallory took a sharp right turn. 'If a customer ever comes up to you and gets mad just ask for the manager on the two-way. They will give almost *anyone* comp tickets. They don't cost anything.'

'Almost anyone?'

Mallory nodded. 'Uhuh. I've seen them hand out comp tickets when there were noisy kids in the back row, if the temperature was too hot or too cold, even if the toilets weren't clean enough.'

'Wow. I had no idea. Before I worked at Central I remember coming in and thinking it was too hot a few times.'

'You should have complained,' said Mallory.

'I guess I should have,' Bree agreed.

Mallory accelerated through an orange light moments before it changed to red. Bree pretended not to notice.

'You don't strike me as the kind of person who complains a lot though,' stated Mallory, sizing her up.

Bree could hardly argue. She had always been a passive person, with little to complain about. She'd been so docile throughout High School that she'd failed to cement any real and lasting connections. She was friendly with everyone, but just in passing. Bree also hated confrontation. That was part of what made her parents' break up so difficult for her, and the main reason she'd been ignoring her mother's calls up until now.

'Yeah… I guess I don't like to rock the boat,' Bree managed to say.

'It's not a big deal. I'll help you find your voice.'

'Thanks.'

'And don't forget Bree, boats are made to be rocked.'

Mallory seemed confident and Bree liked her very much. Today was different. They were spending time together as friends, not proximity bound colleagues. Mallory didn't *have* to offer her a ride home the night before, but she had. Bree was feeling optimistic.

They arrived at a Salvation Army op shop a short time later. Bree's confusion must have been obvious, forcing Mallory to clarify things.

'We're going to find some cool vintage clothes,' she said with a grin.

'That sounds fun,' said Bree, trying to be positive.

'You've never been op shopping before, have you?'

Bree confessed that she hadn't.

'We're going to get clothes that have barely been worn. They're going to be cheap, unique and fresh.'

'Aren't most of these clothes donated after their owners die?' Bree didn't think old clothes could be *fresh*.

'Nah, that's an old wives' tale. Most of them are donated after people get too fat for them, I reckon. I promise it'll be fun.'

Hanging out with Mallory had been a breath of fresh air so far. Bree trusted that this shopping experience would be more of the same. Inside there were twelve long rows of clothes on hangers. The girls blew past the children's clothes and toys and were soon rifling through jackets and tops. Mallory pointed out several great possibilities and confessed a fondness for tassels. Bree noted that some of the clothes had a musty smell.

'Don't worry about that. We'll fix that later,' said Mallory confidently.

Bree smiled and kept flicking through the clothes on the rack.

'So, what's your *thing*?' Mallory asked while holding up a gaudy purple vest.

'What do you mean?' asked Bree.

'Most people that work at the cinema are tragic movie buffs or wannabe filmmakers. Are you like… an aspiring actress or something?'

'No. I mean… I *like* movies… but I don't want to make one.'

'Well what's your thing? Are you studying something or making something or writing something? What's *your* something?'

Bree flicked past some shirts that resembled the Von Trapp children's play clothes.

'I'm going to do Hotel Management next year.'

Mallory scrunched her mouth to the side. 'Could be fun… I suppose,' she offered hesitantly.

'I like the service industry so my Dad and I figured I should aim for the top jobs,' Bree said hoping to impress her new friend.

'Think about the managers at Central,' Mallory said. 'Do you think *they're* in the top job?'

Bree thought for a moment. 'They're probably paid the most.'

'But how much fun do you think that job would be?'

'It's not meant to be fun… it's a job,' stated Bree.

'But jobs *can* be fun. They should be really.' Mallory seemed so sure of herself.

'Not in my experience.'

'That's because you've never worked with me!' Mallory chuckled to herself.

'That's true. I guess… I mean… I suppose what my Dad and I thought was that if you're going to work somewhere that you should *aim* for the top job,' said Bree defensively. She'd never had her goals questioned by someone outside of her immediate family.

'So this is what your Dad wants?'

'No… it's what I want too.'

'Those kinds of positions are overrated,' said Mallory.

'How do you figure?' asked Bree.

'At Central the managers spend most of their time in an office calculating overtime pay and calling in staff when people *claim* they're sick. If something goes wrong, they're the ones that get in trouble. They have to deal with all the bullshit. They only come out of the office if we call them for help on the two-ways or if a customer is upset.'

'But they're in charge,' replied Bree.

'Of *what*? A cinema? Look you don't have to listen to me. I'm sure it's a different story in hotels… but for me I'm happy not to be in charge of anything but myself. You're only young once. I think you should enjoy right now.'

'So, you don't want to be a staff trainer?' asked Bree.

Mallory started laughing and had to use a rack of shirts to support her frame from doubling over. 'No thanks,' she smirked.

'I wouldn't mind,' said Bree in a small voice.

'Trust me it's not worth it. They *overwork* the trainers. They get called in every weekend and guilted into working if they're needed.'

'You don't get called in?'

'Sure, sometimes they'll call me,' Mallory returned with a shrug. She eyed a pair of black jeans before putting them back down.

'And how do you get out of it?' asked Bree.

'I'll tell them I've been drinking.'

'*What?*' Bree's reaction made Mallory laugh.

'Sure! No matter what time it is, no matter what day it is. They can't make you work if you've been drinking. Imagine if something happened! They'd be liable.'

'But they'll think you're an alcoholic.'

'Well I don't tell them that *every* time! You have to be creative though. It makes it more fun. If I'm not in the mood sometimes I just don't answer the phone,' said Mallory as she picked up a short pink skirt and held it against herself.

'I don't mind getting called in now and then,' stated Bree timidly.

'Of course not. You're new and everything at work is so *shiny*. You want to impress them. And last time they called you in for a shift you met me.'

'You don't want to impress them?' asked Bree.

'Nope. It's just a job to me. I'm not going to work there for the rest of my life.'

'So, what's your *something* then?' Bree asked.

'I'm saving up all my money so I can make a break for it.'

This sudden announcement felt bittersweet. Bree was making such great progress with Mallory and she hated the idea that their new friendship had an expiration date.

'Where will you go?'

'Where *won't* I go?' Mallory exclaimed. 'I'm going to disappear.' Mallory lit up like a Christmas tree as she imagined this future for herself.

'I'd love to travel. I've never been anywhere really,' stated Bree. She had dreams that her Hotel Management course would allow her to see the world. She'd also been contemplating an escape from her hometown. Canberra had a small and forgotten feeling at times. It was wedged between the major Australian cities of Sydney and Melbourne, so tantalisingly close that Bree could see the appeal of running away.

'You're welcome to come with me. Anything's possible you know,' Mallory said as she picked up and then immediately put down a pair of white sunglasses.

Bree thought Mallory would make an excellent travel companion. She was tough and seemed very street smart.

By the time they'd finished looking through the aisles of clothes Mallory had a pile of items hanging over one arm. Bree had been surprised to find a skirt she liked as well as a black shirt that fit her perfectly.

They paid only a few dollars for each item, which pleased Bree, as she'd contributed most of her latest pay to this month's rent. They threw the pile of clothes into the back of the car and drove towards to the mall. The parking lot hysteria from the morning rush had subsided and they were able to find space under cover easily.

'I'm going to let you in on one of my little scams, okay?' Mallory said as she shut off the engine.

'Okay.'

'You can't tell anyone about this.' Mallory looked serious.

'I won't.' Concern flashed across Bree's face. *What was Mallory about to confide?*

'Back in the day Central Cinemas used to pay all their employees a cleaning allowance.'

'A... *cleaning* allowance?' Bree repeated.

'Yeah. It was about eight or nine dollars a week and it was just tacked on at the bottom of everyone's fortnightly payslip.'

Bree wasn't seeing the relevance. 'So?'

'So, a few years ago they found a sneaky way around it to save the company money. They made a deal with a chain of dry cleaning places instead. Basically, they set up a corporate account that was designed to cover the laundry needs of *all* of the staff at each location. So, instead of paying you a little extra to wash your shirt every two weeks they created a loophole so they could stop paying everyone's cleaning allowance completely.'

'I haven't heard anything about this.'

'Of course not!' exclaimed Mallory. 'They don't want you to actually *use* the dry cleaning service! They just want it to *appear* available if anyone actually questions it. That's why they don't give you multiple shirts. Because then you could actually wash one while wearing the other. They save heaps of money I'm sure.'

'So, you took the shirt from the guy's change room so we could get it dry cleaned?'

'Yes. But Central Cinemas are *also* going to dry clean our op shop clothes.'

'Won't they notice the extra cost?'

'Nope! I've been doing this for over a year. It's a service that they *have* to provide and nobody else uses. Its still way less expensive to Central in the long run so they won't question it,' said Mallory. 'And if they *did* question it, they'd have to highlight that this service exists in the first place… and they don't want to do that. I know the guy behind the counter and he's happy for the extra business. He lets me use a different staff members name each time.'

'Wow. Pretty sneaky.'

'You have no idea.'

'You said this was just *one* of your scams?'

Mallory raised an eyebrow knowingly and got out of the car. The girls carried the old clothes to the dry cleaner with the orange shirt on top. As predicted the man behind the counter charged the cost to Central Cinemas and let Mallory use an alias.

Mallory took Bree to the food court and they each bought a frozen Coke and a hot dog from Donut King. The guy who'd provided the free donuts the night before wasn't rostered on.

'Told ya it would work,' bragged Mallory.

It was hard for Bree not to be impressed.

When she arrived home that evening her father offered to give her a driving lesson. Coincidentally he took Bree back to the same car park where Mallory had picked her up that morning. She'd considered telling him about the phone call with her mother, scanned her father's face while she'd adjusted her mirrors. Bree turned the phone conversation over in her mind while she practiced parallel parking. She imagined what Carol might be doing tonight while she shifted from first to second gear. Bree questioned whether her mother missed her as much as she claimed to. Most of all she wondered whether her mother regretted running off with Adrian.

'Dad?' she asked, when the lesson was over.

'Yeah?'

'Have you heard from Mum lately?'

Henry scratched his neck just beneath his chin. It felt like he was stalling while he mulled over the appropriate response.

'Listen… Bree… your mother and I aren't really speaking at the moment. I think it's for the best. Maybe in time we can be… *civil*… but right now it's all a bit fresh. I'm sorry kiddo.'

'It's alright. I agree actually,' she replied. 'I could use some space from her right now too.'

'You haven't seen her?'

'I don't want to,' confessed Bree.

Henry let out a sigh.

'That's life, huh? Things will get better.'

'I hope so.'

<h1 style="text-align:center">CHAPTER SEVEN</h1>

Year 12 came to a natural end and summer weather arrived in the Nation's Capital. While life at home was still settling, the workflow at Central was becoming second nature to Bree. One afternoon Mallory came up to Floor during her meal break and invited Bree to a party. They had been hanging out intermittently over the past two weeks and it sounded like a ripe opportunity to improve that frequency.

'It's on Saturday at this guy's house. You should come.'

'Who is he?' asked Bree.

'His name is Pierre. I've never met him but I know some of his friends. It could be fun.'

'Could it?' teased Bree.

'Okay... it *will* be.'

Bree agreed and Mallory wandered outside via the fire escape for a cigarette. As Victor returned from cleaning Cinema Four he cornered Bree at Point.

'Was that Mallory I saw here before?' he enquired.

'Yeah.'

'What did she want?'

'She wanted to see if I was free on Saturday.'

'What's on Saturday?'

'A party,' replied Bree.

'I *love* parties.'

Bree realised that she may have said too much. She had no idea how exclusive the party was and whether Victor could tag along. Bree wasn't even certain she *wanted* Victor to attend. She hadn't spent time socialising with anyone other than Mallory outside of work.

'I'd have to check with Mallory,' Bree said in-between tearing tickets.

'Cool. I'm not working that night so let me know,' he said enthusiastically.

Victor went back down the tunnel to check slides and trailers. Bree felt a lump in the pit of her stomach at the possibility of a confrontation with Mallory. If she had to tell Victor that he couldn't come to the party she was also anxious about how to break that regrettable news to him.

'Um… Mallory?'

'Yeah?'

'I kind of… told Victor about the party.'

'So?'

'I think he wants to tag along.'

Mallory's reaction spoke volumes. She wasn't concerned about adding to the guest list. She'd already invited several other Central Cinema employees.

'You're so funny Bree. It's just a party.'

'I was worried! I figured it was invite only.'

'Pierre didn't invite *us!* The more the merrier I say.'

'Okay… cool.' Bree was relieved, having avoided unpleasantness.

'Actually, I've never seen Victor party.' Mallory was smiling at the thought. 'I'm not even sure he drinks.'

On Saturday Bree sat down to lunch with her father. She'd made them grilled salmon and steamed vegetables, leaving leftovers in the fridge in case he wanted more later on.

'Looks good Bree,' he said.

'And it's better for you than fast food.'

In the days after her parents break up there had been an abundance of take away in their kitchen. Now her father seemed like he was trying to set a good example again. He'd asked Bree questions about work and seemed genuinely pleased when she'd told him about Mallory.

'That's great news. I knew you'd enjoy it there.'

In truth he'd never taken any interest in her work at Toys R Us or Central Cinemas before her mothers' departure.

'You know Bree… if you ever need to talk to me about anything…'

'I know Dad.'

'I worry about you sometimes. With all the changes we've been through lately. Let me know if you need anything, okay?'

'I will.'

Bree was sure her father would say no to her attending a party, so she'd kept him under the illusion that she was going to the movies with Mallory.

'So, what are you two going to see?' asked Henry as he cut his salmon.

'I'm not sure yet. We'll probably decide when we get there.'

'It's a nice perk of the job, isn't it? Free movies?'

'Yeah.'

'We should go see a movie some night too. You and me,' Henry said with a hopeful grin.

'Sounds good.'

Her father had worked as a security guard for most of his life. His current role had him on twelve-hour shifts at a local radio station. Henry told her once that he spent most of the night behind a desk listening to his radio but would patrol the grounds and the outside of the building every hour or so. Bree had been encouraging her father to apply for a job that had regular daylight hours but nothing suitable had materialised.

Henry spoke fondly about his days playing rugby league before he was injured. At the age of twenty-one he'd required a knee reconstruction that had slowed him down and made him uncompetitive.

'Nobody wanted me after that,' he'd said. 'Not even the reserve grade sides.' He'd always dreamed about playing for his beloved Canberra Raiders, who'd been hit and miss for years. They'd had a promising 2003 finals campaign, which had been a great source of joy and distraction for Henry.

Bree had been unpacking the events that had led to her mother's exodus in her mind. She'd considered that her father sleeping all day wasn't conducive to a marriage, which had left his wife to seek out the affections of another. Bree was now experiencing a version of what her mother had endured for years. She'd found that whenever her father was sleeping, she had to become increasingly quiet so as not to wake him up. Bree couldn't condone her mother's affair, but she was starting to understand the kind of loneliness that she must have felt prior to it. She and her father were like ships in the night. It was easier not to tell him about the party. He'd be at work anyway.

'I'm glad you've made a friend,' he said, chewing his food thoroughly.

'Me too. Hey Dad… can I ask you something?'

'Yeah?'

'On the night you found out about Mum's affair… you said *why did it have to be Adrian*… or something like that.'

'Did I?'

'Yeah. I guess I just wanted to know what you meant by that. If you don't mind talking about it with me.'

'No... we can talk about it. Adrian was your mother's friend at work. They confided in each other. Whenever she talked to me about her day she'd mention him. One day I'd asked her if I should be worried... I was trying to gauge whether or not this guy was a threat. She told me it wasn't like that.'

'And then it was,' stated Bree.

'Yeah. I guess something changed.'

Mallory honked the horn at seven o'clock and Bree went out to meet her. As they were backing away from the Walker Court Apartments Bree noticed that the grass beneath their windows was overgrown.

'Hey Mallory? Have these apartments changed at all?' asked Bree. 'Since you used to come here?'

'Nah... they were always run down.'

Mallory drove them back to her place, a three-bedroom house she was renting, to hang out before going to Pierre's party. It was two-storeys high and Bree could see a small balcony with a metal guardrail around it that faced the road. The house was so much more modern than the Walker Court Apartments.

'You live here?' Bree asked.

'Yeah,' replied Mallory.

'By yourself?'

'Yes! Geez.'

'It's huge! How can you afford this?'

Mallory brushed off the question, saying that she had a great deal going. Bree started fantasising about moving into one of the empty rooms in the future, a plan that brought a smile to her face.

'So, is your Dad like... strict?' Mallory asked as they moved through the house on an impromptu tour.

'I'm almost seventeen. He's just being parental.'

Mallory's place was sparsely decorated. The walls were all cream-coloured and bare. She explained that she couldn't hang anything because of her landlord.

'I'm not allowed to nail into the wall without their permission. It sucks.'

She led Bree to a bedroom at the back of the house. Mallory's room contained a single bed, a desk with a laptop and a beanbag, which was covered in clothes. Bree pretended not to notice the bong and lighter by the foot of the bed. Mallory opened the laptop and started playing some music for ambiance. Bree didn't recognise the obscure folk artist.

'Do you want a drink?' Mallory asked.

'If you're having one.'

'Have you had alcohol before?' quizzed Mallory.

'A couple of times.' Bree felt she needed to exaggerate a little, at the risk of being uncool.

'When?'

'Last year. With this guy...'

'Ooh! And the two of you got *wasted*?'

'Not wasted. I mean... I had a couple of drinks with him... a couple of times.'

'Was he your boyfriend or something?' asked Mallory like a shark sensing blood in the water.

'Or *something* seems about right.'

'Well we're going to have some drinks tonight, cool?'

'Sounds good,' replied Bree. She was pleased they were changing the subject. She wasn't ready to talk to anyone about Ryan yet, or their night in his car.

The girls had several glasses of white wine, which Bree confessed she'd never tried. Her friend's lack of rebellion delighted Mallory to no end.

'You're such a *good* girl,' she said with a laugh.

Bree didn't feel like a good girl. Tonight she felt like a liar. She knew that her father would be at work at the radio station until at least six in the morning, but he always stopped in to see her before he went to sleep. This meant she couldn't get *too* drunk. Bree needed the drinking and the party to stay a secret, which meant not leaving a trace of evidence. While she could disguise the smell of alcohol, any sickness or indication of intoxication would definitely give her away.

'Who else have you invited tonight?' asked Bree.

'I just said everyone's welcome. You never know who will turn up really.'

'You should probably stop inviting people to Pierre's party,' chuckled Bree.

'Why? We're doing him a favour.'

It was at that moment Bree's phone rang. While she had a dreadful feeling it would be her mother, it was Central Cinemas.

'Are you going to answer it?' asked Mallory.

'Should I?'

'No. They probably want you to work,' said Mallory, casually tucking her dark hair behind her ears.

Bree muted her phone.

'See? Just don't answer,' Mallory said as she downed a slug of wine.

'I could have told them I'd been drinking!' Bree said with a laugh.

'*YES*! That would have been so funny!'

Mallory laughed so hard that she snorted out loud. Hearing that made Bree laugh even harder. She wouldn't have *really* told her employer that she'd been drinking. At just sixteen years of age Bree was breaking the law with each sip she imbibed. In that moment she didn't care though. She was having a great time with her friend.

Mallory kept prolonging their departure by pouring more and more drinks.

'I really think we should go soon,' Bree protested.

'You've gotta be fashionably late to these things! I'll call a taxi soon, okay?'

Mallory wore green eye shadow. Her jacket had no sleeves and silver studs on the back that formed the shape of a skull. She was going for a punk rock look and it was one of her many op shop bargains. Bree had tried not to stare when she'd watched her friend get ready. She'd always wondered what having a sister would've been like. Bree had wished for someone to swap clothes with in her early teens.

'What I like about fashion is the way you can re-invent yourself,' said Mallory, posing in the mirror. 'If I don't like something about myself then I can dress up to accentuate something different. Plus… who wants to be like everyone else?'

'I think you look really pretty,' Bree replied, feeling a little self-conscious in her plain pants and jean jacket combination.

'You have to say that. You're my friend.'

The party was in progress when they arrived via taxi. The house itself was unremarkable but there was a helpful line of lanterns leading people out into the backyard. *Are You Gonna Be My Girl* by Jet was being blasted as they made their way down the driveway. They could hear some voices singing along enthusiastically. The yard was spacious but people had mostly gathered around a metal bin with a fire in it. A large percentage of the guests appeared to be male but there were a few girls floating around. Bree couldn't see anyone she knew but Mallory strode up and hugged a man with a well-groomed beard.

'This is Dex,' she said introducing him to Bree. 'He's in a band.'

'That's cool. What kind of music do you play?'

'All rock, all the time,' Dex said and rewarded himself with a long sip of beer.

Dex looked like a version of Mark Wahlberg from the film *Rock Star*. He was sporting a mane of black locks and his eyes looked too small for his face.

'The band is *really* good,' Mallory chimed in, 'they're putting out an album.'

'Great!' Bree replied eagerly. 'Like with a label?'

'Nah. We're doing it all ourselves.'

'Cool.'

'Do you like music?' asked Dex.

'Uh… yeah.'

Bree listened to Dex tell her about the album while Mallory fetched them some drinks. His band was called *The Raw Umbrellas* and their debut offering was to be titled *It's Hard to Look Cool in the Dark*.

Soon Victor appeared, wearing a slightly feminine purple floral shirt, cargo pants and a huge grin.

'So great to see you outside of work!' he said to Bree. 'Having fun?'

'So far so good.'

'Thanks for the invite.'

'Sure.'

Bree followed Mallory to the far side of the backyard where the wooden fence was broken in places. The music was at a much more tolerable volume now and she was pleased they would be able to chat.

'You checking out the guys? Anyone catch your eye?' asked Mallory as she sucked on a cigarette and flicked her black flame lighter nonchalantly.

'Not really.'

'What do you think of Dex?' she asked as she took a drag.

'I don't really like beards,' Bree said screwing up her face.

'Why not? They're soft.'

'They're not for me,' declared Bree.

'So, your ex didn't have a beard?'

Bree hesitated. Mallory was fishing again.

'I don't think he could grow one yet,' she replied, careful not to divulge too much.

Mallory offered her a cigarette, but Bree politely refused.

'George is supposedly coming,' said Mallory, changing the subject back to her own love life.

'Are you two getting serious?'

'Pretty serious. I'm not seeing anyone else at the moment.'

Mallory and Bree returned to find Victor holding his stomach. He'd been dared to do shots by one of the guys hanging around Dex.

'I did four shots,' he explained, 'but they were all different drinks.'

'You mixed drinks?' Mallory asked with a laugh. 'You're so crazy Victor!'

'Will you be alright?' asked Bree.

'I think so.'

'Did you see Victor drink those shots?'

'That was hilarious!'

'Hey... where's Pierre hiding anyway?'

'I think he's upstairs with some girl.'

Later, when she went inside to use the bathroom, Bree was surprised to find Lizzy sitting on a blue sofa in the living room. To her right was the man with the shaved head. Bree recognised him as Lizzy's movie date. The two looked cosy. Lizzy's hand was resting comfortably on his thigh, subtle and possessive.

'Oh, hey Bree. I didn't know you'd be here,' said Lizzy when the two locked eyes.

'Yeah... Mallory invited me. Victor's here too, but he's not feeling great...'

'Mallory's here?' Lizzy's hand jumped from the man's leg and she looked outside. 'What the hell George? I thought you said she wouldn't be here,' said Lizzy, shoving her date.

That's George? Mallory's George? Bree knew she had to report back to her friend. She had a sudden knot in her stomach.

Mallory was throwing sticks into the fire when Bree approached her and asked what George looked like. She needed to be sure.

'Tall, shaved head. Nice eyes, cute *butt*. Why?'

'I think he's here. Inside with Lizzy.'

Mallory dropped the remainder of the sticks into the metal bin all at once.

'Interesting,' she said calmly.

Mallory walked to the window and folded her arms. She stood, with Bree by her side, watching as George and Lizzy argued openly. Bree felt nervous that there was an altercation brewing. She'd avoided fights her whole life and hoped that this wouldn't be the first. Mallory wasn't giving anything away. In stark contrast, the scene inside was boiling over. Lizzy shook her head, her hoop earrings dancing wildly. She gave George another shove, which caused his drink to spill onto the leg of his pants. There were murmurs from the other partygoers.

'Are you going to go in there?' Bree asked.

'No. He's got to come to me,' announced Mallory in a measured tone.

Mallory lit another cigarette and meandered back to the fence. Bree studied the scene in the house before inadvertently locking eyes with Dex. She gave a polite smile and looked away. Bree could sense Dex in her periphery trying to get her attention. She decided to follow the grass back to the fence where more of her Central Cinema colleagues had assembled.

'This is Nathan,' said Victor, introducing a Rupert Grint type to Bree.

'Hi... it's...'

That was all he managed to say before throwing up all over the ground.

'Great first impression!' laughed Victor as he gave Nathan another slap on the back. Bree was mortified by the experience but held her composure. Nathan had only just avoided vomiting on his shiny silver shirt.

'Are you alright?' asked Bree.

To her surprise Nathan straightened up and grinned.

'That's better,' he said, wiping his freckled forearm across his mouth. Victor and Nathan started chatting, which allowed Bree to sidle over to Mallory. She was isolated, away to the side, oblivious to the fresh bile. Bree felt badly about the love triangle between Lizzy, George and Mallory. She worried that she should have somehow known and warned Mallory earlier.

'I didn't realise what George looked like,' Bree began, 'and he came in to see a movie with Lizzy. I didn't... I didn't recognise him... otherwise I would have said something.'

Mallory threw her lighter into the air and caught it.

'It's not your fault. And I'm not worried about *Lizzy*.'

Mallory emphasised the word 'Lizzy' as if it was a chore to say the name out loud.

A short time later George joined them outside. Lizzy was fuming and stood alone, blocking the doorway to the house. George's eyes found Mallory and he made a beeline for her. He was solid with muscular arms. Bree hadn't seen them last time because they were hidden underneath a jacket. In the moonlight she could see George's appeal, and understood why two women were fighting over him.

'Hey arse-face,' Mallory said and cocked her head back.

'Hey yourself,' George replied and threw his arms around her.

They kissed. When it was over they acted as though nothing had even happened. Bree wondered if a similar reconciliation was possible with her own parents. *Her mother had strayed. Maybe her father would forgive her in time.* It felt impossible while Adrian was in the picture.

'This is Bree,' Mallory said introducing her to George. 'You two haven't officially met.'

They exchanged a nod. Bree felt a little awkward having seen George and Lizzy together at the movies but was able to move past it. She'd made the conscious choice to stop drinking before she lost control or embarrassed herself. Nobody had noticed that she was nursing the same beer during every encounter and random conversation. Nathan threw up again before calling his brother to come and pick him up.

Bree split a taxi home with Mallory and George. She made small talk with the elderly driver from the passenger seat, while the lovebirds let their bodies do the talking in the back. The driver was polite enough to ignore them.

As Bree was going to sleep that night her face hurt from smiling. It was a feeling she hadn't experienced in a long time. It also occurred to her that she was never introduced to the host Pierre, and that perhaps she'd been a pretty selfish party guest.

<h1 style="text-align:center"><u>CHAPTER EIGHT</u></h1>

Central Cinemas Location Manager Maxine White had phoned Bree before her shift, asking her to come in early for a meeting. Maxine's voice had been so confident and powerful on the phone that it made Bree wary. She called Mallory for advice.

'Maxine's worked at a bunch of places in the mall before Central Cinemas. She won't be here much longer,' explained Mallory. 'She wants a position at the Sydney Head Office, which everyone reckons will be vacant in the New Year. The rest of the management team have all been speculating about which one of them would become Location Manager if she does go.'

'Who do you think it would be?' asked Bree.

'Probably Paul. He's such a suck up. I can't see Rita or Carl rising to the occasion.'

Talking with Mallory didn't help to calm her down. She really had no idea why Maxine would want to speak to her.

A ball of nerves, Bree arrived to the meeting early and knocked on the office door, which was ajar. The Location Manager was sitting at her desk looking formidable.

'Come on in Bree,' Maxine said with a professional smile.

'Hello.'

'I'm Maxine White.'

'It's nice to finally meet you,' said Bree.

Maxine indicated towards a chair and Bree sat down. She assessed that her boss most closely resembled the actress Glen Close, if she was playing the head of a finishing school. Maxine looked very put together.

'I'm sorry we haven't really spoken. I was away at a corporate retreat... it was very rewarding. Since I've been back I guess we've just been ships in the night.'

'Ships in the night... my Dad always says that,' said Bree.

'Does he? Isn't that funny?'

Bree smiled. Maxine wore a dark pink suit jacket with black pants. Around her neck sat a string of pearls that she touched frequently during their conversation. It seemed to be a kind of nervous tic.

'Are you enjoying working here?' asked Maxine.

'Yes, very much.'

'That's great. And everyone is treating you well?'

'Yes thank you.'

'And remind me where you were working before this?'

'At Toys R Us on level 3.'

'Ah yes, I remember that from your file. Bree Fielding...'

Without warning Maxine opened her desk drawer and took out a manila folder. From inside she withdrew Bree's resume and held it exactly halfway between her face and the desk. She went through each item on the resume out loud which made Bree feel as though she was being interviewed all over again. She started to perspire.

'One of the reasons I wanted to meet you was to touch base and see how you're doing. If there was anything I could help with?'

'No. I think I'm okay at the moment.'

'Well, just know that my door is always open to you.'

'Thank you.'

There was a sternness to Maxine. She smiled with her mouth but her intense eyes seemed to look right through Bree.

'You started working with Liam, is that correct?'

'Yes, we started on the same day.'

'I hope he's been settling in as well?'

It was posed as a question that Bree had to answer. She wondered if Maxine knew her son had asked her out on that first day. *Has Liam been ruffling feathers?* she wondered.

'I think he's doing fine.'

'Good.' Maxine seemed satisfied with the answer. She picked up a yellow envelope from the desk and continued. 'There was another reason I wanted to bring you in today Bree.'

'Oh?' Her heartbeat quickened.

'Are you familiar with the mystery shopper program?'

'I haven't been told...' Bree started to respond but trailed off.

'So, there is a program, the mystery shopper program, and it runs in most of the businesses here in the mall. An independent company employs everyday Australians and asks them to check up on the staff. Those results are sent to head office.'

Bree felt her stomach tighten as Maxine continued.

'I was sent their latest report this morning.'

'Okay...'

'They named you personally,' Maxine said as she reclined into her high-back office chair and clutched her pearl necklace. Bree quietly waited as her boss paused dramatically, letting the moment grow longer than necessary.

'They were really impressed with you, and that really impresses me. It's a great start Bree. Keep it up and you'll be a staff trainer before you know it.'

'Thank you very much.'

Bree left the office and almost collided with Paul, who was distracted.

'Sorry Bree.'

Paul was carrying a stack of papers, which he set down by the phone.

'Is everything alright?' Bree asked.

'Its fine… I suppose. I have to hire two new staff is all… so I'm ringing around.'

'If there are extra shifts I don't mind picking up one or two.'

Bree explained that since school had finished she was trying to work as many hours as possible before Christmas. She wanted to buy her father a set of golf clubs. He had sold his old ones a few years before and Bree thought it would be a good idea for him to take up the hobby again.

'I love golf, but I never have time to play. I usually just go to the driving range these days. I'll let you know about the shifts, okay?' said Paul with an appreciative nod.

Bree wondered why they needed to hire two more staff. She'd been afraid to ask Paul within earshot of Maxine after she'd been so complimentary. When Bree started her shift on Floor she decided to see if Shannon knew anything about it.

'Is it common to take on extra help over Christmas?' Bree asked Shannon as she rounded the Candy Bar toward Floor. She knew from her experience at Toys R Us that seasonal staff were a necessity sometimes.

'Nah… we just hire people as people leave,' she replied. 'Why?'

'Paul was looking at resumes.'

'Oh, you haven't heard? Lizzy quit. They have to replace her,' said Shannon, who seemed indifferent to the news. Bree was quite puzzled.

'She did? Why?'

'I'm not totally sure. I've been hearing rumours... something that happened at a party?'

Bree wondered if Mallory might know more. She spent the first session cleaning cinemas with Warren. He quietly ventured from session to session, checking everything was being projected correctly.

'Slides are fine in Cinema Nine.'

Bree smiled at Warren's unintentional rhyme.

'Thank you.'

Bree recognised the voice on the two-way. Matt was working tonight. She made a mental note to say hello later on.

'Did Lizzy quit? For real?'

'Yeah... good riddance.'

'Did you hear that Liam and Andy went to the Casino after work?'

'Andy wants to be a manager I reckon. Maybe Liam can put in a good word with his Mum...'

During her meal break Bree found she'd missed a call from her mother. The latest trend for Carol seemed to be consuming some wine and trying to make contact. Bree had listened to all of her messages to start with, but it had become too painful. They were always full of apologetic tears and hope. Bree had replied only once to tell her mother that she still wasn't ready to talk. That hadn't stopped Carol from persisting. Ignoring the latest voicemail Bree phoned Mallory from the red sofa in the staff room.

'How's it going?'

'Mallory, did you know that Lizzy quit?'

'Ha! Did she?' chuckled Mallory.

'Do you know why?'

Bree stared at a cork noticeboard that was leaning against the wall. Mallory seemed to take a long time to answer the question.

'Let me call you back. I'll see what I can find out,' replied Mallory.

'Ok. I'm on my break so I've got to go.'

'Alright. Later.'

Bree hung up the phone and less than a minute later Matt came into the staff room, drill in hand.

'Oh hey!' he said cheerfully.

'Hey Matt. I heard you on the two-way before.'

'Are you on your break?' he asked.

'Yeah.'

'That's perfect.'

'It is?'

'Yeah, because I need someone to hold that steady while I drill it in.' He indicated towards the corkboard. Bree blushed and helped Matt attach the noticeboard to the wall. It was a tiny bit crooked but neither of them cared enough to redrill.

'How's your shift going?' asked Bree.

'It's an average night,' he answered.

Bree told him she had no idea what an average night in Projection looked like, having only glimpsed the room during that first tour.

'How long till you have to go back?' he asked.

'Twenty minutes or so.'

'Come up and see then. I have to go and put the drill back anyway.'

'I dunno…'

'C'mon. It's kind of great up there.'

Bree was hesitant but agreed. They wandered up the steep incline to the outer Projection room door. They pushed through and Bree waited patiently as Matt punched in the security code. He made no attempt to obscure it from Bree's vision even though she was too polite to peek. Matt opened and held the large door for her. The steady hum of the machinery and the ticking of film sprockets flying through each projector's gate seemed so foreign to Bree. The last time she was up here the cinema hadn't opened yet and things weren't so *in motion*. It was a little overwhelming to Bree.

'It's alright. Just don't touch anything,' said Matt with a reassuring look.

'It's so noisy!' she shouted.

'You get used to it.'

They walked past the glass portholes that peered into each cinema. Bree was fascinated to be eye-level with the screen. Everything was different from above. They reached the middle of the room where a workbench filled one wall.

Attached to either end of the desk were small vertical platters where film could be wound from one side to the other and checked manually. Matt opened a cupboard at the base of the bench and put the drill away next to a collection of what must have been spare projector parts. On the wall was a poster for *The Matrix*. Underneath someone had written the words:

No one can be told what Projection is.

You have to see it for yourself.

'That's cool,' she said pointing to the image of Neo.

'You like that? All of the posters get stored here in Projection for security reasons and sometimes we get bored and put them up on the walls.'

'Security reasons? Why would anyone steal a poster?'

'I don't know. I guess they have a certain value to collectors,' he replied.

Matt pointed out an area near the door where replacement light bulbs rested next to a large supply of film paraphernalia. He explained that the posters arrived in cardboard tubes and were unfurled and placed in a large set of drawers.

'Custom made for movie posters. We keep them here until they're displayed. Hey… come and check this out.'

Matt led Bree deeper down the tunnel. On the wall between the projectors for Cinema Six and Cinema Seven there was a solid stretch of brick covered from top to bottom in promotional flyers. The small movie advertisements went back years and had been arranged in an almost obsessively neat pattern.

'That's my flyer wall.'

'Oh that's *your* flyer wall?' said Bree with a cheeky smile.

'Well… I started it,' Matt said proudly. 'Some of the other projectionists have added things here and there but it's my baby.'

'Interesting.'

'Who is your favourite actor?' he asked.

'Heath Ledger,' replied Bree.

Matt pointed out a flyer for *A Knight's Tale* and she smiled at the inclusion.

As they travelled back to the workbench Bree noticed a small wooden shelf and a mini-fridge tucked away near the sound system for the complex. On top of the shelf was a collection of cereal boxes. She held up one of the many varieties and gestured towards it.

'Did you start this too?'

'I sure did! Don't you think it's a good idea?' Matt seemed pleased with himself.

'I mean… I *guess* so. Don't most people eat their breakfast at home though?'

'Breakfast is a good idea at any time of the day.'

He offered her a bowl but Bree declined saying she would take a raincheck. She liked hanging out in the Projection room but she was carefully checking her watch, knowing that soon she would have to go back to Floor and the reality of work. Matt seemed in his element and his confidence and technical knowledge were attractive to Bree. She asked about his outfit, which consisted of a black polo shirt, black pants and black shoes. He explained that the uniform was designed to make him invisible in the dark of Projection, but people would often spot him through the portholes, especially in the stadium seating of Cinemas Five and Six, which were up a lot higher. As they chatted Bree shared her plans to study, eliciting an approving response from Matt.

'That's awesome!'

'What's your passion outside of this place?' asked Bree inquisitively, remembering what Mallory had implied about the staff at Central Cinemas. She wondered if it was also true of the projectionists.

'My passion? Oh… I don't know…'

Bree sensed some embarrassment emanating from Matt.

'You can tell me. I won't judge.'

'Alright, alright. I like to do… stand-up comedy.'

'Really?'

'Yes.'

'And... are you *good* at stand-up comedy?' While Matt seemed like a nice guy it occurred to Bree that she'd never heard him say anything particularly funny.

'Yeah, I do alright. I'm still working on my material but I'm putting together a show.'

'When it's ready I'd love to see it.'

'I'll be sure to invite you.' Matt seemed pleased with the exchange.

He let Bree watch some of *In the Cut*, which had been classified R. It was a rush for her even though she didn't see anything graphic before her break ended. The night session was beginning and she would be needed back on Floor.

While Bree was cleaning later that night with Warren, she spotted Matt through the porthole and gave him a small wave. He smiled and saluted. She liked flirting with Matt. Warren was oblivious as he scooped up a pile of popcorn that had been poured out mere inches from the bin.

At the end of Bree's shift there was a message on her phone from Mallory asking her to call.

'What's up?' asked Bree, suddenly tentative about the gossip she was about to receive.

'You're not going to believe what I heard,' said Mallory in an excited voice.

'What?'

'Apparently after we left the party Lizzy got *really* drunk. I spoke to my friend Dex and he said she was off her *face*.'

'Oh my God.' Concerned, Bree sat down on the staff room sofa and tucked her legs up underneath her.

'She was hitting on one of Dex's band mates, but he wasn't into it. I think she was probably hitting on a few people.'

'What happened? Why did she quit?' asked Bree.

'One of the guys said Lizzy and Victor hooked up in the toilet!'

Bree said nothing. She was shocked. Mallory was laughing on the other end of the phone. Finally, Bree found her voice. 'How... what the *hell...*'

Hearing Bree say 'hell' made Mallory laugh even harder.

'So, she quit! If it's true, which I think it is, she must have been too embarrassed to come back. Isn't that *hilarious*?' The joy in Mallory's voice indicated the high degree of elation she was experiencing. Bree, on the other hand, was struggling to comprehend Victor's involvement.

'That's crazy. Victor told me his parents were trying to find him a wife! He's supposed to be getting married!'

'He was drinking a lot too,' said Mallory. 'Things happen. I mean... he's not married yet! Maybe he's trying to get it while he can.'

'I can't believe it.'

Victor seemed so sweet. Bree wondered if she had been wrong about him, just as she had been with her mother. Maybe she was an awful judge of character.

'My sweet innocent Bree... it was an eventful night.'

'I guess you don't have to worry about George and Lizzy anymore at least.'

'I don't sweat the Lizzys of the world,' she replied.

Bree heard a male voice in the background talking to Mallory.

'Where are you?' asked Bree.

'I'm out… with Dex,' she replied, as if it was no big deal. The dismissive way that Mallory spoke forced Bree to accept that nothing untoward was going on. She was seeing George exclusively, and the silver lining was that the love triangle was over, which they could both agree was good news.

The two friends said goodnight. Bree hung up and stared at the vacant cork noticeboard in disbelief. How quickly things had changed.

CHAPTER NINE

'They promoted HIM?'

'Yeah… which means I missed out… again!'

'But he's always calling in sick.'

'This place is a freakin' joke.'

Almost two weeks later another bombshell of gossip was dropped at Central Cinemas. The reason that Paul had to hire *two* new employees was revealed in a memo that was placed in every staff member's pigeonhole. Liam White had been promoted to the role of projectionist and would be training and working at the Southern Cinemas location on the other side of town. Everyone was annoyed at the clear favouritism of the choice and the lack of opportunity. Nathan, who Bree learned was a staff trainer who aspired to work in Projection, was particularly annoyed.

'It *sucks*,' he declared to anyone that would listen.

Bree couldn't complain, having only been there a short time. It seemed inconsequential to her, as she didn't care who worked in the Projection room so long as the sessions ran on time. She also felt that relocating Liam would be a good thing overall. The news of his promotion had encouraged an outpouring of stories. People didn't like Liam and were generally happy he was leaving.

'I can't believe he's getting promoted,' declared Shannon when she read the notice.

Even Warren, who was always so neutral, was seen shaking his head at the news.

Bree was in a great mood because after hassling Paul repeatedly, tonight was her first shift in the Box Office. She would be receiving training from Mallory, despite the fact that she wasn't technically a staff trainer.

'I hate Liam. He has such a punchable face,' Mallory said after the first burst of patrons had cleared out of sight.

Bree didn't want to create conflict and did her best to mellow out her friend. 'But there's no point complaining to the Location Manager about her *son*, is there? Did you really want to be a projectionist anyway?' asked Bree.

'I don't know... I like being up there with George...' Mallory smirked.

'Gross! I don't need to hear about the places you spend time with George.'

'It's pretty dark up there Bree! And almost no one ever interrupts. If you and Matt ever get together...'

'Matt? What makes you think I like *Matt*?' Bree said defensively.

Mallory's smile widened. 'I wasn't sure a minute ago but based on *that* reaction I think I might be right!'

Bree's cheeks flushed. She'd given away her feelings without meaning to. She tried to formulate a response but before Bree could say another word the phone rang.

'Katie speaking,' said Mallory.

Katie? Why is she using a fake name? Bree waited in a confused state until the phone call ended. It was yet another senior citizen that wanted to check session times with a real person as opposed to calling the automated service. After the call Mallory informed Bree that she always answered the phone in Box Office using an alias.

'That way if a customer is calling up to complain about *Mallory* they won't think they are talking to Mallory... even though they are. Then I don't pass on any complaints about myself and keep the managers off my back.'

'Do many people complain about you?'

'A few. It's mostly about my attitude though and I'm not about to change who I am.'

Bree liked learning from Mallory and found her training style, while unorthodox, was effective. Although she kept insisting that she had no interest in training staff permanently.

'It's a few extra dollars an hour,' offered Bree 'Maybe that would come in handy.'

'It's not about the money. Do you know what they did at the last Staff Trainer's meeting? Paul handed out juggling balls and they all tried *juggling*.'

'Why?'

'It was supposed to represent the challenge of juggling duties on shift... or some shit like that.'

'Ugh... that sounds kind of dumb,' Bree said, screwing up her face.

'It does sound dumb, doesn't it? They do stupid stuff like that all the time. I already know how to juggle by the way. And everything I know about being a trainer here makes me *not* want to do it.'

Mallory answered the phone again. 'Angela speaking.'

Bree served customers consistently during the night and found it to be much easier than Candy Bar. There was nothing to suggestive sell or upsell to the customers but there were a series of vouchers and codes to learn. The only time Bree became flustered was when her printer ran out of paper and she couldn't change it herself. Mallory made some customers wait while she showed Bree how to do it. The rest of the night flowed on without incident.

'Box Office is the place to be,' stated Mallory.

From her comfortable chair Bree had to agree.

Paul had only needed to pop his head in a couple of times to give them change or see how long the line of customers was. He called them his 'Box Office Girls' and made a loose promise to pair them up again soon. Bree loved the idea. Mallory was right; Box Office was a good shift to have, and it was made even better with a friend for company.

Mallory showed Bree a cardboard box that was kept in the corner of the room.

'This is the complaints box,' Mallory said as she tipped it towards Bree. 'Whenever someone complains you are supposed to print out a response letter... the template is saved on the computer... and answer their complaint on behalf of management. So, let me show you one.'

Mallory grabbed a complaint from a woman named Gemma that stated her session of the film *S.W.A.T* was out of focus on the right side of the screen.

'So, how do we know if it actually *was* out of focus?' asked Bree.

'We don't. We get complaints like this every other day. If we spent time chasing up what actually happened we wouldn't get anything done. It probably was though.'

'Well... why didn't the projectionist fix it?' asked Bree.

'Who knows?'

Bree wondered whether the projectionist on duty might have been George. If Mallory had been in the Projection room distracting him from his job that might explain why the film wasn't screened correctly.

'Sometimes Central Cinemas is to blame, sometimes it's the complaints that are wrong. But since we can't spend time checking we just have to put out one fire at a time.'

'And we reply to the complaints?' asked Bree.

'You got it.'

Mallory showed her how to fill in the template on the computer and together they apologetically answered Gemma's letter about the session. Mallory printed their reply out and tossed it inside an unsealed envelope. She then placed it into the cardboard box.

'Now this gets taken from here to a tray in the office. Paul or Rita will put a comp ticket in there and mail it off. They don't even look at the complaints anymore.'

The phone started ringing as they were cleaning up and Mallory instructed Bree to answer it.

'Use a fake name and ask what they want. If you don't know what to do just put them on to me,' she said with encouragement.

'Hello… *Zara* speaking, how may I help you?' Bree said as confidently as she could. She didn't mind taking on the role of someone else.

'Hi Zara… this is Lizzy. I guess you're new? So, I used to work there and I need to speak to a manager about my last payslip. It's all wrong.'

Bree became immediately flustered and tried to disguise her voice.

'Sure thing. I'll put you through.'

Bree put Lizzy on hold, which was the one thing she knew how to do. Mallory showed her how to transfer a call to the office and Bree complied, thankful when the blinking red light had vanished.

'Who was that?' asked Mallory.

'Lizzy.'

'Whoa, really? What did she want?'

Bree told her.

'Oh man... I should have answered the phone! I would have asked her what happened at the party!'

'I'm glad you didn't then. She must be so embarrassed.'

'Have you seen Victor?' asked Mallory as she tidied up her desk.

'No.'

'He's walking around like a stud. This Lizzy thing has been good for his reputation.'

'Shannon's ex-boyfriend was here last night.'

'Cameron? Was that his name?'

'Yeah. He was here with another girl. I think she works at McDonalds.'

'I still can't believe the way he and Shannon broke up. Crazy...'

As the mall started to close the same Donut King employee wandered into the foyer of Central Cinemas with leftovers from the day. He looked at the staff on Candy Bar but then headed for Bree when he spotted her sitting in the Box Office.

'Hi again. Did you want some of these? We always have too many,' he said with a smile.

'Oh, thank you,' she replied with a nod. 'My Dad was happy when I brought them home last time.' Not only had her father enjoyed the donuts, he'd taken them to work with him that night.

'*Another* perk? Unbelievable!' he'd exclaimed.

Bree wandered around to the foyer to collect the donuts because they wouldn't fit through the small glass gap in the bottom of the Box Office window. It had only been designed to slide money and tickets back and forth.

She returned to Mallory who once again refused the free treats.

'I think maybe donut boy has a crush on you.'

'He's just being nice. He probably handed out donuts to lots of stores.'

'He probably made extra ones because he saw you working!' joked Mallory. 'It's a shame really.'

'Why is it a shame?'

'Because he doesn't have a chance with you. You're too into Matt!'

Bree threw her head back feigning frustration. 'I thought we were past this!'

'No,' said Mallory standing up, 'and I'm pretty sure you've got a chance too.'

'Do you think?'

'He'd be an idiot not to want you Bree.'

Bree was filled with butterflies. She felt vulnerable advertising her feelings, but was ultimately happy she could finally talk to someone else about her developing crush on Matt. She might have confided in her mother, if the situation were different, and she was still too nervous to speak to her father about boys.

That Sunday night her father called in sick and parked himself on the couch. Bree made him tomato soup and poured it into an ocean blue mug that was at the back of the cupboard. She'd recognised it straight away as the mug her mother had always used for her morning cup of tea. When she brought it out to her father, he also acknowledged its significance.

'This was your mother's cup,' he said with a sigh.

'Yeah. Sorry… I couldn't find any soup mugs.'

'She must have left it, huh?'

'Uhuh.'

Bree imagined what her mother was doing at that moment. Maybe she now favoured a red mug, one that Adrian had purchased for her. Bree didn't know what Adrian looked like but she pictured a generic blonde man with a full head of hair, the opposite of her father, cradling her mother on a sofa. Maybe she was watching the same thing on TV right now. Carol had stopped calling the apartment's landline altogether. Bree assumed her parents were not speaking to each other at all anymore. She was feeling positive about it, knowing that a clean break was the best thing for everyone.

'It was supposed to be *in sickness and in health*, you know?' said Henry in a frustrated tone.

'I know Dad.'

'Sorry… I'm just…'

'It's okay. I'm mad at her too. But we'll be alright.'

'Yeah… and I guess we get to keep this soup mug.'

Bree smiled, knowing that her father was on the mend.

CHAPTER TEN

In early December 2003 Maxine went away and everyone at Central Cinemas seemed to relax and appreciate her absence. The Canberra weather was delightful, and the cinema was regularly filled with patrons. As acting Location Manager Paul was in a great mood and went for long lunches in the food court, promising he was on his two-way and could be reached if they needed anything. The staff thought he might have been interested in one of the women at the coffee shop nearby, which he seemed to frequent on a daily basis.

While for Bree driving lessons and domestic adjustment continued outside of Central Cinemas, she felt the most alive when she was there. She continued to volunteer for extra hours and sometimes was rewarded with a cruisy Box Office shift. After their day shifts finished Mallory and Bree would often keep hanging out. They would wander into movies, eat at the food court or chat at Mallory's place. Her father's security shifts had become more erratic, and Bree was happy to have someone to spend time with while he slept in and let his body adjust. He was always in a better mood when the house was quiet and he could get a solid seven or eight hours.

One afternoon when Bree was cashing out her Candy Bar till she was interrupted by Mallory, returning from one of her regular cigarette breaks.

'Do you want to hang out in Projection with me and George?' she asked.

'That depends. Will you keep your pants on?'

'Oh alright... for *you* I will,' joked Mallory.

After she balanced her till Bree met Mallory in the change room.

'I don't want to wear that gross orange shirt any longer than is absolutely necessary,' Mallory said firmly and tossed it into her bag.

'I'm sure George won't complain when he sees you in *that*.'

Bree was referring to the short red plaid skirt that Mallory had changed into. She'd also added knee high socks to complete a kind of casual schoolgirl look, although she was yet to select a top.

'Oh this? Yeah... he might notice,' said Mallory, standing casually in her black bra.

'And are you planning on adding any more layers? Or... no?' joked Bree.

Mallory stuck her rude finger up while simultaneously sticking out her tongue. Bree laughed at her friend's expression. She took her own orange shirt off and smelt it.

'Might have to take this to the dry cleaners,' said Bree.

Mallory stepped in front of the mirror. While scanning her reflection she gave her stomach a pat.

'I'll lend you one if you want. I have some spares at home.'

'Why does that not surprise me?'

There was a noise outside the change room door. Mallory grabbed her singlet but didn't put it on. Before Bree had a chance to dress, Mallory did a short shimmy past her and pushed the door wide open. Sitting on the sofa reading a book was Warren, who was about to start his shift. When he looked up and saw the girls in bras, Bree barely covering herself up, he turned redder than a tomato. Bree faced away and slipped on a t-shirt as swiftly as she could. Warren took off his glasses and started to clean them nervously.

'Warren you perve,' said Mallory quickly. 'Are you cleaning those so you can get a better look?'

'No... I wasn't... I didn't see anything,' he shot back, putting on and then adjusting his glasses awkwardly.

Mallory turned away and pulled on her singlet. Then, just as Warren was becoming comfortable, she lifted her top up again and flashed her bra at him. Clearly embarrassed, and out of his depth, Warren held his book up in front of his face.

'Did you like that?' asked Mallory, raising an eyebrow.

'No... I mean... *yeah*... but,' he stammered, resting the book in his lap.

'It's alright. I'll take it as a compliment.'

Mallory put her index finger seductively into her open mouth. Warren didn't know where to look. He was rescued by a fully dressed Bree, who swung in from the change room and ushered Mallory away towards Projection.

'Leave him alone Mallory,' said Bree.

'He loved it,' she boasted.

George had wedged the Projection room door open for them with a cardboard box. When they entered the room he was busy lacing the projectors so the girls casually explored the tunnel alone. They turned up the volume on a small speaker at each projector and monitored random scenes from *Cabin Fever* and *Scary Movie 3*. They went through a pile of new posters, unrolling them one by one from their cardboard tubes. Mallory determined that the vinyl material ones would be worth the most money.

'The paper ones would just rip over time.'

As they passed the cereal shelf that Matt had constructed Bree smiled, and was caught in the act.

'What are you grinning at?' quizzed Mallory.

'Nothing.'

There was a lot of machinery in Projection that George told them sternly not to touch. He wasn't as easy-going as Matt.

'We'll be good,' promised Mallory, and she gave George a lingering kiss.

Soon the girls had walked the length of the room and found themselves at an unmarked door at the other end.

'Where does this go?' asked Bree.

'Let's find out.' Mallory had that wicked look in her eyes, and it was accentuated by the red eye shadow that she'd applied to compliment her skirt. She opened the door and revealed a concrete staircase that went down one flight.

'Come on,' she said, motioning to Bree.

'I don't want to get in trouble.'

'We'll be fine!'

Mallory stuck a rogue brick against the door to hold it open and started down the stairs. Bree followed carefully into the unknown.

At the bottom of the staircase there were two taupe coloured doors that faced each other. Bree took the lead and tested the closest door.

'It's locked.'

'Oh well... that's that,' laughed Mallory.

'Yeah... well, we're not going to break it open,' reasoned Bree.

'I'll try the other one then.'

Mallory pressed her shoulder against the second door, the handle turning freely, and the two were blinded by sunlight. They could see a walkway that led around the far side of the mall to a car park.

'It's just a fire exit, I guess. But where does that locked door lead?' asked Mallory, indicating towards the first door that Bree had failed to access.

'No clue.'

They concluded that the mysterious door could only lead back towards Central Cinemas, although they were unsure how it connected with the complex. They tried to mentally map out their location.

'We're on the same level as the cinemas now... underneath the Projection room,' stated Bree.

'But there is nowhere for this door to lead to... because where we're standing right now if you walked through this doorway you would be *inside* Cinema Five or Six,' replied Mallory.

'Maybe there's a secret room *between* the two cinemas?' noted Bree.

'Okay... but for what purpose? It can't be very big because those cinemas have the stadium seating in them. What are they hiding in a tiny room like that?'

Neither of them had a suitable answer. When they returned to the Projection room they asked George.

'I have no idea what you two are talking about,' he said, staring blankly ahead.

Mallory explained the location of the door.

'I never go out that way. Nobody does. I didn't even know there *was* a fire exit down there, let alone a mystery door,' said George as he threaded some film through rollers on a wall mounted bracket.

Mallory kissed him goodbye as Bree waited patiently by the main Projection entrance. As she held the door ajar she looked up at the concrete staircase that she'd spotted on her very first day at Central. It beckoned to Bree to explore it. Soon Mallory wandered back over to her.

'While we're up here... where do you think that goes?' asked Bree. She pointed up the elusive stairs and Mallory's eyes lit up.

'Oooh. Let's find out!'

After the disappointment of the locked door, they both retained hope that this second mystery zone would be worth exploring. Mallory took her friend's hand and they ascended the stairs promptly. That was a quality she loved about her new friend. Whereas Bree might have stopped and hesitated in the face of this obstacle, Mallory was a woman of decisive action. Bree needed that push sometimes.

At the top of the flight of stairs there was a single unlocked door that led into an air conditioning room. The door was raised off the ground and when it was opened they had to step over a concrete slab at the base. They were standing one floor above the Projection room, but this area wasn't nearly as wide or deep. At first Bree was disappointed that it wasn't something immediately better, but ultimately both girls were enjoying the rush of being somewhere that they weren't allowed to be. It helped that Maxine was away, and neither felt like they were actually going to get caught. Oversized industrial air conditioning units dominated the room. They were making a loud churning noise as they provided cool air to the ten cinemas below. The lack of space meant the girls had to snake their way around them. Bree and Mallory stepped over some cables and around corners as they explored. There were control panels occupying some walls but almost every other surface was caked in dust and cobwebs.

'Are you willing to go through one more door?' asked Mallory dramatically.

She was standing just ahead of Bree at an exit marked:

DANGER: RESTRICTED AREA.

It seemed too good to refuse. Mallory tried it and found it too was unlocked.

'Well, we've come this far.' Bree said with a tentative smile.

On the other side Mallory and Bree found themselves on an open platform that accessed the roof of the entire mall. The cinema complex was three storeys up, the Projection room was on the fourth floor and now, adjacent to the air conditioning room the girls had a view of the

Canberra skyline five storeys high. It was remarkable, captivating and terrifying all at once.

'Holy crap!' Mallory tested the door handle on the outer side. It didn't budge. 'It's only unlocked from the inside. We'd better prop this open. Unless you want to stay out here?'

'No thanks!' replied Bree. She'd seen some more loose bricks in the air conditioning room and grabbed a few. Bree wedged an excessive amount into the doorway, ensuring they would be able to escape once their rebellious exploration was over. Her phone interrupted, indicating a text message.

Hi honey. Do you think we could talk some time? I'd really like to. Please call me back. Mum.

Bree put her phone out of sight in her pocket. As they walked out towards the edge of the platform, she was hit by a sudden and unshakable sense that this was all wrong. It was windy and her hair whipped up into her face, adding to the drama of the scene. Bree contained it using a tie from her wrist. Mallory's hair was seemingly too short to bother her. Either that or she was transfixed by the view.

'I don't think we should be out here!' Bree shouted to Mallory, who had already fearlessly walked straight over to the edge. It wasn't fenced off, but there was a discouraging concrete ledge that spanned the length of the platform. With no other protection Bree knew that there was a very genuine danger of falling five stories if they weren't careful.

Mallory looked over the ledge to the ground below. There were various types of roofing between them and the lower levels. It would be a very painful fall, featuring many uneven and damaging surfaces. Mallory spat into the distance and they watched her saliva sail through the air and splat against the metal two floors down. They could only just see the obscured view of the car park and dozens of distant people navigating trolleys back to their cars. The wind seemed to intensify.

'We should head back in,' suggested Bree, edging herself in the direction of the door.

Ignoring her, Mallory swung her legs over and straddled the concrete ledge.

'What are you doing?' shrieked Bree.

'It's *fine*! Come over here.'

Bree cautiously stepped over to Mallory. She paused next to her friend and they both stared out into the distance. Bree didn't want to look down.

'We shouldn't be up here. This is a restricted area.'

'We're here now,' said Mallory with indifference. 'Now hold my hands.'

'Why?'

'Just do it. Don't be such a wuss.'

Mallory held out both hands and her friend took them. She looked back over her shoulder towards the cars below and then into Bree's eyes.

'Mallory? What are you doing?'

'Do you have me?' she asked.

Without waiting for Bree to answer Mallory leaned back until her arms were stretched straight out in front of her. She was light and Bree was able to support her until she threw her head backwards maniacally and kicked her legs out in front of her. Bree struggled as Mallory's body went slack.

'Stop it!' Bree squealed as she tried to pull her friend away from the edge. The shocking jolt that came when Mallory had first leaned back was affecting the way they now held hands. Bree found herself wishing she had a better grip.

'Mallory...'

The world muted around her as Bree concentrated. She braced her feet against the ledge to ensure she didn't falter under the strain of her friend's weight. After a minute or so of silence the wind picked up again and Bree descended into a panic. This had to end.

'Come on Mallory! You're going to fall!' Bree had started to shake slightly under the pressure.

Mallory opened her eyes. She was staring at the clear Canberra sky, lost in a strange meditation. Using the ledge for additional purchase, Mallory straightened herself up with her legs, and leaned forward again into a seated position. Bree was relieved when they were both out of harm's way.

'Why did you do that?' Bree demanded. 'What if I had dropped you?'

'I'm glad you didn't,' said Mallory, offering a feeble smile.

'Are you *crazy*? Do you have some kind of death wish?'

'No. But I want you to know that I trust you now,' said Mallory, and she threw her arms around Bree.

'You didn't trust me before?'

'I thought I *could*... but now I know I can.'

'Don't ever do that again,' commanded Bree.

'I won't.'

They hugged tightly. When they pulled out of the embrace Bree saw a small tear in Mallory's eye. She'd never seen a glimpse of vulnerability in her before this moment. Mallory quickly wiped it away and Bree decided it was best not to mention it.

'Time to go home.'

Mallory nodded in agreement and they walked back through the air conditioning room, down past Projection and away from Central Cinemas. Hanging off the ledge was unlike any trust exercise Bree had ever experienced, but she'd held on, which meant she'd passed. *What was Mallory thinking?* Bree worried that she might never know. Her heart was still racing but she knew they were closer because of it.

'You know, I'm glad we don't know what's behind that random door,' said Bree when the girls were safely in Mallory's car.

'You like the mystery?'

'Yeah.'

'Well don't get used to it. I'm going to find out where it leads,' said Mallory. 'Loose ends like that drive me nuts.'

Mallory was stubborn and headstrong. Bree believed that one day soon they would both know what was eluding them behind that door.

'If anyone can get us in there it's you.'

CHAPTER ELEVEN

Bree didn't want anyone to know it was her birthday. At seventeen years of age there wasn't anything new she was allowed to do that was forbidden the day before. She'd still have to wait a full year to legally drink, not that she'd been letting that stop her lately. Mallory had encouraged her to partake on occasion but Bree had always stopped herself from losing control. The only thing she was excited about was the opportunity to get her driver's licence. Bree was confident that all of the extra hours practicing with her father were finally going to pay off.

Her birthday fell on the same day as the staff Christmas party, which felt like another big reason not to say anything. Bree didn't want to be the centre of attention if she could avoid it. For her past sixteen birthdays she'd been able to blend her celebration in with Christmas, happily keeping the spotlight away. Her father had the night off and although he said he would have preferred doing something together like going to the movies, he was happy to chauffer Bree to the party instead.

'This might be the last time I have to drive you *anywhere*, hey?'

'Fingers crossed,' replied Bree.

Her father went quiet, perhaps wanting to say more but failing to find the right words.

'Are you alright?' asked Bree, just as the silence was becoming uncomfortable.

'It's just… you're growing up. I need you to take care of yourself. If anything happened to you I'd never be able to forgive myself.'

'Nothing's going to happen to me Dad,' she replied.

'Be careful with your drinks. Don't let them out of your sight.'

'I'll be fine!' cried Bree.

'I know you will… just keep talking to me, okay? Try and keep me in the loop. I'm not going to want to hear *everything* you're doing… believe me… but I need to hear the important things. If you *want* to talk… you know?'

'Uhuh…'

They drove quietly for a stretch of time. The streets of Canberra featured too many roundabouts, which constantly slowed them down and gave Bree more time with her thoughts. She could understand where her father was coming from. Her mother had hurt him, and he was trying to take precautions to make sure Bree didn't do the same. Communication was a reasonable request of a father to his only daughter and it made her feel a little guilty for having omitted the truth so often recently.

'Are you heading home after this?' she asked, changing the subject.

'I should probably straighten up the house a little,' he said as they drove.

'Is it even messy? It looked okay to me,' replied Bree.

'It's just that… I was thinking about moving some of the furniture around. Changing things a little, you know? A bit of a fresh start.'

'That sounds like a fun Saturday night,' she joked.

'When you're a bit older you'll want to stay in and clean up your house too,' said Henry reflectively. 'Funny how your mindset changes.'

They parked at the Italian Club, where Central Cinemas had rented a function room for the party. There were heaps of cars there already, which made Bree thankful for the lift.

'I guess you'll be having Italian food then,' he said.

'What will you have for dinner?' asked Bree.

'Well… I might treat myself to a pizza or something. It being a special occasion and all.'

Henry reached into his wallet and took out two hundred dollars.

'I didn't know what to buy you Bree. Happy birthday,' he said, forcing the money into her hands.

'It's too much Dad, really.'

'No, no. I want you to have it. I've been putting aside money since you started paying me for the rent. It's yours anyway. You should get yourself something. You deserve it. It's been a... a rough year.'

'Thanks Dad.'

Bree gave her father a hug and walked into the party.

'*Look what she's wearing...*'

'*I know, right?*'

'*She's not going to win Employee of the Year... that's for sure.*'

'*Neither are you!*'

The room was buzzing with conversation when she arrived. Bree had texted Mallory earlier in the evening and asked her what fashionably late time she would be showing up. To her surprise Mallory announced that she would be spending the night with George, and that neither of them would be attending. Bree decided that she wouldn't let Mallory's dismissive attitude ruin her first Christmas party at Central, and that she would have fun on her own.

Lose Yourself by Eminem was roaring from a nearby jukebox. She found a group of staff shooting pool opposite the pokies. Andy was gyrating in between shots, his pool cue doubling as a dance partner, while playing against Nathan.

'If you miss this shot you owe me twenty bucks Nathan!' called Andy.

'Shut up so I can take it then!' he replied.

Bree wasn't sure who was winning as she inched over to Victor to say hello. He'd elected to dress in a patterned lime shirt and white pants. On his head he wore a bright orange fedora.

'Whoa Bree! Your first Christmas party! Welcome,' said Victor.

'Thank you.'

'You look great!' he declared.

Bree was wearing a dark blue dress and it occurred to her that most of the staff were used to seeing her in work clothes. She thanked Victor again.

'Are you drinking?' he asked, indicating to the beer in his hand.

'No I'm only sixt... *seventeen*,' she returned. He didn't seem to notice the slip up.

'Maybe next year!' he replied.

The management team looked out of place in casual clothes. Rita had opted for a Christmas jumper while Carl, in the ultimate sign of anti-social behaviour, had brought a book to the party. Carl reminded Bree of Hugo Weaving's Agent Smith from *The Matrix*, because she'd never seen him smile. Bree said hello briefly but knew neither of them cared to be there.

'Merry Christmas,' offered Rita, while Carl remained stoic.

Maxine was walking around in a Santa hat, with Paul following her like a puppy. She was handing out gift cards to the staff.

'Thank you Maxine!'

'Aren't those gift cards from corporate?'

'Yeah, Head Office sends them down every year, right?'

'Yeah... so why is Maxine handing them out like SHE paid for them?'

'Just wants to take the credit I guess!'

Bree was happy for the gift, no matter who was ultimately responsible for it. She wasn't surprised that her father had given her cash. He'd been too busy to put up their Christmas tree, let alone go shopping for her birthday.

Moving through the function room Bree said hi to Shannon, who was flirting with the bartender. He looked a little bit like Jeff Goldblum with acne. Shannon was wearing a purple dress with a matching shawl.

'This is my friend Bree!' she squealed at him.

'Hi,' the man replied politely.

'Do you need a drink?' Shannon seemed like she was also determined to have a good time, no matter what. She let out a loud 'woooo' and started to dance on the spot. Bree declined the offer of a beverage and left Shannon at the bar.

The only effort to decorate the space came in the form of orange Central Cinema balloons, which were tied in bunches around the room, suspended over the tables. Bree spotted Warren standing by the dance floor awkwardly. He held a glass of Coke with a striped paper straw in it.

'Having fun?' Bree asked.

'Yeah.'

Warren stared at the floor, adjusting his glasses, and Bree politely excused herself. She concluded that he might still be carrying some embarrassment about seeing her in a bra.

Bree had been watching the door, waiting for Matt to walk through it. When he finally did, she was so glad to see him that she hugged him right away. Bree figured that the extra affection could be attributed to the nature of the event. If Mallory had been present, she might have raised an eyebrow, or drawn attention to them, but nobody else seemed to question it. Bree was thankful in that moment that her friend was absent.

'Hi Bree, you look pretty,' said Matt.

'Thanks,' she replied, trying not to blush. It meant so much more coming from him than it did from Victor.

Matt had arrived with another projectionist named Lou. He explained to Bree that Lou, who was much older, had stopped working many years ago due to arthritis. He'd been invited along each year since his forced retirement as a kind of lifetime member of Central Cinemas. He looked frail, but in his youth might have once resembled Martin Sheen, were it not for his noticeably large nose and ears.

'He lives near me so I pick him up sometimes,' added Matt. 'He never stays the whole night anyway… always sneaks away to get a taxi.'

'I like to play the pokies,' confessed Lou.

Lou made obligatory small talk with Bree and Matt before wandering off towards the bar and gaming area.

'I actually took over from him, so we've spent a lot of time together,' said Matt. 'Lou's a pretty funny guy. Lots of stories about the good old days of Projection.'

'Speaking of projectionists, have you heard how Liam's training is going?' she asked.

'Yeah… I know a few of the guys over at Southern Cinemas. Some of them are covering at Central tonight while we have this party. Liam's making an impression, that's for sure.'

'Is he?' Bree's interest had been piqued.

'Yeah, he's throwing his weight around. Thinks he's all that. Liam knew how to lace projectors before he'd even started working there. He's been groomed for the role by his Mum. I heard he really messed up at a few other jobs so I guess there's a bit of pressure from her to make sure he doesn't do it again.'

'Really?'

'Yeah… Maxine personally vouched for him. I guess he used to be a bit of a troublemaker. Or so the rumours say…'

'So, if Liam messes up and they hear about it at Head Office that could seriously damage Maxine's chances of getting promoted, right?'

'Wow. I'm impressed. You've really been listening to all of the office gossip, haven't you Bree?'

'Bits and pieces,' she said with a coy smile. 'You can't always believe those pesky rumours though. People will say anything for attention.'

'And Central Cinemas is a hive of attention seekers, looking for something juicy to spread around.'

As they chatted Bree remembered to ask Matt about the mysterious door at the far end of Projection, hoping he might know more about it. Unfortunately, he had no idea where it led either.

'I'm with George on that one. I never go out that way… and I don't know if anyone else uses it.'

Matt walked Bree over to the bar where they asked Lou about it too.

'Haven't the foggiest,' he replied.

After dinner, which consisted of basic pizza and pasta options, came the award ceremony. It was the only time during the evening that the music stopped and everyone had to pay attention to the front of the room. Maxine stood tall by the bar, Paul heeling at her side.

'This year was one of our best, and I wanted to personally thank each and every one of you,' she said, resulting in a light smattering of applause. Shannon gave a brief cheer from the bar. 'I know it can be a hard job at times. It's busy… people can be rude… sometimes you have to clean up something particularly gross…'

There was a murmur through the crowd of employees. Someone at the back yelled 'Nathan!' and everyone laughed. Bree made a mental note to find out what exactly he'd been forced to clean up.

'Well, while it's hard at times,' she continued, 'we're like a family. Thank you all so much for your amazing work this year and have a wonderful night. You deserve it.'

The muddled applause dissipated as Paul took the microphone. He straightened a red bow tie at the top of a festive light green shirt.

Bree looked around but couldn't see Rita or Carl, who had most likely opted for an early exit. She also noted that Old Lou, who had walked around shaking every hand he could find, had since vanished as well.

'Thank you Maxine,' said Paul. 'Now let's give out a few awards, then back to the party.'

Shannon continued cheering enthusiastically behind Bree.

'We'll start with the award for customer service. You all know him… you all love him… This year's winner is Victor Patel!'

Based on the reactions in the room, Bree could tell this was expected. She could hardly debate against the decision, as Victor was nothing if not excellent at customer service. He accepted a golden statue of a figure holding a star, which looked suspiciously similar to the trophies available at the engraving store on Level 2 of the mall. Victor gave a short thank you speech and stepped aside.

Paul announced that the next award was for effort, which seemed like a vague category. It became clear that the management team had invented a new honour specifically for the evening.

'This next employee has been a model of consistency,' said Paul. He held out the shiny golden statue with both hands as if it were an Academy Award.

'This years effort award goes to Shannon Chambers!'

There was a responsive clap from the gathered employees but Shannon wasn't paying attention. She was talking to the bartender again. Nathan had to tap her on the shoulder and reiterate that she'd won an award.

'Oh my God!' she screamed as she clambered up to receive the statue. She started to cry, partly because of the amount of alcohol in her system and partly due to the gratitude she was feeling. Bree's earlier comparison to Gwyneth Paltrow felt particularly apt. Shannon gave a speech that went on for too long. When Paul felt that adequate time had been spent on her, he ushered Shannon away from the microphone. Bree considered that the award was probably bestowed because of her contributions to Candy Bar sales and choc-top creation and was well deserved.

'Just two more employee awards gang, bear with us.'

Matt positioned himself next to Bree.

'Having fun?' he asked in a low tone.

'Yeah… did Lou sneak away on you?' asked Bree.

'I think he did. Classic Lou. So, who do you think will win Employee of the Year?'

'Um… you?' she suggested, subtly bumping her hip into his.

'Oh yeah? You think that highly of me, do you?'

'Why not? You seem to know what you're doing,' said Bree.

Paul called out the next award as the 'Rookie of the Year.'

'Hey! You'll be eligible for this one,' said Matt.

'I've only been working for about half the year though. There would be a few others that would be eligible too.'

'But you're the *best*,' replied Matt.

Bree bit her lip.

'This year's Rookie of the Year is... Bree Fielding!'

She couldn't believe it. The whole room became so loud and bright that Bree thought something had exploded. Matt cheered and gave her a hug. She moved to the front and accepted the award from Paul. Maxine smiled at her.

'Thank you all... so... *so* much,' she managed to say. 'This is very unexpected. Thanks for making me feel like part of the team.'

Bree received a brief applause as she floated back to Matt in a daze.

'I won!'

'You sure did.'

'I can't believe it. I've never won an award like this before,' said Bree, grasping the prize.

'You should thank me because I voted for you.'

'Did you?'

'Nah... not really. But I would have!' replied Matt.

Bree playfully hit Matt on the arm. Unexpected applause on her birthday had been particularly nice. She'd never felt so validated by a workplace before.

'The final award of the night is the biggest of them all. The award for Employee of the Year!'

Shannon screamed a cheer that was much louder than the room was anticipating. Maxine squinted in her direction.

Paul opened an orange envelope, which was apparently a new feature specifically for the big award, and announced the name.

'Employee of the Year goes to Andy Cooper!'

Andy put both his hands over his mouth and practically flew up to collect his statue. He hugged Paul and then went out of his way to embrace Maxine, who didn't seem to appreciate the additional affection. Then, to everyone's surprise, Nathan passed Andy one of the orange helium-filled balloons. A few people laughed knowingly. Bree didn't understand its significance.

'Come on mate… do it,' pressed Nathan.

'Oh man… I didn't think I'd *win*… alright… alright!' replied Andy, and he loosened the base of the balloon. Some of the guys at the back of the room started clapping. To everyone's surprise Andy proceeded to inhale a healthy dose of helium before giving his speech.

'This is so fantastic!' he said, holding up the award, his voice now a comically high pitch. The gathering of employees became hysterical, the room filling with a cacophony of laughter. 'My thanks to the management team. One day soon I hope to join your prestigious ranks. Now let's party!'

Nathan was laughing so hard that he was crying.

'A bet's a bet,' said Andy as he moved back into the crowd. Both Maxine and Paul clapped politely and the music was turned back on.

'I guess Andy lost that game of pool then,' deduced Matt.

'He must have. That was hilarious!'

'So, where are you going to put it?' asked Matt.

'Excuse me?'

'Your award.'

'Oh… I guess it will just go in my room somewhere,' said Bree, clutching it with two hands. It was lighter than it looked. She wondered what her Dad would say when he saw it. This really had been a memorable night. A part of Bree wished Mallory had been there to see her win, but considered that she might have spoiled the moment by diminishing the statue's worth.

The evening crested with Shannon becoming a sloppy mess thanks to an abundance of free drinks. Maxine had departed, leaving Paul in charge. He seemed instantly annoyed with the responsibility. Bree, seeing Shannon in a state, offered to take her to the bathroom where she could recuperate.

'I don't usually drink so much…' she said as they moved towards the toilets, arm in arm. Shannon was bigger than Bree and it was hard to coax her stumbling body in the right direction. They ran into a couple of plush chairs before correcting their course.

'Let's play the pokies!' said Shannon suddenly.

'Not tonight,' replied Bree.

As they bumbled along Bree scanned the faces in the room and spotted a late arrival. George, with a freshly shaved head, was talking to Matt by the pool table. He spotted Bree, excused himself from Matt and walked over.

'Hey Bree,' said George. 'Congrats on the award.'

'Thanks.'

'Do you need any help with Shannon?'

'I think we'll be alright,' Bree replied.

'Soooo alright…' chimed in Shannon as she tried in vain to keep a straight face.

'Hey… so have you seen Mallory tonight?' he asked. 'She said she might be hanging out with you and then coming to this all *fashionably late*. You know how she is. Anyway… is she around?'

Mallory was using Bree as an excuse to lie to George. *But why?* She calmly nodded and held open the door for Shannon, who gratefully went inside the lavatory. Bree had to think fast.

'Yeah… she and I were together earlier. She popped by and was only here for a little while.'

'Okay. So, she left?' asked George.

'Yeah.'

'Never mind. Good luck in there,' said George, regarding the Shannon situation. He walked back over to Matt while Bree took sanctuary in the female bathroom.

She held Shannon's long blonde plait of hair out of her face as she vomited into the nearest toilet bowl. As Bree knelt down, her eyes caught sight of the Rookie of the Year award, sitting on the tiles. Winning it had been such a good feeling.

Bree texted Mallory and told her that she'd covered for her with George. The reply was a short *Thanks*.

Where were you really? Bree texted.

She wanted to ask: *Why did you lie?* but she resisted. Bree received no response. Mallory owed her an explanation.

CHAPTER TWELVE

On Christmas Eve Bree went over to Mallory's place and was surprised to find a present waiting for her. It was an envelope, similar to the orange ones used at the Christmas party to announce the big awards, and it was staring up at her from Mallory's bed.

'You didn't have to do that,' said Bree in disbelief. 'I didn't get you anything.'

'You don't have to! And this is actually for your Dad.'

For my Dad? Bree opened the envelope and found a voucher that could be redeemed for a set of golf clubs at Rebel Sport.

'That's amazing. He'll love it, thank you so much.'

Bree hugged Mallory. She had expressed her plan to purchase a Rebel Sport gift card that night with a view to buy her father the golf clubs for a reduced price in the Boxing Day sales. It was nice to see Mallory had been paying attention. It was a very generous gesture.

'Since you're going to the mall anyway do you want to watch a movie tonight?' asked Mallory. 'I still haven't seen *The Texas Chainsaw Massacre* remake.'

'If you want.'

'Will you drive? I'd like to smoke.'

Bree had passed her driving test just after her birthday and happily agreed to drive Mallory's Ford Cortina, knowing it was a short and familiar distance to work. Mallory picked up the bong that lived next to her bed. She took a zip-locked bag of marijuana buds from the bottom drawer of her desk and positioned herself on the beanbag. Bree felt a little odd sitting higher than Mallory on the bed, so she shifted, landing cross-legged on the floor. The apparatus was packed with care. Mallory lit the marijuana and started to inhale the smoke through the glass tube at the top. Bree was fascinated. She'd never seen someone use drugs up close like this.

'Do you ever get high?' asked Mallory as she exhaled smoke wildly into the air.

'No, not really.'

'Do you *want* to?'

'I don't know. I like to be in control,' replied Bree.

'You'll still be in control. This will just open your mind a bit more. You'll probably cough a little but then you'll laugh a lot.'

'Um...'

'You don't like to laugh?' asked Mallory as she nudged Bree.

'I have to drive us to the movies. I can't smoke and drive.'

'We can go to the movies any time! We're always there anyway... and you've got the voucher for the golf clubs. Let's *not* go. Let's get high together! Come on... it's Christmas Eve.'

'I don't know what I'm doing. I've never really smoked anything. I don't really know how to...'

'I'll help you though it. Come on, it will be so great!'

Mallory was very convincing. She offered to watch a movie with Bree on her laptop and had plenty of snacks in the kitchen. Eventually Bree succumbed to the pressure. Mallory was right; they didn't have to go anywhere.

'Alright, fine. But this isn't going to be something I make a habit of, okay?'

'You got it Bree.'

Mallory repacked and lit the bong for Bree. Once again smoke billowed inside the glass tube.

'Inhale,' prompted Mallory.

Bree nervously held the smoke inside her for as long as she could. She felt a burning sensation in her throat and coughed loudly. Then Mallory had her repeat the process. There was an unpleasant taste in Bree's mouth.

'Did you have fun at the Christmas party then?'

'Yeah,' replied Bree. 'You must have heard by now… I won Rookie of the Year?'

'Well it was between you and Warren, and he has the personality of a bag of flour.' True to form Mallory didn't share Bree's enthusiasm for the achievement.

'Hey Mallory?'

'Yeah?'

'Can we talk about why George thought you were with me that night?'

'Yeah, thanks for covering for me by the way,' said Mallory, as she took another hit from the bong.

'So, where were you?' asked Bree.

'I was with Dex.'

'Again? I thought you wanted to be with George?' It was confusing for Bree. She hoped Mallory wasn't cheating on her boyfriend. She hated being caught up in the middle. After her mother's affair Bree didn't want to watch that kind of fallout happening with her friend.

'I *do* want to be with George. It's just that Dex and I like to get high. And George doesn't want me smoking. So, I can't do that with him.'

'Well… don't use me to lie about it anymore, alright?'

'That's fair enough. Sorry Bree. I should have given you a heads up.'

Mallory handed her the bong as a means of apology and Bree took another hit. It was a relief that she wasn't cheating on George, only lying to him about her recreational drug use: the lesser of two evils.

'Hey… do you remember that Donut King guy that drops off stale donuts?' asked Mallory after a time.

'Yeah. And they weren't stale by the way. You'd know that if you ate any of them.'

'Whatever. So that guy? That was Pierre. From the party.'

'Pierre is the Donut King guy?' Bree was stunned with Canberra's social network. Everyone knew everyone.

'Yeah. Weird, right? Well anyway, he kind of gave me an idea.' Mallory looked like the cat that got the cream.

Bree cocked her head. She hoped Mallory hadn't given Pierre her phone number or anything, as she was still hoping to pursue something with Matt.

'What if we could get free stuff from other stores in the mall too?'

'Sure, I'd like a bunch of free stuff. Who wouldn't?' said Bree as she gave an unexpected chuckle. The weed was taking effect.

'What if we could trade the free movies we get at Central for other things? That would be good, wouldn't it?' asked Mallory.

'Like what?'

'Food, clothes, whatever! It's a big mall but we work somewhere that everyone wants to go. Free movie tickets are something staff in every shop would like to have. We arrange for them to get into sessions for free and they arrange free stuff for us.'

'How do we get them in for free? You can't just *let* them in. There are security cameras, they'd need a ticket,' stated Bree.

'What if they just walked up and handed you a business card? You could rip something like that for the cameras at Point…'

'I don't think so Mallory. This sounds like a good way to get fired. I like my job.'

'Alright… say you don't just let them walk in. Let's say they have valid tickets. Then there's no way you'll get in trouble.'

'Wait… they have valid tickets? Well then I'm not doing anything wrong. I don't get it…'

Bree wondered if she was more confused because of the drugs. She had become very conscious of a place at the rear of her head that felt like it had been activated. She imagined smoke swirling to the back of her skull. It felt as if the weed had turned on some invisible light that was usually off. Dormant thoughts were suddenly becoming accessible.

'If someone comes up to the Box Office with comp tickets what do you do?' Mallory asked as she tied up her black hair.

'Swap them out for actual tickets for the night,' replied Bree, trying to track Mallory's train of thought, 'to the session of their choice.'

'Right. Okay… so you don't know *how* they *got* the comp tickets though,' said Mallory.

'I don't get it…' Bree squinted at Mallory as she tried to focus.

'We could use comp tickets and trade them with other stores for gift vouchers. That's what Maxine did to get the gift vouchers that she handed out at the Christmas Party.'

'I thought they were from Head Office.'

'Were they?' asked Mallory. 'I heard she swapped comps for them.'

'Did you get one?' asked Bree.

'Yeah it was in an envelope. Carl handed it to me when I was at work the other day.' Mallory didn't seem to care for the Christmas gift.

'Cool.'

'Look… comp tickets don't have any value to us, because we can get free movies any day we like. But for the average mall employee a comp ticket is a great get.'

'Right, so you want to *steal* a bunch of comp tickets? I can't do that.'

Mallory hopped up and opened the top drawer of her desk. She took out a wooden box that looked like something Bree had made as a high school project once. Mallory passed it over to her.

'What's this?'

'Open it,' directed Mallory.

Bree complied by sliding the lid away. Inside was a stack of at least fifty complimentary tickets from Central Cinemas.

'Mallory! Did you steal these?'

'Nope.'

'Then how do you have all of these comp tickets?'

'I'll show you.'

Mallory produced a pile of paper and shoved it towards Bree. They were templates from the Box Office. Mallory explained that she had been replying to non-existent complaints on her Box Office shifts and effectively sending herself complimentary tickets courtesy of Central Cinemas management team.

'This just started because I wanted to see if it would work. And then it did,' mused Mallory.

Bree read some of the fake complaints. *Cinema was too cold. Teenagers were too noisy. Missed the beginning of the film. Screen seemed out of focus. Toilets were too dirty.* Each letter had resulted in a pair of complimentary passes.

'Remember what I said? The managers don't even check the complaints. They just throw in the comp tickets and drop the envelopes off at the Post Office. Sometimes they make a Box Office staff member mail them… like me.'

'You mailed these to yourself?' asked Bree.

'Yeah,' replied Mallory. 'Some of them anyway. It was surreal.'

'So, you tricked them out of these?'

'Kind of. I didn't really steal these though. They were given to me.' Mallory looked sternly at Bree. 'I've never shown these to anyone before. Don't make me regret it, okay?'

'Another one of your scams, huh?' Bree wondered how much deception one person was capable of.

'It could be one of *our* scams… if you want it to be.'

'I mean…'

'I trust you now Bree.'

'I know,' she replied, thinking back to that day on the roof.

'You're not going to throw me under the bus over this, are you?' asked Mallory.

'I guess not…'

'If you think about it this is actually good for Central Cinemas in a way. It's a victimless crime. Those seats we're giving away would be empty otherwise. And if people come in and buy stuff from the Candy Bar they'll make heaps of money selling overpriced popcorn. Money they wouldn't have had otherwise.'

'But they'll notice Mallory. They must track how many comp tickets they give out.'

'They haven't noticed so far. I've been doing this for months. If they start to, or somebody says something, we'll stop straight away.'

Bree picked up a handful of comp tickets and checked the expiration dates. They were valid until December 2004, a full calendar year away.

'You won't tell anyone about this, will you?' asked Mallory as she slid back onto the beanbag.

'No.'

'Promise?'

'I won't,' said Bree, 'but... how would this even work? I mean, how would you even approach another store and trade comps with them?'

'It's easy. I'll do that part if it worries you.'

Mallory seemed supremely confident. She was five steps ahead.

'I don't think it *will* be easy.'

'Well it *was*,' replied Mallory, folding her arms.

'What do you mean?' asked Bree as she slid the lid back onto the wooden box.

'I've already done it.'

'You have?'

'That's how I got your Dad the Rebel Sport voucher.'

'*What?*'

'Yeah.'

'You're either a genius or a super villain,' offered Bree as she stood up.

'I'll take either,' said Mallory with a smile.

Bree laughed until she heard herself snort, which made her self-conscious. She excused herself to use the bathroom. She looked at the clock in the hallway on her way.

7:20pm.

It was still early. Her father was finishing work at midnight, which left plenty of time for Bree to shower and disguise the smell of drugs. She'd been doing most of the laundry at their apartment too, so there would be little chance of him discovering the truth about their impromptu marijuana session.

She thought about Mallory's offer to make it *their* scam. It seemed that everything was in place already. Mallory would probably continue with this scheme with or without her input. Bree concluded that it would be best if they were both involved so that she could protect her friend and ensure Mallory wasn't caught out. Two heads would be better than one.

When she'd finished in the bathroom Bree felt lightheaded and hungry. She washed her hands and felt her phone buzz in the pocket of her jeans. It was her Dad touching base. Suddenly Bree noticed the clock on her phone.

8:27pm.

Had she been in the toilet for over an hour? Bree returned to the room and sat down quietly. Mallory's blood shot eyes seemed to stare through her.

'Hi,' Bree managed to say, albeit cautiously.

'What?' Mallory shot back, confused.

Bree was getting paranoid. It didn't *feel* like she had been gone for that long, but she had no idea. She'd never been under the influence of weed and thought she might have been hallucinating. She started to laugh uncontrollably at the idea that she'd been in the toilet for an hour, which in turn made Mallory laugh. Bree took a full five minutes before she could actually form a sentence.

'What time is it?' she asked Mallory.

'It's like half past eight. Why?'

'How long was I away?'

'What?'

'How long was I in the bathroom just now?'

'I don't know. I wasn't timing you!' said Mallory feeling confused.

Bree got up and checked the clock in the hallway.

It still said 7.20pm.

It had stopped! Bree returned to the bedroom and burst out laughing again. Once more she failed to articulate to Mallory why she was so amused and each time she tried to it made her laugh even harder. Soon both girls were making each other cackle so much that they cried tears of pure joy.

Bree messaged her Dad that everything was fine. She was looking forward to their Christmas together. Bree would present him with the voucher that Mallory had provided. She may have manipulated the system in order to make it happen, but it was going to be the perfect gift. Bree decided to throw caution to the wind.

'Okay… I'm in.'

'You're in? That's excellent.'

I must have imagined it. Bree had felt a strange intuition at the start of her shift. She could have sworn she'd spotted her mother, obscured among the faces in the foyer. When she'd looked again the figure wasn't there, and she'd determined that the sighting must have been false. Bree dismissed the phantom as best she could, supressing her feelings and throwing herself into work.

'Feature is fine in Cinema Four,' Bree said confidently into her two-way radio.

'Thanks,' replied George from the Projection room.

Bree went back to the podium to rip tickets, allowing Warren a chance to clean the male toilets. It was Nathan who had called in sick that night, causing Rita to reluctantly work in the Box Office. She claimed it was easier to call in Carl, another manager, than a regular staff member due to everyone going away over New Years.

A second previously absent figure materialised when Liam wandering up the stairs. Bree hadn't seen him since his promotion to Southern Cinemas. He was dressed in a coat and accompanied by a thin blonde girl wearing a jean jacket over a black dress. She looked like an anorexic Reese Witherspoon with baby doll eyes. Liam approached with a swagger when he noticed Bree at Point.

'Well, look who it is!' he said with his arms raised in the air like an impressed game show host.

'Hey Liam.'

'How are things?'

'Fine.'

'Bree, this is Daniella,' Liam said indicating towards the blonde. Bree thought she looked intimidatingly pretty up close. 'Daniella, Bree.'

'Hi.'

'Nice to meet you.'

'Daniella works with me across town.'

'How do you like it there?' asked Bree.

'It's *so* much better I think,' replied Liam. 'Everything is newer and Southern Cinemas are nicer. They have me doing Projection at the moment, but I'm transitioning into the management team this year.'

She hated the way Liam was bragging in front of his date.

'Sounds like you're enjoying it,' said Bree.

'It's great. You should come and try it out. I think I could get you into the Projection team after I move into management. I'll have a say you know.'

'Oh?' This came as a big surprise to Bree. She'd turned Liam down when he'd asked her out and now he was essentially offering her a promotion.

'Is Projection something you want to do?' he asked.

'It looks like a lot of work,' replied Bree hesitantly, wondering if Liam truly had such influence. She'd been intimidated each time she'd ventured up to the Projection room. The thought of juggling ten projectors by herself gave her anxiety.

'You don't shy away from work... Rookie of the Year. Congrats on that by the way.'

Daniella looked impatient. Liam's face changed, recognising her shifting mood.

'Think about it. If you come over now while you're seventeen we can train you up as an eighteen year old. You have to be eighteen to do Projection in case they want to screen an R-rated movie.'

Bree wondered how Liam knew how old she was. *Had he seen her resume?* Perhaps Maxine had left it out and he'd stolen a glance.

'Okay, I'll think about it,' she replied.

Liam handed over their tickets.

'*Love Actually*, that's in Cinema Six down the end,' said Bree. 'Enjoy the movie.'

Daniella shot a distrustful look back at Bree as they walked down the tunnel. Warren returned from cleaning the toilets. He looked surprisingly sweaty, but Bree decided not to ask him why. Some messes are best left with those that find them.

'*What happened to Shannon at the Christmas party?*'

'*You saw her... she was super drunk.*'

'*Was that George arriving at the end of the night to take her home? Isn't he dating Mallory though?*'

'*Who knows... George is a bit of a player if you ask me...*'

As the final sessions of the night started Bree was loitering alone at Point. While checking her phone a man threw his hands over her eyes from behind, causing her heart to skip a beat.

'Guess who?'

She assumed it was Liam, and felt immediately uncomfortable, visualising a dirty look from Daniella just out of view. Bree panicked and ducked under and away from their grip. When she'd spun around she was surprised to see it had been Matt. He was dressed in a crisp short-sleeved shirt and jeans.

'Jesus...'

'Nope just me,' he replied jokingly.

'Don't do that to me!'

'Sorry, I didn't mean to startle you.'

'It's not you… I mean… I didn't know it was *you*. Liam is seeing a movie tonight too and I thought that you were him,' said Bree as she tucked her shirt back into her slim fit black pants, trying to maintain her composure.

'You seem to be working Floor every time I see you. Have they trained you on Candy Bar and Box or do they not trust you with money?'

Bree pulled a face. 'Ha ha. I've done Candy Bar and Box thank you very *much*.'

'Is this your first poster shift?' asked Matt.

'What's a poster shift?'

'On Wednesday nights the Floor staff member that's on til midnight has to change the posters. New movies start on Thursday… some movies are finishing up… and you have *no* idea what I'm talking about, do you?'

Bree shook her head. Matt took her to the office and together they collected the keys to the scissor lift.

'We have a *scissor lift*?' exclaimed Bree, not entirely sure what that meant.

'We'll use it last,' promised Matt. 'Let's do the easy stuff first.'

'You're going to show me how to change posters?' she asked. 'You're not even working tonight.'

'It would be my pleasure. I used to change the posters all the time when I worked on Floor. I'd better make sure you know what you're doing. I wouldn't want you to besmirch the legacy of the poster shift!'

'Nobody uses the word *besmirch* anymore.'

Matt smiled. He escorted Bree up to the Projection room and they went through the cardboard tubes of posters that had arrived that week. There were a handful of really eye-catching new ones. Bree picked five of them and they returned to the foyer. Matt checked which films were finishing and they located all the posters that needed to be replaced. He showed Bree how to unlock the display boxes and together they installed the newest ones that she'd selected. Some patrons even stopped and checked out the posters as they came out of their sessions, which was pleasing.

'Who is *The Rock*? Is he a rapper or something?' asked Bree as she changed the signage on *Welcome to the Jungle* from Coming Soon to Now Showing.

'He's a wrestler. You don't watch wrestling?' asked Matt.

'Not really my thing. How is the stand-up comedy going?' she asked, as they started to take down an old cardboard standee.

'I've done a few gigs and got some laughs. I'd say I'm improving each time.'

'Isn't it scary?'

Bree wasn't the biggest fan of public speaking. The idea of everyone staring expectantly gave her the creeps.

'The first time it was. It gets easier. Your skin gets thicker. You start to know what to expect and the adrenaline is really good. Making a room full of people laugh feels amazing. It's a rush.'

'And if nobody laughs?'

'Then I need to write better jokes.'

Matt and Bree carefully put away the old posters even though he was sure they'd be thrown away in due time.

'You don't want them for your flyer wall?' she asked with a grin.

'Now Bree, you know that my wall is for *flyers* only. If I hung up huge posters like this I'd be out of room immediately.'

'And what will you do when you actually run out of space? Will the wall be complete?'

Matt scratched his chin. 'I'm not sure it will *ever* be complete. I hope that after I've left Central Cinemas-'

'And you're touring your famous stand-up comedy act?' she interrupted.

'Uhuh… after I've left to *succeed* at comedy I hope that the next generation of projectionists continue this noble tradition!'

'If there still are projectionists, of course. You might all be replaced by automation robots by then.'

'Yes, you're right,' replied Matt with a smile. 'When Central Cinemas can afford the latest tech.'

'I can see it now. The projectionists of the future will be eating cereal and admiring your unfinished flyer wall,' said Bree sliding her hands in front of her to accentuate how vast the wall could grow to be.

'Well, from little things…'

'What?' asked Bree, urging him to finish his thought.

'Big things grow.'

'That's true.'

'It's a fairly famous saying,' stated Matt.

Bree wasn't familiar with it but she liked the expression. She hoped that with each small interaction she and Matt were growing something between them too.

Soon there was only one thing left to change. It was an oversized vinyl banner for *Mystic River* that hung on the wall above Candy Bar.

'This is where the scissor lift comes into play,' said Matt with a grin.

He led Bree down a passageway where the device was waiting. All of the backstage service corridors in the mall looked the same and she was reminded of how things had started with Ryan, pressed against a similar brick surface. She banished the memory from her mind. The scissor lift consisted of an open top metal box on wheels. It was incredibly heavy but Matt was able to roll it into the foyer with Bree steering at the front.

'I've never even seen this before. Why would they buy this? Surely not just for changing the posters,' said Bree, thinking out loud.

'They probably need it for the lights too,' reasoned Matt.

'Those never get changed!'

'You're right. I think projectionists are supposed to change those but it's a real effort to wheel this out, as you can see. And it's time consuming.'

'But the ceiling looks so much worse when it's dark,' argued Bree.

'Who's coming to the cinema to look at the ceiling? When enough bulbs go out we'll do them all in one go,' reasoned Matt.

Once it was situated directly underneath the banner, they withdrew four large metal legs from inside the basket. Matt connected them at each side of the scissor lift, locking it safely into place. It looked much sturdier with the supports attached.

'Do you need a licence to use this?' she asked.

'Well... I don't have one... but I guess you technically *should*. Wow... nobody has ever asked me that before.'

'So... should we still use it?' asked Bree warily.

'Yeah, of course. I've used it dozens of times. We'll be careful... don't worry.'

He dashed around the Candy Bar and plugged a long red extension cord from the scissor lift into the power point. Matt clicked open the metal gate that housed the platform and held it open for Bree.

'How are you with heights?'

Bree thought of her recent trip to the roof with Mallory. This was child's play compared to that.

'Totally fine,' she said and climbed up into the lift. Matt seemed impressed with her bravado and joined her. The metal box was not designed for two people and they had to stand very close together. There was electricity between them, and Bree could once again smell his cologne.

'The key, once you get it from the office, goes here,' said Matt as he inserted a silver key into the control panel of the machine. 'Then you have to hold both of these buttons together to go up.'

The panel had three red buttons on it. Matt pressed and held the top two and the scissor lift rose at a medium pace. The initial jolt came as a shock to Bree and she placed one hand on Matt's arm to steady herself.

'Sorry,' she said, releasing his bicep.

'It's all good.'

They came to a stop within arm's reach of the banner. Matt took the plastic pushpins out of the vinyl corners that he could reach and then whipped the banner away from the wall in a rough movement. It flapped and fell to the tiled floor below with a thud.

'That was heavier than it looked,' she said.

'Yeah. Sometimes they are difficult to hang up on your own. That's it. We're done,' proclaimed Matt as he held down the bottom two buttons.

They started to glide back down to the floor below. The ascension had been a lot louder, as if the scissor lift was straining. In contrast descending was whisper quiet. For a moment Bree felt as though she was being brought back down to Earth by Superman, in a fluid movement like she'd seen in the movies. Matt opened the gate and stepped out of the metal box. He then held it open for Bree who followed him down onto the tiles.

'What did you think of that?' he asked.

'It was pretty dusty up there.'

'Well yes… as you know the scissor lift doesn't get used much, so dusting doesn't really happen either.'

They decided against replacing the old banner with a new one and wheeled the machine away, leaving an empty wall space above the Candy Bar.

'It was nice hanging out with you,' he said as they returned to the podium at Point.

'It was, wasn't it? I'm pretty great,' joked Bree.

He forced a smile. Matt's calm and even temperament started to change. He was suddenly nervous. 'I want to kiss you so badly,' he blurted out.

Bree blinked hard as though she couldn't believe what she was hearing. No guy had been so forward with their intentions since Ryan.

'Hang on… you want to kiss me… *badly*? That doesn't sound very inviting,' she said supressing a laugh. Bree was trying to take some of the tension out of the moment.

Matt was turning red but to his credit he squared off his shoulders and placed one hand on Bree's hip. It felt good to be held. He took a deep breath and leaned in for a kiss. Bree instinctively closed her eyes in graceful anticipation.

'*BAM BAM BAM BAM.*'

The moment was lost. Someone was knocking against the sealed fire door mere metres from where they were standing.

'*BAM BAM BAM BAM,*' the bashing intensified.

'I'd better check it out,' said Matt quickly.

Bree followed him cautiously towards the noise. There was no way of knowing who was on the other side without opening it. *Should she call out? Would they even answer?* Bree tried to rationalise that it had to be someone that would know about the door. *Maybe a patron that had left something in a cinema?* Matt pressed confidently against the metal crash bar and unlocked the fire exit door. It was raining heavily outside and there, standing in her oversized black raincoat, was Mallory.

'Finally,' she said and stepped into the complex.

'Mallory? What are you doing here?' asked Bree.

'I came to see you.'

There was a bittersweet moment as Matt realised he would not be kissing Bree tonight, badly or otherwise. He thought it best to excuse himself from the situation.

'Well, I was just going anyway,' he said. 'Have a good night.'

'Thanks for your help… with all the posters,' said Bree.

'No worries.'

'And… *everything,*' she said quickly.

'It's all good. Night Bree… night Mallory.'

Matt disappeared around the corner, looking a little defeated. It had taken courage to tell her how he felt, and Bree valued that.

'He was acting really weird,' said Mallory. 'Was he bothering you or something?'

'No he was… just being helpful.'

They checked each empty cinema one by one. It was the job of the midnight shift to do a final sweep of the building before the doors were locked for the night. Shannon had once left a patron in the toilets and caused quite a panic when the trapped woman had phoned the police for help. Understandably she couldn't work out how to escape the complex on her own accord once the roller doors were secured. When Bree and Mallory walked into Cinema Six they were startled to find two patrons lingering in the back row.

'Oh *crap!*' said the man as he spotted them.

The woman lifted her head out of the man's lap and he covered himself as quickly as he could.

It was Liam and Daniella.

Bree couldn't believe it. Liam pulled up his pants and Daniella rose from her knees. Mallory's mouth hung open like a broken suitcase.

'Oh my God.' Mallory had started to chuckle.

'Sorry, sorry,' said Daniella as Liam buckled his belt. It wasn't clear who she was apologising to.

Though they were both embarrassed to be caught in such a state Liam seemed to be able to compose himself. Daniella re-applied her lip-gloss and the squatters made their way down the stairs and out of the cinema.

'Don't tell my Mum about this or else,' commanded Liam as he walked past the girls with his date.

'Your fly is down,' replied Mallory with her signature raised eyebrow. Bree didn't say anything.

As the roller door sealed Central Cinemas like a tomb Mallory lifted her hands to her head in amazement.

'That was crazy. I can't believe that just happened. Are you going to tell Maxine?' she asked.

'Of course not,' replied Bree. 'How would you even bring something like that up with her?'

Mallory bit her lip and then turned to her friend. 'Can *I* tell her?'

'No!'

'Come on, *please*?' grinned Mallory.

'Absolutely not!'

'Fine… you're no fun.'

'Was there a reason you dropped by to see me tonight?' asked Bree.

'Oh yeah. I'm here about the mystery door at the end of Projection,' said Mallory.

'What about it? Did you work out where it leads?'

'Well, I was thinking about where it *should* lead. It should lead underneath the stadium seating in either Cinema Five or Cinema Six.'

'Okay…'

'So, I was talking to George about it and he told me there's a panel on the side of the wall that comes off. It leads inside and *underneath* the seats.'

'And you want to have a look?' asked Bree.

'No time like the present.'

Mallory and Bree found the panels with relative ease. The material on the wall of the stadium seating matched so seamlessly that if you didn't know to look for them, you'd walk right past them. Bree had done so at least a hundred times without thinking twice. Mallory used a screwdriver that she'd borrowed from the Projection room and removed the panel in Cinema Five first.

'This is so exciting. We're finally going to find out what's behind those doors!' exclaimed Mallory.

'I hope so. What do you think is in there?' asked Bree.

'Something they don't want us to see.'

'Really?'

'Well what do *you* think they're hiding?' asked Mallory.

'I honestly have no idea. I'm not sure they're hiding anything.'

It was like being in a scary movie. The deserted complex, the eerie silence and the sense of the unknown thrilled Bree. Once the panel had been removed they shone the torch that Bree had been using all night for her cinema checks into the opening and saw a series of wooden support beams caked in dust.

'I guess people don't go under here much.'

'Why would they? It's gross down there,' said Bree.

It was so much dustier than the ceiling. The many wooden beams were staggered to build up the stadium seating levels and each new row obstructed their view of the back wall where the mystery door ought to be.

'I can't see it. One of us will have to get in there and have a closer look,' said Mallory.

'Don't look at me!' shrieked Bree, who was starting to feel genuinely scared. The usual ambiance of quiet music was absent and staring into the dark hole was giving her an uneasy feeling.

'Fine, I'll do it,' said Mallory bravely.

'I don't think you should go in there either.'

'It's fine Bree. There's nothing down there but dust.'

Mallory took the torch from her friend, holding it with her clenched teeth, and went feet first into the opening. She found a series of cut out grooves and ledges made from wood that she was able to use to clamber down.

'Be careful,' advised Bree.

Mallory made it look easy. Bree presumed that no one had scaled those ledges since the initial construction work. She watched on in quiet fascination as Mallory jumped down to the concrete floor. She removed the torch from her mouth. The light revealed several discarded fast food wrappers and another lifetime worth of dust on the floor. Mallory stepped carefully over the wooden frames that connected the support beams at ground level and soon all Bree could see was her torch flickering around in the otherwise sinister distance.

'There's no door here,' she yelled back to Bree, 'just a brick wall.'

Mallory managed to find her way back and ascended without incident. They sealed up the panel and the pair moved on to Cinema Six.

'Your turn,' she said, turning to Bree.

'You're not serious?'

'I've got your back. You can do it.'

They removed the panel and set it aside. Below Cinema Six's seating was the mirror opposite of Cinema Five.

'I still can't believe what Liam was up to,' laughed Mallory.

'I didn't get a good look,' said Bree.

'Don't worry… I don't think you missed much!'

Bree composed herself, took a deep breath and stepped into the darkness. She placed her right foot on a wooden beam and, as she was shifting her body weight, it cracked beneath her. She tumbled down, suddenly in a collision course with the concrete below.

'Bree!' yelled Mallory.

She'd managed to hold on, catching another wooden beam as she fell, but in doing so Bree had dropped the torch to the ground. The sudden ricochet of the light bouncing in the dark had made the moment seem more dramatic than it was. Bree squinted and gradually made her way towards it in the dim light.

'I'm okay.'

'Geez, watch your step,' called Mallory from the opening, which from Bree's perspective inside the stadium style seating resembled a window. It offered the only light source besides her torch, and she was thankful for it.

Now bursting with adrenaline Bree scooped up the torch and made her way carefully on a path to the far wall. There was no opening or doorway. It was solid grey brick all the way along. The mysterious room must have been on the other side but there was no way to access it from here. She made her way back to Mallory and climbed out.

'Nothing.'

Mallory was disappointed.

'That's where it should be! That means there is only one way in? So, it's a sealed space with brick walls. Maybe we should just go up to Projection, down the back stairwell and kick that mystery door down.'

'It's late Mallory and I'm getting tired. I've got to get home.'

'Can you drop me off too?'

'Sure.'

As they said goodbye to Paul in the office he thanked Bree for amending the posters.

'I spotted some of the changes… they look really good. Maybe if you're interested you can do a midnight shift on Floor again next week?' he offered.

'Sure, I can do that.'

In the car on the drive home Mallory played a game where she would ask a question about their lives and then the next song that came on the radio would give them the answer.

'Will we ever find out what's behind the mystery door?' she asked.

They waited patiently for the current song to end. As she drove along Bree kept an eye out for kangaroos. Under the cover of the Canberra night the marsupials became confident and were often a hazard for drivers. Bree's father had warned her about them during their lessons. *Angels Brought Me Here* by Australian Idol winner Guy Sebastian was the next song on the radio. The girls tried to decipher its message and struggled to find lyrics that applied to the mystery door.

'It's not a perfect science,' said Mallory, defending her radio game. 'Ask something else.'

'Will Matt ask me out?'

'Oooh, really? Interesting! I *knew* you had a thing for him!'

Bree wished that Mallory hadn't interrupted them earlier. She wasn't mad at the time, but now she felt like she'd missed out on something that could have been great.

The next song was *Big Yellow Taxi* by Counting Crows.

'I think he's going to ask you out,' stated Mallory.

'How do you figure?' asked Bree, listening to the lyrics.

'Because you're one of the good ones.'

CHAPTER FOURTEEN

February started with some bad news from her father.

'I was let go,' he reported.

'What happened?' asked Bree.

'They just didn't need me anymore. They cut hours across the board and security had one extra person.'

This meant that Bree had become the sole breadwinner for the family by default. She could see the strain her father was now under. His eyes had become sad in the same way they had when her mother had left.

'It will get better,' she told her father. 'You'll find something soon.'

Henry confessed to his daughter that he didn't want to work at anything other than security and that no one seemed to be hiring.

'But you can do something else. Maybe it's time for a change,' suggested Bree.

'This is who I am. I'm a guard… I'm a protector. This is in my DNA.'

'Sure, but like… I'll still love you if you work in a bowling alley or a supermarket or wherever. You don't have to keep doing this just because you're good at it. You'll be good at the next thing too.'

'Maybe.'

'I know it's scary Dad,' said Bree. 'A lot of things are changing… but that's life, right? Things change.'

'I guess we'll see what comes along next. Maybe you're right. Maybe this is for the best. We've been like ships in the night for too long.'

'I'm sure it is,' agreed Bree.

'And… um… speaking of for the best,' said her father, 'I've been talking to your mother.'

'You have?'

This was an exciting development. Bree wondered whether the loneliness of the holiday period had driven them to communicate. It all depended on whether it was over with Adrian. Maybe her mother was finally coming home. Their reconciliation might mean that they could all move somewhere else together and Bree could put her time at the Walker Court Apartments behind her.

'I've asked her for a divorce. Formally.'

'Oh.' All of her internal speculation was blown to smithereens.

'I believe it's for the best.'

'And what did she say?' asked Bree.

'She's agreed. We're making plans to meet with a lawyer soon.'

'Okay.'

'I just thought you should know Bree. In case she calls you or messages you about it. You should know what's going on.'

'No… you're right. Thanks for keeping me in the loop.'

Things were changing. Financially they weren't struggling yet but Bree knew that when she started her Hotel Management course they *could* be. She decided to defer her studies until her father got a job. Henry didn't love the idea but eventually agreed with Bree. There was no point commencing her course if she had to drop out part way through. When the school year began Bree picked up steady day shifts with Mallory, who had dropped out of school the year before, and had no plans to return.

'Did you see that girl Nathan was with?'

'No…'

'I think she works in the mall. I'm sure I've seen her before.'

'Maybe he's looking for another job.'

'So, do you keep in touch with your parents at all?' Bree asked Mallory during a particularly slow Thursday afternoon behind the Candy Bar. She'd never really volunteered any details about her family and Bree had become curious.

'Not really. They live interstate.'

'Whereabouts?'

'South Australia.'

'Do you ever go back and see them?'

'As infrequently as I possibly can.' Mallory's disinterest in this line of questioning was obvious.

'When was the last time you were there?' asked Bree.

'When my brother went to jail.'

'Why did he-'

'I'd rather not talk about this Bree,' she said, interrupting the conversation.

'Okay.'

Bree had been building towards opening up about her own family dilemmas. The conversation felt clandestine, like she'd been prying into the secrets of Mallory's past. Bree nodded and restocked the chips.

'Hey Bree?'

'Yeah?'

'Do you know a guy named Ryan Kellerman?'

The name provoked an immediate cluster of memories for Bree. She froze hearing his name come out of Paul's mouth. *How does he know Ryan?*

'Uh… yes. I know him.'

'Cool. I'm guessing you two worked together at your last job?'

'Yes.'

Bree's palms had started to feel clammy.

'Great. What was that like?'

'Um… how do you mean?'

'Is he a good guy?'

Bree thought about the passive way Ryan had ended things with her. After their night in his car he'd ghosted her. His fleeting contact and the lack of shifts at Toys R Us had led her to apply for another job. She'd never imagined hearing his name inside the walls of Central Cinemas.

'Sorry… why are you asking me whether Ryan is a good guy?'

'Oh, sorry… he's applied for a job here. I just figured because you two had some history I'd see if you thought he'd be a good fit.'

History. Bree could feel herself turning red. She didn't want Ryan working at Central, but she didn't know how to say that without revealing their complicated past.

'Um…' she stammered.

Paul furrowed his brow in search of an answer, which caused Bree to panic.

'I don't think we worked together much. I can't really remember him,' she said.

'Alright, well I'll just see how he goes in the interview.'

'Uhuh,' she said as she ducked out of the office.

Ryan is coming.

Bree was full of nervous energy. *Maybe this is a good thing* she thought to herself. *Maybe it will be different with Ryan this time around.*

As a day worker Bree found that she almost never saw certain employees. Those who only worked on weekends faded from her mind completely. Victor and Warren were strictly night and weekend workers as they both went to school. Due to the brief exchanges during crew handover she felt like she became a stranger to most of the staff. It was just like High School all over again. She dealt with her colleagues in short polite interactions that never amounted to much. Socially Bree's world had started to revolve around Mallory.

Shannon took over from her occasionally on Candy Bar or came in early to make choc tops but there was no time to bond on such shifts. Shannon was too busy meeting her production quota to chat anyway. George and Maxine were the usual projectionist and manager team during the day. Bree missed Matt. She wondered if he was heading up to the Projection room via a back way or another secret door that she wasn't aware of. The two hadn't spoken since their near-kiss and Bree wanted to get out of the limbo she now found herself in. She kept looking out for Ryan's job interview with Paul, but he too remained elusive.

One afternoon a memo was put up in the staff room congratulating Andy, who had been promoted to the newly created position of *Head Staff Trainer*. He started doing mid-shifts that were scheduled to straddle the day and night, where he bossed Bree and Mallory around. Bree wondered how different her life at Central

Cinemas would have been if he'd trained her on that first day instead of Lizzy. Maybe they would have had a better rapport.

'If you've got time to lean you've got time to clean,' Andy would bark when he caught them talking at the Candy Bar.

Mallory was excellent at ignoring him and feigning interest whenever he spoke. Bree often had to bite her tongue to keep from laughing at the obscene gestures she would make behind his back.

'If you want to become a staff trainer Mallory you'll need to keep the place tidier than this!' Andy would decree.

Mallory would wait until he'd strutted away before leaning in to whisper to Bree. 'He already got the promotion. Why is he still being such a kiss-ass?'

Soon some fresh staff were hired at Central Cinemas. Bree loved not being the newest employee. Tristan was a Korean student that was now supporting his family in the wake of his father's early retirement. Bree noticed that Tristan had the exact same haircut as John Cho on the poster of *Harold & Kumar Go to White Castle*. He was attending night school and heavily suggested to Bree that she should do the same, commenting on how easily she would fall behind otherwise.

'Don't compare yourself to him,' said Mallory. 'Let him run his race and you worry about yours.'

Nathan's brother Joel had started working at the cinema too. His red unkempt hair was longer, but he also resembled one of the Weasleys from *Harry Potter*. He barely ever spoke to Bree except to ask her how to get free things.

'So, we can just *have* soft drink?' asked Joel.

'Yeah, but only in these tiny plastic cups.'

'And we get free tickets, right? I don't have to rely on Nathan anymore?'

'That's right.'

Bree also met Paul's younger sister Kasey, who was extremely friendly and open. She was well aware of the nepotism involved in her hiring and Kasey openly compared herself to Liam, who she'd met at a previous job.

'It's going to be tough for me… being the sister of a manager,' she said to Bree one morning. 'Plus Liam seems to have ruined it.'

'Well, you seem much nicer than him…'

'That wouldn't be difficult!' chimed in Mallory as she walked past the Candy Bar, broom in hand.

Bree and Kasey shared a laugh, although she wasn't sure how long Mallory had been eavesdropping on their conversation.

Kasey, who reminded Bree of Zooey Deschanel from *Elf*, was a casual employee and only came in when she felt like working. Even though she was often called to cover sick leave, Kasey often declined.

'You don't get the annual leave perks… but the money's alright,' she informed Bree.

There was one notable absence. With the influx of new blood Bree assumed that Ryan's resume must have been overlooked. She needed to know for sure.

'Hey Paul?'

'What's up Bree?'

'I just wondered… Ryan Kellerman… did you end up interviewing him in the end?'

'Ryan? Yeah we did. We hired him. He's just finishing up at Toys R Us before he starts with us. Should be soon. He's given notice.'

'Okay… thanks.'

'He seems nice, by the way,' observed Paul.

Adding Ryan to the Central Cinemas roster complicated things for Bree. She was now vacillating between her emerging feelings for Matt and her brief but important history with Ryan. This was all new territory. She liked Matt but they'd never even kissed, and he was nowhere to be seen. Bree had been wondering whether he was avoiding her. On the other hand, she'd had so much chemistry with Ryan. If they could get back on track maybe they could pick up where they'd left off. On one level she felt like she was betraying Matt by thinking about what *could be* with Ryan. *But if Matt actually liked her wouldn't he be pursuing her right now?* Bree decided that when she saw Ryan again she'd know. If there were something between them it would be impossible to ignore.

Of all the people she'd met while working at Central Bree was most glad to have met Mallory. Her friend made the decision to delay studying an easy one. The two spent hours together at work scheming and coming up with personal jokes. Mallory had been right: work could be fun.

In the evenings Bree would go home and spend time with her Dad. Without shift work to go to Henry had started to clean the house obsessively and had been rearranging the furniture on a weekly basis.

'How's the *feng shui?*' he'd ask.

'I have no idea,' Bree would reply.

Her father had started to use several dating services, which Bree had struggled with at first. This strange new era seemed to be born out of boredom more than anything. He would show her pictures of women on his computer and ask her what she thought. It was always a little uncomfortable, and Bree took a long time to realise that what her father really wanted was her permission to date again. When the concept finally clicked for Bree she was much more accommodating about the change.

'Do you think she uses too much make-up?' he'd ask.

'I don't know.'

Henry pulled up another profile.

'What about her?'

Bree excused herself from most of these conversations and reminded him that he should be looking for a job, not a girlfriend.

'I'm applying for things,' he protested.

'Like what?'

'Security stuff…'

'But that's still shift work, right?' asked Bree.

'Most of it.'

'Can you apply for some non-shift work too? It would be good to see you at night.'

'Would it? You're off with Mallory a fair bit… I'm by myself here. Excuse me for thinking that some company might be nice.'

'I'm just saying that…' Bree had started to perspire. This conversation was becoming confronting. 'Do you want to watch some TV?'

Her deflection worked and they sat down in silence. Bree knew that her father would settle down once he started working again. While it would be good to see his mood improve, his love life wasn't really her primary concern. Bree had her own budding teenage desires to contend with. Ryan was heading back into her orbit any day now. Bree was excited about the future and this time she was in the driver's seat.

'That Kasey chick is pretty hot.'

'You know she's Paul's sister, right? That's like saying Paul is hot!'

'As if.'

'She's pretty hot though… yeah.'

'There's a party this weekend. You want to go?'

Mallory always knew about upcoming parties. Sometimes she drove around with Bree until they *found* a party. It never mattered that they weren't invited. If there was a big enough turn out they would blend in with the crowd. And they were two dressed up teenage girls, which meant nobody ever asked them to leave.

'Guys *want* girls at their parties. It's a no brainer,' reasoned Mallory.

She was an expert at giving the impression that she belonged, no matter where they were. Mallory was a true chameleon.

'Sounds fun,' replied Bree.

'Cool. I'll text you.'

Bree was spending every weekday at work and every weekend with Mallory. She was starting to see her father's point, but she was having such a good time. It felt amazing to be out in the world, living her life and being a teenager. Canberra didn't hold many secrets for Bree anymore. She longed to explore a new city, and discover the world for herself. Mallory was right to save her money for an escape, and Bree had started following her example. In the back of her mind she had been contemplating what it would be like to defer for *another* year after this one and travel with Mallory. She hadn't brought it up with her father or her friend but was holding onto Mallory's invitation.

Anything's possible you know...

In the background, Bree had thrown herself into their complimentary ticket scam. She'd willingly counterfeiting dozens of imaginary complaints over the last few months. Mallory had filed them, sourced the free passes and had been meeting with other stores in the mall. The whole operation had been executed just as Mallory had promised: without detection. Their plan to trade goods for complimentary tickets was on track.

CHAPTER FIFTEEN

'Take a seat dear.'

Bree sat down and placed her hands in her lap. She was still confused as to why she'd been called into the Location Manager's office. Maxine walked around behind her and closed the door. It was as if all of the air in the room escaped when it sealed. Bree felt like she'd just stumbled into some kind of camouflaged trap.

'I'm going to ask you a question and I need you to be honest with me.'

'Okay.'

She hoped it wasn't about Liam and Daniella. *Had Mallory said something after all? Had the rumour reached their Location Manager?* Maxine's eyes bore into hers, checking Bree for weakness like some kind of human lie detector.

'Bree did you take any money from the office that didn't belong to you?'

'Money from the office?'

Stealing? Bree was shocked at the unexpected accusation. Her jaw dropped open and for a moment she was stupefied. She loved working at the cinema and would never want to jeopardise it. Bree realised that Maxine was suspended before her, waiting for an answer.

'You can tell me if you did,' she stated matter-of-factly.

Bree hoped her silence didn't make her seem guilty in Maxine's eyes.

'No! I would never!' Bree felt her face flush and when she spoke she was alarmed at the anger dominating her words.

'Alright calm down,' Maxine said as she fondled her pearl necklace. 'There has been a theft... *two* thefts really... from Central Cinemas.'

It suddenly occurred to Bree that she might know the culprit. She hoped that Mallory had nothing to do with this, that these actions weren't the result of one of her many little *scams*.

'The same amount of money has gone missing from the office on consecutive Wednesdays. The reason I am talking to you about this is because you were working on both those days.'

Maxine had highlighted the two Wednesday shifts in question on a small desk calendar. The shifts were almost two months ago, back before Bree was permanently doing day shifts. She realised that Wednesday nights had been her poster shifts and that she would have been working on Floor.

'I wasn't handling money on those nights, was I?' she asked.

'No... you were rostered on Floor. But that isn't a complete alibi. You were here, and unfortunately that puts you on my radar.'

The room felt like it was closing in on Bree. She'd never been involved in anything like this before. She wondered if this was how Carol had felt when her father had accused her of having an affair. It was so direct and awful that she felt an unexpected pang of sympathy for her mother.

'I didn't take anything I *swear*. I have no idea what you're talking about,' said Bree placing one hand over her heart, as though she were suddenly under oath.

'It's alright Bree. I just needed to ask you. But know that this is only the beginning of the investigation.'

Maxine leaned back in her chair and stared off into the distance. The movement would have been more effective if her office had included a window. Instead it appeared to Bree that she was analysing a corporate poster that was plastered on the wall next to her desk.

'The police have been called,' she said with a knowing nod. 'They will be taking all of the suspects over to the Police Station for formal interviews.'

'I'm a *suspect*?'

'Yes. There are a few of you. I can't name names… you understand. I wanted to give you a heads up because you will be required for your interview before you go home today. Paul will come in early and walk you over during your shift. Is that okay with you?'

'I suppose so,' said Bree. She tried to remain calm and reminded herself that she hadn't stolen any money.

'*Somebody* did this,' Maxine's gaze lingered for a sign of betrayal in Bree that she could not easily find. 'I'm going to find out who it was.'

Bree thought about her time at Central Cinemas. With the exception of some exploration into restricted areas with Mallory she'd been a model employee. Bree compartmentalised the complimentary ticket scheme, deciding it was a grey area. She contemplated telling Maxine about the way she'd snuck away and added fifty dollars of her own money to balance the till on her first Candy Bar shift. Then Bree realised that this act might make her look incompetent rather than loyal.

'You were Rookie of the Year last year and so I know it's more likely than not that you're a good employee. But it's important to stomp out rebellious and criminal behaviour immediately, and without exception,' stated Maxine with a soulless look in her eyes.

'I agree,' said Bree.

'It's no secret that I'm applying for a position at Head Office… and I'm not going to walk into that job in Sydney without a perfect management record here. Finding the missing money will be a top priority,' said Maxine as she tapped the table with her index finger. 'Now head back to work and wait for Paul. He'll be along shortly for you. And don't talk to anyone else about this, okay?'

Bree nodded.

Maxine opened the door and Bree left in a hurry. *She probably doesn't know about the complimentary tickets. She can't know... otherwise she would have said something by now.*

Bree was distracted for the rest of her shift. Mallory had called in suspiciously sick that morning. Bree couldn't help but wonder if her friend was in any way responsible for the theft. *Had that been the Wednesday night that Mallory had materialised with a torch to look under the stadium seating? Was she working the week after that as well?* Bree remembered that Matt had been there too. That was the night they'd almost kissed. *Could he have been responsible?* She tried to focus on who else had been there. Andy perhaps? Maybe Victor? Bree couldn't be sure. She couldn't recall the particulars. Bree wished that she had someone to talk to about it.

At three in the afternoon, as Bree's shift was drawing to a close, Paul walked out of the office looking tired. He stood with Maxine in the foyer for a few minutes. They looked sombre and kept conspiratorially glancing in Bree's direction. Her two-way radio beeped softly behind her. It was running out of battery. In her distracted state she'd forgotten to place it on the charger at the back wall of Candy Bar. Bree unclipped it and set it down in the charging station. The light turned red, indicating that a charge was in progress.

There wasn't a patron in sight. Bree would have welcomed a customer instead of this pensive alternative. She'd been pretending to clean for the last ten minutes. Paul wandered up to Floor but did not make eye contact with Bree. He'd always been so pleasant to her in the past. She longed for a look or a glance that said *I believe you* or *I know you didn't take that money.* Instead he hastily vanished from view, leaving Bree wanting.

The next few minutes seemed to pass in slow motion. Even though Bree knew she was innocent she was worried that she would be reprimanded, or that she would be framed and that the money would be found in her locker. Her mind had been running wild with all the worst possible outcomes. *What if someone had been targeting her from the beginning? She'd been short fifty dollars during her first shift in Candy Bar. Did she have an enemy at Central Cinemas? Maybe she'd been caught on camera.*

Bree needed this job. Her father was depending on her. Even though deep down she felt that her fear was irrational Bree couldn't stop herself from worrying.

Paul returned to Candy Bar with Shannon and Andy following in a line like lemmings.

'Are you ready to go Bree?' asked Paul.

'Yes.'

'Let's make our way over then.'

Much to Bree's surprise Shannon stepped behind the Candy Bar to cover for her, while Paul and Andy accompanied her out of the cinema. *Andy, the Head Staff Trainer himself, was a suspect too!* This revelation allowed Bree to breathe a little easier. If he'd been implicated as well then there was nothing she could have done to avoid the same scrutiny. She turned around and looked back at Shannon as they were leaving. Bree was surprised when she was offered a broad smile from her colleague. Shannon gave her a thumbs up too. It was so reassuring to have an ally during that moment.

Andy seemed offended by the investigation and as they walked he whispered to Bree.

'This is such bullshit, hey? What a witch hunt.'

Bree said nothing. She looked down, trying not to make eye contact with anyone in the mall as they walked.

The trio made the journey into the daylight and across the street. The sun concentrated its most penetrating rays on them, as if nature itself was trying to sweat out a confession.

The plain white Police Station was directly opposite the mall. Though it had been there for years Bree felt like she was seeing it for the first time. Soon they were sitting in individual leather chairs and awaiting their inevitable interrogation.

Even though he'd opted not to speak, Bree wished Paul would. The deliberate silent treatment the manager employed seemed to magnify the importance of the crime in question. She'd been alone on Candy Bar and the isolation of the day had been endless.

Andy went in first. He wasn't at all nervous. When he was out of sight Paul took out his phone and started to text while Bree shifted uncomfortably in her chair. She'd never been in any trouble with the Police before. This was forcing her to take stock of her recent choices. In the time since Mallory had confided in Bree about the complimentary ticket scheme they had both filled in *dozens* of false complaints. The passes were arriving often. Bree had suggested they use a PO Box in the mall, but Mallory thought that was a waste of money.

'They'll *never* check the addresses. And it's like I said... I'll probably be the one mailing them,' Mallory had said with supreme confidence. 'I usually am.'

'But it's like... a *literal* paper trail that will lead them to your place. If they ever *do* question it... if they go looking for someone... they'll know to look at you!' argued Bree.

'It's going to be fine. Trust me. My name isn't even on the lease at my place,' confessed Mallory.

'It isn't?'

'Don't worry about it. It won't come back to us.'

Mallory had swapped the tickets for gift vouchers across at least nine stores in the mall and was showing no signs of slowing down. She continued to covertly meet with unsatisfied employees and sell them on the idea of a mutually beneficial trade. So far they had split the incoming vouchers evenly, although Bree had yet to actually use any of hers. She had benefitted from all of it, even if she wasn't as involved as

Mallory was in the operation. They were still partners in crime. As Bree sat there next to Paul, a feeling of guilt growing, her phone rang.

Mallory.

She couldn't answer it. Bree didn't want to implicate her friend. She hung up the phone and looked over at Paul. He was staring at her, which she found alarming. Bree worried that he'd seen Mallory's name on the screen.

'Did you do it?' Paul asked her.

'Of course not.'

Paul gave her a nod, his face changed back to the jovial expression that she was accustomed to. 'Some of the staff heard about your Dad losing his job. They think you might have done it because of that.'

'*Some* of the staff?'

'Well... people gossip... you can't help that.'

'And what do you think?' asked Bree. 'You believe me, right?'

Paul gave her a reserved smile. 'I don't think it's in your nature. But someone stole three thousand dollars and that's why we're here.'

'*Three thousand* dollars?' parroted Bree. She couldn't believe it.

'The safe was short fifteen hundred dollars for two straight Wednesday nights.'

'I've never even been *near* the safe. That's in the manager's office,' she protested. 'It's always locked when I'm in there.'

'Yeah... I know.'

'So, what am I doing here?'

'If you were on site on both of the nights in question then you're a suspect. Sorry. I'm just following Maxine's instructions.'

Bree pondered how an employee at Central Cinemas had managed to steal three thousand dollars from a locked safe. She'd heard that the only people that could even open it were armed guards that regularly couriered money directly to the bank. Stealing that much seemed beyond a simple *scam*. She hoped that Mallory was innocent but until she spoke to her friend Bree knew she couldn't be completely sure.

While she sat in the waiting area a memory stirred up in Bree. She recalled a moment from her early teens when, no doubt wanting something insignificant like lip-gloss, she'd stolen coins from her mother's purse. Bree remembered the joy she'd felt when she'd shown off her purchase and the extreme guilt that had followed when her mother had enquired about the financing behind it. She had broken into tears and confessed immediately. Bree didn't appreciate the memory announcing itself now.

They sat on the white plastic seats for about five more minutes. Some officers passed them without comment. Andy resurfaced and walked out of the Police Station alone. Paul made no attempt to stop him. Andy's irritated demeanour looked unchanged by the experience.

'You're up,' declared Paul.

Bree walked in through the security door. The carpeted floor was a dark blue colour that matched the pants of the officer in front of her so well that he had the appearance of a floating torso. The man had a goatee and Bree estimated his age to be about forty. He somewhat resembled Kevin Smith, the Director of *Clerks*, but more svelte with an attractive olive complexion. They ended up in a small interrogation room and sat on opposite sides of the desk. The walls were white painted brick on all sides, and there was no two-way mirror like Bree had seen in so many movies. The Police Officer started a recording device that was attached to the table.

'The time is three forty in the afternoon. It is the tenth of March 2004. I'm here with Bree Fielding who is currently employed at Central

Cinemas in the mall. Miss Fielding can you confirm your date of birth please?'

Bree stated her date of birth.

'So... hang on... are you *eighteen* years of age?'

'No. I'm still seventeen.'

The Police Officer sagged into his seat.

'This interview is suspended. Miss, we can't conduct any formal interview with you without an adult or legal guardian present.'

'Oh.'

'Nobody told you that?'

'No... I was only told about this today,' said Bree.

'Alright, could you write down your mother or father's details for me? In case we need to talk to you again?' he asked.

'Okay.'

Bree wrote down her father's name and number. In the past she would have certainly wanted her mother by her side during such a stressful time. In making the choice she was forced once again to think about how sad it was that her family had fractured six months earlier.

'Thank you for your time. You're free to go.'

He stopped the recorder. Bree was perplexed but happy to be allowed to leave the room.

She was escorted out to Paul who walked Bree back across the street to work. Her shift was almost over and he acknowledged that she could leave early, as Shannon was happy to cover the rest.

'It was a pretty quick interview,' said Paul, as they walked through the mall together.

Bree explained that there was no interview due to her age.

'Well, that's something. I doubt we'll need you for a second interview. The Police are pretty sure they know who did it.'

'They are?'

'Yeah... it should all become public knowledge soon. I'm sure you'll hear about it down the gossip pipeline. Thanks for your co-operation Bree.'

She was annoyed with Paul in that moment. She'd literally been walked to the Police Station like a criminal and now he'd casually confessed that they might already know the culprit. Paul was clearly unsympathetic to her feelings. Bree said nothing more to him on the subject.

In the staff room Victor was ironing his orange work shirt. He stood next to the ironing board looking informal in a white singlet and black pants.

'Hey Bree. How's things?' he asked when he noticed her.

Bree didn't want to talk about it. She dismissively said that things were 'fine' and grabbed her belongings. When she was a safe distance from work she called Mallory.

'Did you do it?' asked Bree after explaining the situation.

'Of course not! Just *taking* money has never been my style.'

Bree believed her. She could hear the honesty in Mallory's words.

'I just didn't like the way that felt today... like... I'd been caught doing the wrong thing.'

'But you haven't done anything Bree. Not really.'

'What we're doing... with the complimentary tickets...' she trailed off.

'It's perfectly legitimate. We're working within their system. Anyone that complains gets a free ticket. We're just more *aware* of that than the average patron. Just like the dry cleaning scam! If people knew about it they'd do it all the time. It's the same thing with the comps. We just have the information,' explained Mallory. 'Don't worry Bree. Everything is still fine. I'm watching out for you.'

CHAPTER SIXTEEN

'I heard it was like eight thousand dollars.'

'Whoa! So, who took the money then?'

'I reckon it was Rita. Either her or Carl. They had the access.'

'Nah… I think it was Paul. His sister probably helped him steal it.'

Bree got called into work that weekend and decided that it would be a good idea to pick up the shift. Paul had seemed desperate on the phone and while she would have enjoyed the revenge that came with declining, she did want the extra money.

'Who am I on Floor with?' Bree asked Paul, as she collected her two-way and schedule for the night.

'Ryan.'

'Ryan?'

'Yeah. He started last week.'

This was the moment she'd been waiting for. When Bree arrived at the podium for work he hugged her. The move took her off guard. He still looked the same, like a boyish Paul Rudd. Ryan's arms felt good around her and she knew it would be a memorable shift.

'I'm so glad we're finally getting to work together again Bree,' he said when their embrace was over.

'It should be fun.' Bree couldn't stop smiling. 'Who called in sick?'

'Andy. I've been training with him and Victor. You shouldn't have to show me much though,' he bragged. 'I've been picking things up pretty easily.'

'So, what brings you to Central anyway?'

'Well in the new year my hours at Toys R Us ran dry.'

'The same thing happened to me,' said Bree. 'They… just stopped calling.'

'Yeah… you get it. They iced me out. So, I started to look for another job,' explained Ryan.

'Cool.'

'The funny thing is… after I told them I got the job here they started giving me shifts… like they were trying to keep me. But I wanted to leave.'

'Yeah Central is better,' said Bree.

'Well… I'd heard you were here. So, that was the push I needed.'

'Oh… yeah?'

'Yeah. You look good.'

During the night Bree found Ryan to be quite a charmer. He'd recently become very tanned, almost to the point of sunburn, which made his white teeth stand out even more. When Nathan came up to help on Point they had a chance to clean together. Ryan explained his new love for the beach as they swept up popcorn in Cinema Four.

'Have you ever surfed?' he asked with a handsome grin.

'No.'

'I started in Sydney over the summer. I'll have to take you sometime. It's the *best*.'

Bree enjoyed his passion and playfully flirted back. While they were cleaning they played a game. Ryan would stand a bottle of water or soft drink upright and then hit it with his broom as hard as he could in the direction of the bin. He never once got it in, but Bree found it amusing to watch.

'I'm just having an off day,' he explained. 'I'm usually pretty accurate with a golf club.'

'Oh, I'm sure you are,' teased Bree. 'But we're not on a golf course and that's a broom.'

'You're distracting me!' he said throwing her another smile.

Bree blushed and turned away. They could only play cinema golf in the two bigger cinemas with stadium seating. While they were cleaning Cinema Five Bree noticed Matt behind the porthole in the Projection room and gave him a wave. He smiled at her but didn't wave back.

'Is that George up there?' asked Ryan.

'No... Matt's on tonight.'

'I don't know him... but George plays really great music.'

'Well... if you wanted Matt to play something specific... I guess you could request it.'

'You reckon?'

Bree nodded. Ryan took his two-way and called through to the Projection room.

'Go ahead...' replied Matt.

'Do you have any of George's CD's up there? Maybe could you put on some Franz Ferdinand or something?'

'Um... I'll see what I can do.'

'Thanks man,' replied Ryan.

Bree and Matt still hadn't really talked since Mallory interrupted them. She had thought about that missed opportunity and had often wondered what that kiss would have been like. Matt disappeared from view and the music came to an abrupt halt. Seconds later *I Try* by Macy Gray came on and Matt returned to the projector on the other side of the porthole. He had a cheeky grin on his face.

'I guess George took his CD's home,' grumbled Ryan.

Is he playing this for me? Does he like me? As Bree swept up a box of spilt candies she felt completely awful for having flirted with her ex moments before. She hoped she was interpreting the song's meaning correctly, and that Matt truly was sending her a sign.

While Ryan was at Point he seemed to be constantly texting people. He wasn't trying to hide it at all. If it wasn't an emergency then staff weren't meant to be on their phones. They were supposed to leave them in the change rooms, but nobody actually did. Everyone just hid them in their pockets, in case management were watching them on the security cameras. *Had Andy neglected to tell Ryan about the mobile phone rules during training?* Bree decided to bring it up.

'Some friends of mine are coming to the movies tonight. They were asking if I was working,' he explained. 'They might come in and say hi.'

Then, without warning, Ryan placed his left hand on Bree's right butt cheek and gave it a squeeze. The moment was over quickly and she was stunned. There was no one around to witness it and all Bree could think to do was to skulk away, pretending she needed to check the trailers.

Initially Bree was numb. *Had that actually happened? Does Ryan think he can just grope girls like that?* When Bree moved down the tunnel she felt Ryan's violating eyes watching her. *Had she somehow invited that attention?* She hadn't meant to. Bree looked back and caught him leering. The spell that Ryan had cast was completely broken. He wasn't as charming as he thought he was. He was some kind of predator and he'd revealed his true self. Bree was ashamed for feeling any attraction to him. She wondered if anyone would believe her side of the story. She'd told Paul that she didn't really know Ryan, downplaying their familiarity. Nobody knew their intimate history. She could still feel his phantom hand on her. Bree stepped into the darkness of Cinema Seven and cried.

She managed to avoid talking to Ryan for the majority of the night after that. Bree spoke over the two-way radio and informed him which cinemas she was cleaning, but only walked past Point on her way to check the female bathrooms. When she needed help she couldn't bring herself to ask. Instead, as if hypnotised, Bree absent-mindedly swept all of the popcorn underneath the seats. She'd seen some of the lazier staff members, including Nathan and his brother Joel, push popcorn underneath the seats every time they cleaned. Bree imagined that she saw Matt watching her from the porthole above, but when she looked up there was no one there.

At the end of the night Bree was checking the slides and trailers when she spied a group of six guys wearing polo shirts with popped up collars walk past Ryan. He made no attempt to stop them, instead nodding in approval. Bree marched back to Point.

'Did those guys have tickets?'

'Oh… yeah… yeah they did,' Ryan replied.

Bree pivoted on the spot and watched them walk down the tunnel and go into the doors of Cinema Eight. She turned back to Ryan.

'So, if I go in there and ask them for tickets, they'll have tickets?'

'You're cute when you're angry,' he said, still grinning.

'Stop it!' replied Bree forcefully. 'Do they have tickets?' she shot back, now immune to his charm.

'That's what I said.'

Ryan was challenging her authority and that made Bree want to catch him in a lie. *He thinks he can just do whatever he wants and that the world will bend for him.* She sped furiously into Cinema Eight and found the group settling into their seats in the back row. Bree shone her torch towards them.

'Hi there,' she said fearlessly addressing the entire group. 'Did you guys have your tickets on you?'

There were other patrons in the cinema watching the interaction, but Bree didn't care. The group of guys looked at each other for a moment. The one closest to Bree spoke first.

'The guy out there tore our tickets.'

'That's fine,' she said with a polite smile, 'if I could just see the other half of the stub? He should have given it back to you.'

The entourage looked at one another and then back at Bree.

'I've dropped mine,' said one as he pretended to check the pocket of his jeans.

'You've all lost them in the last sixty seconds?' she asked condescendingly.

'I didn't say that...'

They put on a show for Bree as they faked their way through a search of their surroundings. In the end, as she had suspected, none of them could produce a single ticket stub.

'If you guys don't have tickets I'll have to ask you to head out of the cinema and back to the Box Office. You can purchase them there.'

Bree delivered the instructions so confidently that she felt proud of herself. They complained and grumbled at first but then one by one they stood up and obliged. Bree followed the last one back to Point. As they passed Ryan, they whispered something to him. She couldn't hear their words but she could tell that she was now the enemy.

'What did you do *that* for Bree?' You embarrassed me!' Ryan's anger was unmistakable, and certainly a shade she hadn't witnessed.

'You can't just let your friends in like that. It's not cool.'

'Ugh... why do you even care?'

'I care because it's my job! You're a dickhead! You think you can do whatever you want all the time? Well you can't,' shot back Bree. She was still full of adrenaline from confronting Ryan's acquaintances.

'Is this because I...'

He stopped himself. Bree could tell that Ryan was the kind of guy that was used to girls seeking out and appreciating his affections. Here in a moment of bravado Ryan had crossed a line. He knew it, but he would never admit it.

'Do you have something to say to me?' she asked.

'No,' he replied meekly.

There was no apology. Bree stared him down, almost begging him to continue. She was ready for a fight. Ryan decided not to challenge her and instead took the opportunity to walk away and clean the male toilets. Nobody had checked them in hours.

'Feature is starting in Cinema Four.'

Matt's voice over the two-way had a calming effect on Bree. She felt like each call and response they carried out during the night was like that wave through the thick glass porthole. There were rarely mistakes with Matt, who was one of the more professional projectionists. Others did not have such a clean sheet. There had been a legendary fault just one week earlier when two sessions had to be cancelled due to human error from George. Word of his monumental blunder had spread rapidly throughout the staff.

'When film prints are shipped to a cinema they arrive in pieces called spools,' Mallory had explained. 'The projectionist has to ensure the spools are the right way around and then attach them to each other in the correct order. If they mess it up the film will be projected upside down and back to front on the screen.'

When George had built up the two new film prints he had emptied both cases completely and left all of the spools on the floor. His mistake, which was only discovered as the films screened during their first session that day, was that he'd accidently swapped the third spool of an action film with the third spool of a romantic comedy. To compound the error there had been a reviewer from *The Canberra Times* seated inside Cinema Two. He wrote a hilarious piece about the mistake in the paper that was briefly shared on the staff room noticeboard. George was given a formal warning from Carl, who was managing that day and had to cancel both sessions. It seemed like an expensive mistake. Bree figured that days like that were probably contributing factors to explain why Carl never smiled.

'That's not the worst mistake I've heard of,' Mallory had reported. 'Apparently Old Lou once played a *very* adult movie to a cinema full of kids. It was bad. The opening sequence of *American Beauty* is pretty graphic. The management team gave out a whole lot of comp tickets that day!'

Bree was glad Matt was there, shielding her from such abusive customer complaints with his competence. She now felt foolish for wanting to pursue something with Ryan. He was all wrong for her. *Why couldn't she see it sooner?*

Two of Ryan's friends wandered back up to Bree. They had tickets to *The Butterfly Effect* this time, so she let them in. A minute later one of them exited the cinema, passing her again and disappearing from view. Bree wondered what he was up to. *Perhaps he needed to go to the bathroom, or had forgotten to get a snack from Candy Bar?* They breezed past in pairs. Each time they did their tickets had already been torn. Bree realised straight away that they were trying to trick her for a second time with a well-worn scam. They had purchased only two tickets for the group of six and were sneaking people in one at a time, pretending they each had a ticket but using only the original two between them. The tickets were already ripped because Bree had torn them in the first place. She was infuriated with their deception and walked into the cinema, leaving Point unattended. The movie was just starting but she didn't care. Bree might have let it go if it weren't for Ryan's earlier behaviour. These guys were now a proxy for him, and they would feel her wrath on his behalf.

'Do you guys have tickets?' she asked calmly, shining her torch against her torso to illuminate her work badge.

'Are you *serious* lady? Don't you have anything better to do?' moaned a guy wearing his trucker hat backwards.

Bree insisted that they comply and threatened to have the projectionist stop the movie if they refused to. She wasn't sure Matt could actually *stop* the movie at her request, but Bree spoke assertively and the group were once again caught out. Slowly they revealed two tickets between the six of them.

'Two of you may stay. I need the rest of you to leave.'

The group hesitated as if they were silently weighing up their options.

'If you don't leave now I'll get the mall security guards to escort you out,' she said in a menacing tone. Bree had heard that if patrons were rowdy, she should contact security. She'd never actually had to before.

Once again they were escorted from the cinema. On the way one of them swore at Bree. The guy in the backwards hat deliberately spilt his large popcorn all over the carpet and then spat on top of the debris. Ryan looked awestruck that his friends were leaving yet again.

'What's going on now?' he asked Bree.

'They were sneaking in.'

'Really?'

'They only bought two tickets between them.'

'So, you kicked out my boys?'

'Your *boys* were breaking the rules,' replied Bree.

'I can't win with you, can I?'

'That's your problem right there. You think that it's just about winning or losing. It's not. This is about right and wrong. You did the wrong thing.'

'And you did the *right* thing, did you?' Ryan asked incredulously.

'I did what needed to be done.'

The group refunded their two tickets and left the complex. Bree stared at Ryan and waited for an apology that she knew would never come. He was an inconsiderate idiot, and Bree now knew it.

'Well?' she demanded.

'Well, what?' he asked, rolling his eyes.

'I never realised you were such a jerk until this moment,' said Bree. 'You're not going to apologise to me, are you?'

'I've got nothing to apologise for. And I didn't think you'd be such a *bitch* either, but here we are!'

That was the limit for Bree and she hurried away. She could feel tears forming in her eyes again and she didn't want to cry in front of Ryan. He might have considered that a victory and she couldn't abide that. Bree didn't know where to turn. *Was the manager's office too serious for this?* If she walked in there now Bree knew that she'd be making a formal complaint. It was overwhelming. She didn't want to be at work anymore so she headed to the staff room.

Bree called her mother who picked up on the second ring.

'Hello?'

'Mum?'

'Yes Bree, it's me. Are you alright?' her mother asked, concern in her voice.

'I'm upset... this guy at work is just being such an arsehole.'

'At work? Oh... honey I'm sorry. Men... can be difficult. There are a lot of bad ones out there.'

'He grabbed me… like I was a piece of meat!' exclaimed Bree.

'That's not okay. Bree, you can report him for sexual harassment, do you understand? Don't let him get away with that.'

'I didn't. I called him out on it… I got really mad,' said Bree.

'Are you alright though? Is there anything I can do?'

Bree had stopped crying.

'I think I'll be okay Mum. I was just… I needed to talk to someone about it.'

'Will you report it? If you don't say something then he'll think that he can do that kind of thing again.'

'I'll think about it,' Bree replied.

'Look… I know it's not easy. Sometimes you have to speak out and say the uncomfortable thing. Otherwise it will keep happening.'

'I know.'

'You can always reach out to me. I realise that… *this*… all of this hasn't been easy but I'm here no matter what.'

'I miss you Mum.'

'I miss you too.'

'I have to go… I'm at work and I'm not even on my break,' said Bree suddenly, realising her absence would soon be noticed.

'I'm only a phone call away,' replied Carol.

'Thanks.'

Bree said goodbye and hung up. As she crashed through the change room door she ran right into Matt and knocked a slice of re-heated pizza from his hands.

'Oh God, I'm so sorry!'

'It's all good. Five second rule, right?' said Matt as he quickly picked up the food. The pizza had landed right side up and could be salvaged. Matt could tell right away that she was in a state. 'Hey, what's wrong?'

'It's Ryan… the guy I'm working with,' said Bree.

'The one requesting Franz Ferdinand?'

'That's the one.'

Matt sat down on the table while Bree sat on the sofa. She wanted to confide in Matt. She explained how Ryan let his friends into the cinema but left out the part about him squeezing her rear. As a potential suitor she wasn't sure how Matt would react if he heard about that detail. She also didn't feel she'd be able to say it out loud.

'Well, that's not good. He's only new, isn't he?' asked Matt. 'Maybe we should say something. What do you think?'

'I don't know… Paul is working tonight and I feel like Ryan will get a slap on the wrist and I'll feel like an idiot.'

'Maxine is in her office. She's working on advanced rosters. Let me talk to her and I promise we'll get a result.'

Bree looked into Matt's coffee-coloured eyes and believed him. She nodded and stood up. Matt hopped off the table and threw his arms around her. It was exactly what Bree wanted and she hugged him tightly. She contemplated kissing him, just to get it over with, but the moment felt extremely unromantic.

'Hello Projection?'

Ryan's voice over the two-way burst their bubble and the hug concluded. Bree turned her two-way off so that when Matt answered there wouldn't be any high-pitched feedback.

'Hey you remembered!' Matt said with an impressed smile. He raised his radio to his mouth. 'Go ahead.'

'Um… Cinema Three has stopped.'

Matt flew out of the staff room without another word. Instinctively Bree followed him around the corner and up the incline towards Projection, even though she was completely unqualified to help. She caught the door to the Projection room before it closed and followed Matt down to the third unit on the left.

'Hello Projection? Could you take a look at Cinemas Three?' repeated Ryan.

'I'm on it,' Matt replied, without unclipping the two-way from his belt.

The film had tightened around a roller and snapped, causing the projector to stop. It had triggered a beeping sound that indicated the film was no longer running over one of the sensors correctly. Matt went into work-mode and quickly repaired the damage with a custom made metal splicing tool. Matt fixed the two ends with sticky tape and then brought the handle of the device down, cutting fresh holes into the sprockets of the 35mm film. He held the film between his fingers and double-checked his work. Satisfied, he re-threaded the projector and re-started the film. The whole process took less than two minutes.

'Feature's restarted in Cinema Three,' he announced over the two-way.

'I should get back,' said Bree, who was a little nervous to be up in the Projection room without permission.

'I'll talk to Maxine,' he promised with a smile.

'Thanks Matt. I appreciate it.'

'You're welcome.'

Bree returned to Floor, finding Ryan looking unhinged.

'Where *were* you? I had to deal with a bunch of angry customers in Cinema Three.'

'It was fixed in two minutes. Relax,' she shot back.

Ryan looked confused, clearly wondering how Bree knew how swiftly it was resolved. *Let him wonder* she thought to herself and strode away down the tunnel.

CHAPTER SEVENTEEN

When the night was over they completed their final film checks. Bree had been strategically avoiding Ryan for hours, leaving him at Point for most of the night.

'And feature is fine in Cinema Seven.'

'Thanks Bree.'

Ryan walked down the stairs first and headed towards the office to return his two-way. Matt intercepted Bree in the foyer.

'Listen, I spoke to Maxine. She knows what Ryan did but ultimately it's your word against his.'

'Oh. I thought that might happen.' Bree felt sure that this intervention was only going to make things worse. 'So… what happens now?' she asked.

'Well we're going to have to hope that he implicates himself. If he admits it then she can fire him but if he denies it then there's nothing much we can do.'

'Fire him?' repeated Bree.

'Maybe.'

'Is she talking to him right now?'

'Yeah… but she wants me to bring you in too. Don't say anything unless Maxine asks you to, okay? We're just going to stand there and put silent pressure on him.'

'Okay.'

'I'll be right there with you,' said Matt.

She nodded. Matt was good at putting her at ease, despite the situation. Bree liked his calming presence.

'What are you guys talking about?' asked Joel, who was watching them from the Candy Bar, a curious look on his face. His red hair was backlit by the popcorn machine, making it look fairly angelic.

'Nothing Joel... don't worry about it,' replied Matt.

'Is it about the theft? Who do *you* reckon took the money?'

'It's not about that,' said Matt quickly, and they walked away.

When Bree and Matt walked into the outer office Ryan was already sitting in front of Maxine. She waved them in.

'Close the door behind you please.'

Bree and Matt obeyed. Ryan was looking straight at Maxine, as if they were engaged in an unspoken staring contest. There were only two chairs, and they were both occupied. Bree and Matt stood behind Ryan out of necessity, and it came off as a kind of bold power move. Ryan was visibly nervous and twitched slightly under the additional scrutiny.

'I've asked Matt and Bree to act as witnesses here,' said Maxine as she looked at Ryan with a piercing gaze.

'Okay...' Ryan crossed his arms in front of him defensively.

'Is there something you'd like to confess to me?' asked Maxine. Bree remembered what it was like to be in that seat and didn't envy the stare that he was receiving from their boss.

The room was extremely quiet as Ryan shifted on his creaky chair uncomfortably.

'Not really.'

Maxine leaned forward and interlocked her fingers in front of her face. 'This is going to be your only chance to come clean. Admit to me what you did tonight and this will go a lot easier for you.'

Ryan paused and then exhaled one long breath. Time seemed to slow as Bree considered that Ryan might not know which incident he was here for. *Was he about to reveal that he'd been inappropriate with her? In front of Matt?* Bree held her breath as Ryan spoke.

'I let them in,' he mumbled.

'Speak up please?' barked Maxine.

'I let my friends in,' confessed Ryan.

Maxine nodded. It felt anticlimactic to Bree. Ryan was going to get scolded and nothing more. She felt anger boiling within her, bubbling up towards her mouth. Before she could stop herself, she was speaking.

'And you assaulted me,' said Bree suddenly, surprising herself with the admission. She wasn't going to say anything but speaking to her mother had informed her decision. It was the right thing to do and Bree knew it.

'What was that?' asked a perplexed Maxine.

Suddenly the whole sordid incident poured out of her. She told Maxine and Matt about her history with Ryan, culminating in the events of that evening. Maxine took copious notes as Bree spoke. When she had finished her assassination of Ryan's character Maxine exhaled. Bree felt lighter.

'Do you have anything to add?' Maxine asked Ryan.

'No.'

'I'm very disappointed Ryan. This is not acceptable behaviour. Now head on home. We'll discuss this further next week.'

Ryan stood and gave Bree a repulsive look as he turned around. 'This isn't over,' he said between clenched whitened teeth.

'That's enough,' said Matt quickly. 'You brought this on yourself.'

Ryan left in a huff. They all listened intently as he slammed the door to the outer office behind him. Bree took a long and deliberate breath, pleased that she hadn't cried during the ordeal.

'Thank you for bringing this to my attention. He'll be informed that we're not keeping him on,' said Maxine.

'Can you do that?' asked Bree. 'I mean… *legally?*'

'Ryan was on probation, so yes. If he'd been here another couple of months then it might have been more complicated. As it stands I don't need to supply a reason for terminating his employment. You did the right thing reporting it early. We don't need people like that at Central Cinemas.'

'I'm really sorry… I didn't want to cause such a scene,' admitted Bree.

'You have nothing to apologise for. This wasn't your fault,' said Maxine. 'When I was your age I wish I'd had the courage that you've just displayed. You're very brave to come forward like that.'

'Thank you.'

'I'll type up a report and I'll need you both to sign it.'

'Okay,' said Matt.

'And don't worry Bree, this will remain confidential,' assured Maxine.

Bree felt guilty. She didn't want to drag Ryan's name through the mud, even if he might have deserved it. She hadn't really wanted him to get fired either, but that seemed unchangeable now. Matt led her away from the office, and he waited patiently as she collected her things from the staff room.

'I'll walk with you to your car if you like,' Matt offered.

'Thanks. That would be nice.'

They passed Joel and Tristan who were standing at Point, deep in conversation. Joel's brother Nathan was on the phone nearby, waiting for a ride home.

When they reached the vehicle, Matt and Bree lingered just in front of the bonnet. She'd had borrowed her father's car and was enjoying driving alone. Matt hadn't put on a jacket and looked cold as he leaned against a concrete barrier.

'Summer's over,' commented Bree, as Matt rubbed his arms for warmth.

'Yeah… the weather's been really weird lately.'

'Hey… thanks for helping me get through all that Matt.'

'It was no big deal,' he replied.

'It *was* actually. He was just so… inappropriate with me,' said Bree.

Matt's face furrowed as he expelled all of the air from his lungs. The warm vapour quickly hovered away into the cool night sky. Matt looked like he was trying to control his reaction.

'I care about you Bree, and it hurts me that someone could make you feel so awful.'

'I know you do.'

'Ryan's done at Central Cinemas. He won't be back,' he said in a measured voice.

A single tear formed in Bree's right eye but she wiped it away. Matt noticed and gave her a sympathetic look, before shivering again.

'You seem really cold,' she said.

'Yeah, I should get back in. I have to stay late and do a test screening tonight.'

'You do?'

Matt explained that sometimes the projectionist on duty could elect to remain behind after hours to quality check a film print. It was a nice opportunity to preview a movie before the general public under the guise of a technical screening. It was always done at the discretion of the manager on duty, who sometimes stayed back to watch too. Matt informed Bree that neither Maxine nor Paul had opted to stick around.

'Tonight I'm screening *50 First Dates*. You heard of it?'

'Yeah, it looks funny. So, you're going to watch it alone?' asked Bree.

'Would you maybe... like to join me? It will go til around two in the morning though...'

'That could be fun.'

'If it takes your mind off this rubbish night.'

'Okay...'

Bree locked the car again and they went back up to the Projection room. Henry would be fast asleep by the time she got home but she texted him anyway, under the pretence that a bunch of staff members were staying back late. *Just a half-lie* she told herself.

'I'll have to leave you here in Projection for a little bit while I make sure Maxine has left for the night. She knows *I'm* hanging back but she might have an issue with me inviting anyone else.'

'I understand,' replied Bree.

'It's going to be a bit eerie up here on your own. It's weird and quiet without all of the projectors making noise. But I'll be back as soon as I can.'

'Okay.'

As the door closed behind Matt everything in the Projection room was absolutely still. Bree roamed the length of the flyer wall and was struck by how many unique artworks Matt had collected. It was a labour of love that almost nobody would ever see. She took out her digital camera, which was in her bag, and snapped a few different pictures. It was difficult to capture its size and beauty. Bree walked to the far end of the corridor and wedged the door open with a brick. She travelled quickly down the stairs and checked the mystery door. It was closed, which didn't surprise her. Bree tried the handle but it wouldn't budge. She went back upstairs, removed the brick, closed the door and waited patiently for Matt.

'Sorry, sorry,' he said as he raised his hands. 'She wanted to chat about Ryan.' It had been at least ten minutes.

'What did she say?'

'She's going to fire him... well... not renew his contract anyway. Maxine was asking about you too.'

'Oh... okay. I'm good now.'

'That's what I said.'

Bree knew that the decision to remove Ryan was ultimately for the best. He had contaminated her environment so effectively during a single shift. Bree shuddered to think how bad things might have been if he'd passed his probation. Prolonged exposure to Ryan would have been toxic.

Matt laced up the projector as Bree watched on in awe. His movements were so smooth.

'You're really good at that,' she said.

'Thanks. It's easy once you get the hang of it.'

She stepped closer to him. 'Can I have a go?' asked Bree.

'Sure.'

Matt slowly unwrapped the film and set it up for Bree. He guided her hand through the green plastic rollers, around the projector and back to the metal platter. Bree intentionally positioned herself between Matt and the film. His arms pushed past Bree and she could feel his breath on the back of her neck.

'Now here is the gate... this is where the film has to line up so it's projected correctly,' he said as he bumped into her slightly.

'Uhuh...' she managed to say.

The tension between the pair was too much. Bree looked back over her shoulder to face him. He read her intentions clearly and the two finally kissed. It felt so natural when Matt dropped his arms around her waist and pulled Bree close. She wanted to erase everything that had happened before that moment, allowing impulse to take over. They didn't test screen a film that night after all, but they did stay back late.

CHAPTER EIGHTEEN

*'No… he didn't quit, he was fired.'*4

'Why? Did Ryan take the money?'

'That happened before he was even working at Central!'

'Well I don't know… I never even met the guy!'

Since the inception of their complimentary ticket scam Mallory had continued to escalate their secret operation. She had recently made arrangements with the manager of an electronics store in the mall. Mallory and Bree were to be part of the small team performing stocktake duties. They were tasked with coming in after hours and calculating how much stock had been stolen by comparing the inventory in the store to the amount ordered and sold. Mallory had traded a pile of her free tickets for the opportunity, but she hadn't explained her reasoning to Bree.

'So, how much are they paying us to count stock?' asked Bree as they walked through the adjoining service tunnels at the back of the electronics store.

'It's twenty-five dollars an hour.'

'So… do you… *like* this manager guy or something?'

It was a plausible reason for this gig. Her friend seemed to be in a relationship with George, while also covertly dividing her time with Dex. Mallory chuckled at the accusation before answering.

'No! It's not like that.'

'So, what are we *doing* this for? The money's not that great.'

'It's stock-*take* Bree. We're taking the stock.'

'How?'

'You'll see. It's all been arranged.'

Mallory introduced her to the manager when they arrived at the back entrance. Bree knew right away that this man was not her friend's type. He was a heavy-set gentleman who kept checking out Mallory's arse. She seemed aware of the attention but never once acknowledged it. They counted the stock with three other people as planned and the task took two hours. When they were done the three random helpers were paid and went home while Bree and Mallory lingered. The manager produced a trolley with several boxes in it.

'Alright. As promised you gave me two hundred dollars' worth of that movie money so you may take two hundred dollars' worth of electronics,' he said as he leaned against the trolley with both his forearms. 'At the marked price.'

Mallory selected some new release films, headphones and a portable DVD player. She didn't ask for Bree's input, instead choosing some movies on her behalf. They took the goods and hid them inside cardboard boxes. Mallory took charge, wheeling the cargo down to the service elevator and leading them to the loading docks. From there they were able to make it back to her car without passing in front of a single security camera. It was a very successful heist.

The girls were hanging out late into the night, this time in the deserted car park beneath Black Mountain Tower. They sat on the front of Mallory's Cortina, staring up at the man-made structure before them. The huge tower soared out into the dark night, where clouds danced past their field of view.

'Can you imagine how good it's going to be when we can trade with *any* store in the mall?' asked Mallory. 'We'll never pay full price for anything ever again.'

'I can't believe you were able to organise this. I mean… he just gave us that stuff.' The haul had been thrown into the backseat of the car.

'All he has to do is report that it isn't there. It's accounted for in the stocktake but the store thinks someone stole it earlier in the financial year. No one will be looking for it. He said I could come in and return these movies when I'm done with them but I think I'll sell them on EBay.'

'I reckon he just wants to see you again,' stated Bree.

'He *did* specify that I should come in when he's on…'

'You're always running some kind of scam, aren't you?' asked Bree, half impressed and half surprised with Mallory.

'Always. If you're not the one doing the scamming then you're the one getting scammed.'

'Do you want to be the queen of the mall or something?'

'God… the queen of the mall? I've never heard of *anything* more depressing. No.'

'Then what do you want out of this?' asked Bree.

'There's a world beyond the mall. Beyond Canberra. I still want to disappear into it, I guess. I'm just saving money for now and when I have enough I won't *ever* come back to this town again.'

Bree looked closely and saw a buried pain behind Mallory's eyes.

'Come on. Let's get something to eat,' said Mallory.

Together they drove out to a late-night food truck called *Checkers* for sustenance, although everything on the menu featured grease. The clientele were an extremely random collection of bodies. Some were drunks, lining their stomachs to soak up alcohol while others were unassuming types that stood happily to the side. *Checkers* was located across the road from the Belconnen Labour Club, an establishment full to the brim with poker machines.

'Hi Bree. Hi Mallory.'

The girls were surprised to find Warren and Tristan from Central Cinemas standing adjacent to the food van devouring individual paper cups filled with hot chips.

'What are you two doing here?' asked Mallory.

'We were studying together and we thought we'd get a feed. Nothing else is really open around here,' replied Tristan. 'You look pretty tonight Mallory.'

'Pft whatever.'

Bree and Mallory ordered two greasy burgers and ate them in Mallory's car. Tristan gave them a wave when he and Warren departed together.

'I'm not sure that food truck is sanitary,' said Bree as she checked her burger for hairs.

'It's fine! Live a little,' commanded Mallory as she took a ridiculously large bite.

Bree had been thinking about the sadness she'd glimpsed in Mallory that evening. She wondered if she could coax something from her friend now, while her defences were down.

'It's been really crazy getting to know you. In a good way,' started Bree. 'Have you… always been like this?'

'Like what?'

'Don't be offended but… reckless… I guess?'

'Wow. *Reckless*? I'm not sure I follow.'

'Well… like… I keep thinking about the way you're operating on this whole other level. You're like five steps ahead. The way you're growing the complimentary scam. And the way you're stringing along George…'

'Is there something you want to ask me Bree?'

'No... I mean... yes *and* no. I've been thinking about that day on the roof for one thing. Did you want to fall?'

'No.'

'So, what happened? Do you need to talk about something?'

'No, I don't.'

'Don't tell me it was a trust exercise Mallory. What was going on that day? Why can't you just be honest with me about things? I don't want to be lied to,' said Bree.

'Okay, ask me something. Anything. I'll tell you the truth.'

'Why don't you ever go back to see your family in South Australia? What happened?'

'You want to know what *happened*?' asked Mallory.

'Yeah. I mean... you're jaded and you hate it here in Canberra. But you're all alone. You don't talk to your family and from what I can tell I'm your best friend.'

'You *are* kind of my best friend, aren't you?' said Mallory, a smile creeping across her face. It was as if she hadn't really stopped to think about it before now. Neither could deny that the two had grown close.

'You're my best friend too,' said Bree. 'I don't mean to interrogate you. It's just... I want to know you.'

'Back home I used to hang out with this girl named Valentina,' said Mallory.

'Why did you stop hanging out?'

'She died.'

'Oh my God. I'm so sorry. What happened?'

'We were in school together. Valentina had a defective heart. Her parents knew and never told her. They wanted her to have a normal life and not spend every day worrying. We were in High School... and we were running on the oval one day for P.E and she just collapsed. That was it.' Mallory made a motion with her hand that looked like she was dropping something invisible.

'That's awful,' said Bree. She reached out and sympathetically placed her hand on top of Mallory's.

'They drove an ambulance up onto the oval but it was already too late.'

'How old was she?'

'Fifteen.'

Mallory scrunched her burger wrapper up and threw it into the grease-stained bag.

'She shouldn't have been running but nobody knew. I confronted her parents about it afterwards. They were in shock, I guess. The whole school was in shock. She was beautiful and popular. Everyone liked Valentina. She was so much fun. She didn't deserve to die like that.'

'There wasn't anything you could have done. You didn't know,' said Bree.

'But I *should* have known. *She* should have known! It was her heart after all! Her parents should have told her and it's their fault she's not here.'

Mallory had clenched her fists in anger. Bree had never seen this side of her.

'She should still be here,' Mallory muttered.

Bree didn't know what to say. She imagined the hurt and the confusion that Mallory must have felt in the aftermath of that horrible day. She considered how it would feel to lose someone that meant so much, and during such a formative period of life.

'That's why I hate it there. I see Valentina everywhere in my hometown.'

'Thanks for telling me.'

'Thanks for listening, I guess. Life is too short not to get the most out of it, you know? But you have to look out for yourself.'

'I understand Mallory. When you save enough money… and you leave… I'll miss you,' said Bree.

'Maybe we'll have enough money by then to leave together. What do you think about that?'

This was exactly the sentiment Bree wanted to hear from Mallory. It had been a long time since she'd suggested they travel together, and she'd been afraid that the offer wouldn't be articulated again.

'Explore the world, huh?' Bree smiled happily at the idea.

'Together?' asked Mallory.

'Together.'

'We can be anyone we want,' said Mallory confidently.

'It's going to take a *big* pile of money to travel the world being anyone we want. What kind of scams are you cooking up for our future?'

'Good ones. When I'm ready to share them you'll be the first person I tell.'

While they sat in the vintage Cortina watching the patrons from the Labour Club stumbling out into the night Bree filled Mallory in on her evening with Matt.

'So, he wanted to screen a movie?' asked Mallory.

'Yeah, but we never wound up watching one.'

'I told you that hooking up in the Projection room was fun. Where did you do it? On the work bench?'

'I'd rather not talk about… where…' said a blushing Bree.

'But you did?'

'Yes.' Bree smiled uncontrollably.

'Awesome! About time. So, are you two an item now?'

Mallory shifted in her car seat as she waited for an answer.

'I don't know.'

'It's cool that we're kind of both dating projectionists. Maybe George can do a test screening for *me* some night,' said Mallory with a sly smile.

Then Bree spotted them.

Her mother stepped out of the Labour Club arm in arm with the man that had broken up her parents' marriage. It was the first time Bree had seen him. Adrian was tall and thin, with thick glasses perched above a fairly bulbous nose. With the exception of this one oversized element he was an attractive guy. Her mother beamed at him. Bree could see she'd been drinking. Her face was flush the way it had been after she'd consumed a few glasses of wine. They looked content as they wandered in the opposite direction together.

'Let's get out of here,' said Bree. 'I should get home to my Dad.'

The seed of that test screening idea must have festered within Mallory for the next month because as the school holiday period approached a new scam was born. She cornered Bree in the staff room one afternoon to verbalise it.

'Sometimes Central runs a late night movie marathon of three consecutive films that start at midnight. Sometimes they'll get a popular new film to entice people to come. It's always full of annoying teenagers and they always want to cause trouble.'

'*We're* annoying teenagers that always want to cause trouble,' joked Bree.

'You know it! Everybody gets locked in and watches their three films in a row. Since they can't go anywhere the Candy Bar always makes a lot of money,' Mallory explained to Bree. 'Especially with the stoners.'

'Don't most people just fall asleep?'

'It's hard to sleep with a movie blasting at you. So, George is going to put his hand up and volunteer to work, and you and I are going to make sure we both have the night off too. And the next morning of course.'

'Okay… so you want to watch three movies in a row?'

'We're going to have our *own* little movie marathon in a different cinema. An empty one.'

'And George has agreed to this?' asked Bree.

'Not yet, but he will. I'm very persuasive when I want something.'

As it turned out George was fine with it. He liked having Mallory around while he was at work and enjoyed it even more when she spent time with him in the Projection room. Bree never asked for the details about what they got up to, but Mallory seemed to delight in telling her.

On the evening of the marathon Mallory picked up Bree at nine-thirty at night. Even though she'd told her father all about the event he was still a little annoyed. He'd been unusually sullen, having missed out on a job that he thought he should have been given.

'You went to that late night film check a few weeks back… now you're going to see three movies?'

'I'm trying to make friends. The Central Cinemas staff are nice… and you know Mallory. She'll be there.'

'I've barely met her,' stated Henry.

'Well, we should change that.'

'Well... yeah. If she's a friend of yours then I'm sure I'll like her.'

'I'm just being social.'

'Look... I don't want to prevent you from having friends. It's just that...'

Sensing the real cause of his frustration Bree tried to be supportive. 'You've been doing those casual shifts. Maybe they will turn into more,' reasoned Bree. Her father had picked up some odd hours here and there at the Labour Club where Bree had spotted her mother with Adrian. She had been increasingly nervous that a run in was inevitable.

'I don't know. It's just been difficult seeing how well you're doing... with work... and friends. I guess it's just hard for me to sit around at home while you're such a success.'

'Things will change. They always do.'

Henry smiled at his daughter.

'You're probably going to sleep in all day tomorrow too,' he moaned as Bree headed for the door. 'At least you're not taking the car.'

'Try and relax Dad. I'll make you pork chops tomorrow night, if you're interested?'

'I'm always interested in pork chops. And the Raiders are playing the Knights tomorrow. Want to go to Bruce Stadium with me?'

'I'd love to.'

Bree kissed him on the cheek and met Mallory in the driveway. Her best friend had avoided any and all communication with her father, but as he stood in the doorway of their apartment waving impatiently at her, Mallory was pressured into waving back.

'Was that so hard?' asked Bree as the car reversed.

'I don't like to associate with families. They always ask me about my family. It's nothing personal. I just don't want to talk about them.'

'It's cool.'

Bree could see her father watching her in the side mirror. He kept staring until she was out of sight.

Mallory led Bree out to the back of Candy Bar where they found dozens of energy drinks that had been seized from marathon patrons.

'Every year people try and bring in supermarket food,' said Mallory as she snatched several bottles and placed them into her bag. 'They forget that they can't bring glass into a cinema and we confiscate them.'

'Mallory!'

'What? They'll never come back for it. All of this is fair game.'

'But we're not even working tonight,' Bree protested. 'Don't those belong to the staff who have to stay up?'

'Look around, Bree. There are so many bottles of energy drink that nobody is going to notice.'

Bree shook her head. As always Mallory was in a league of her own. She knew every crack in the system and exactly how to exploit it.

They hung out with George for a little while in the Projection room before midnight and drank several of the energy drinks. Bree liked George for Mallory. The two seemed to make each other happy. The Lizzy incident was a distant memory now and Bree knew instinctively that she should never bring it up, the same way she knew not to mention Mallory's mysterious outings with Dex. Maybe they were more innocent than Bree was making them seem. Perhaps Dex was on the verge of getting her backstage passes to a bunch of gigs in exchange for movie tickets. Either way Bree would have to trust her friend.

Mallory took out her lighter. Craving a cigarette the two girls went upstairs to the roof on Level Five. Bree watched as Mallory tried to blow smoke rings out into the night air. The Canberra weather was calm but the view from the restricted balcony was still terrifying to Bree, who stayed a safe distance from the edge.

'Is that weed?' she asked, noticing the unusual scent.

'Yeah. You want some?' Mallory held it out, offering it to her friend.

'Why not?' said Bree as she took a hit. She considered that the effect of the drug would wear off in a few hours when the movie marathon came to an end. Mallory was the designated driver so Bree felt like there was no excuse for her, the passenger, not to partake.

'I'm such a bad influence on you, aren't I?'

'I wouldn't do anything I wasn't comfortable with,' stated Bree.

'Speaking of which… I wanted to talk to you about something.'

'What's up?'

'I was talking to some people and I told them how we can organise these test screenings late at night.'

'What people?' asked Bree.

'Just some of my connections. *Mall* people… I guess you could say,' said Mallory with a shrug. 'Friends of friends.'

'Mall people makes them sound… *seedy*. Like they live in the mall after hours.'

'Okay fine… not mall people then. Think of them as people that could help us get things we want.'

'*We* can't organise test screenings… projectionists can…'

Mallory wrinkled her nose. 'Well… George will help us.'

Bree looked out over the car park at the collection of vehicles that had settled in for the event. The movie marathon was more popular than she'd realised. It spoke volumes about how little there was to do in the Nation's Capital.

'So, what did these *people* have to say?'

'Well,' Mallory began, 'hypothetically if we were to put on one of these test screenings... some of these... *people* thought it might be good if we...'

'What? Just spit it out!'

'Recorded the film and made them a copy,' said Mallory.

'*What*? You want to start pirating films?'

'I wanted to run it by you Bree. I wanted to see what you thought.'

'But like... who wants to buy our dodgy copy of a film?'

'I don't know. They do. Does that part matter?'

'No Mallory. It's not a good idea.'

'It's not like it would be traced back to us. The camera would only record the screen. You wouldn't even be able to tell what cinema it was filmed in.'

'And then what? How on Earth do we sell that? What's the next step?'

'*We* don't have to worry about that part. We just give the tape to this guy I know and we get paid.'

'I mean... Mallory... it was different when we were filling up empty seats. If we have a stolen copy of the film out there that means people don't even come into Central Cinemas. Now we're hurting the business, aren't we?'

'So, you don't think we should do it?'

'No.' Bree folded her arms.

'And what if we just did it… one time. Like a one-off job?'

'I don't think we should risk it.'

'Okay… don't be mad but I thought tonight's screening would be a good time to try this.'

'Mallory!'

'I said *don't* be mad! I already kind of said yes!'

Bree exhaled deeply and tried to compose herself. It was a stupid suggestion but Mallory was like a dog with a bone when she got an idea in her head. Bree conceded, knowing that appeasing her friend would put a stop to it. At least Mallory was still at the stage where she ran ideas by her. She wasn't a total loose cannon. Bree intended to keep her in line.

'One time alright? We are only doing this *one time!*' said Bree wagging her finger in front of Mallory.

'You're the best Bree! Oh my God I forgot to tell you!' Mallory's eyes had gone wide.

'What?'

'Remember when you went to the Police Station? The money that went missing two Wednesdays in a row?'

'Yeah?'

'They found out who did it!' said Mallory with a little shriek.

'Who?'

'Andy.'

'Really? *Andy?*'

'Yeah. Well, at least they assume he did it. Some money appeared in his bank account that was pretty similar to the amount that was taken.'

'The Police were watching his *bank account?*'

'Yeah! What an idiot. Why would you put stolen money into your bank account? I guess maybe they couldn't prove where the money came from exactly but Paul and Maxine confronted him and asked him point blank about it.'

'And?'

'He didn't confess but they asked him to resign and he did!' squealed Mallory, who seemed to draw sustenance from the ongoing drama.

Andy. The prodigal son of Central Cinemas. The Employee of the Year. Bree couldn't believe what she was hearing. She was suddenly thankful to have lucked out with Lizzy as a trainer.

'Oh my God! He did it?'

'Would he resign if he was *innocent*? Yeah he must have done it!' reasoned Mallory.

'That's insane.'

'Maybe that was part of the deal… if Andy agreed to resign and return the money they wouldn't press charges.'

'I would've loved to have been a fly on the wall during that meeting,' said Bree.

'Well, we can speculate all we want but we're never going to find out. Who would we even ask? Maxine? I don't think so.'

Bree imagined the office door closing behind Andy. She pictured Paul standing behind him as Maxine accused him of theft. Bree knew that those confronting scenes with Ryan in that office would probably stay with her for the rest of her life. She never wanted to be on the end of one of Maxine's stares again.

'Mallory… we're only going to do this *once*, right?'

'That's right. Just tonight.'

They settled into their seats and opened up even more stolen energy drinks. Before George started the film Mallory took out a small video camera and tried to position it between the seats a few rows ahead of where Bree was sitting. She checked the angle and shook her head.

'It could be better.'

Mallory wedged her camera down more forcibly and it stayed in the seat gap on its own. She stood hovering over the device and waited until the trailers started. When the opening titles for *Kill Bill: Volume 2* commenced Mallory hit record and then returned to sit with Bree.

'We probably shouldn't talk much,' she whispered as she sat down, 'in case our voices get recorded.'

Bree nodded in agreement. 'That would be pretty incriminating,' she whispered in reply.

The movie marathon experience allowed teenagers a legitimate place to keep hanging out after hours. It didn't really matter what films were playing. They roamed the foyer and the tunnel freely. Once they were locked into the complex for the night nobody was checking tickets anymore. Several teenagers interrupted Bree and Mallory's screening by poking their curious heads in. They'd take a quick look at the screen and then leave when they couldn't spot any of their friends in the cinema. Nobody noticed the camera, which was hidden beneath a jumper.

At the conclusion of the movie Mallory stood up and checked the device.

'It ran out of batteries,' she announced.

'Oh.'

Bree and Mallory realised that they hadn't really thought this through and had to laugh at their failed attempt.

'This doesn't count,' said Mallory.

'It wasn't a very good movie anyway,' added Bree, who had wanted to watch *Eternal Sunshine of the Spotless Mind*.

On her way out of the cinema Mallory spotted a mobile phone that must have been left behind by a patron earlier in the evening. She checked the screen and saw that it had several missed calls.

'I'll put this in lost property later,' said Mallory as she switched the device off and pocketed it.

The girls left the complex through the fire exit where Mallory had been smoking the first time they'd met. It was the same door that her friend had banged on, interrupting Bree's first kiss with Matt. It was on the other side of that very door that they found Liam, leaning against the railing opposite the bins, wearing a dark suit. He looked like he'd reinvented himself, his hair now changed from his natural blonde to a dark colour. Liam now resembled Christian Bale from the film *American Psycho* more than ever. He took a long drag on his cigarette when he saw them and enjoyed the confusion on their faces.

'Evening. Nice to see you both again,' he said finally.

'It's morning actually,' stated Mallory, sarcasm in her voice.

'What are you doing here?' asked Bree.

'Well I'm a manager *and* a projectionist now. They asked me to cover the office tonight. You didn't see me earlier, did you?'

'No,' replied Bree.

'Well I saw you two. I saw you heading up to the Projection room, which I thought was odd. You never came into the office to ask me for tickets to the movie marathon so I wondered what you were doing here. I had the Floor staff keep an eye on what cinema you went into.'

Tristan and Warren were working on Floor that night. They had become fast friends and, evidently, happy to help Liam rat them out. There was a knot in Bree's stomach. Liam paused dramatically, taking another puff.

'*You're* managing tonight?' asked Mallory.

Liam nodded and exhaled via the side of his mouth.

'I know about your little screening,' said Liam as he flicked ash onto the ground, 'and I don't care. You didn't tell my Mum, or anyone else, about my... *date* with Daniella so I figured I owed you one.'

'That's cool,' said Mallory. 'Thanks I guess.'

'Just *one* though. This one. I wouldn't make a habit of pirating movies girls. The next time you're caught out you'll definitely be fired. Maxine has a zero tolerance policy on theft.'

'Is it *really* theft though...' started Mallory.

'Yeah, one hundred percent it is. If you take a cake from a bakery you've stolen their product. Central Cinema's product is film. You're literally taking it away with you on that tape. That's the definition of theft.'

Mallory clutched at her bag defensively. *Was she afraid of Liam? Or was she just protecting the camera?* He turned to Bree, took a final puff and stubbed his cigarette out against the wall.

'Don't worry about it Bree. I know it wasn't your idea. You should probably be more careful with your associations.' Liam smiled evilly at Mallory.

'Aren't you the *rude* one? Come on Bree,' said Mallory.

Liam chuckled as they left.

When they returned to Mallory's car it smelled horrible. They couldn't immediately place the scent but as they reversed out of their car park they saw a smouldering bag of rubbish that someone had stuffed underneath the car. Half of the black bag had burnt away, exposing an assortment of putrid items.

'Gross!' squealed Bree, as she opened the windows.

'It was probably some shithead teenagers,' declared Mallory.

She hesitated with the car in reverse. The headlights illuminated the smoky plastic bag.

Bree imagined that whoever did this had intended for the car to explode. The girls were supposed to find a burning wreckage but the attack had been unsuccessful. *Thankfully cars don't just explode like they do in the movies.* Unfortunately the smell would linger for days and they would associate the lingering scent with their failure.

'Do you think George will get in trouble?' asked Bree.

'Nah, he just thought we were watching the movie.'

'You didn't tell him we were pirating it?'

Mallory shook her head.

Bree was astonished. She felt guilty, Liam's words still ringing in her head. They'd been lucky. By not spreading gossip about the location manager's son Liam had absolved them of their crime. Mallory had been too brazen for her own good. Bree decided it was beneficial that George didn't know the truth, and that seemingly they'd avoided detection from everyone but Liam.

'I just hate that Liam was the one to catch us out,' said Mallory.

'Yeah it sucks. But what can we do? It's over now.'

CHAPTER NINETEEN

The staff meeting felt unending. Even Paul, who loved administration in all its forms, seemed to be losing focus as Maxine rambled on and on. Bree scanned the foyer. Mallory, who was seated directly next to her, was wearing a hoodie. She'd arrived late to the meeting and sat down without a word. Bree couldn't see her eyes and wondered whether she was still awake at this early hour of the morning. She didn't want to crane her head to check, just in case she alerted Maxine to her friend's sleeping and got Mallory in trouble.

'So, please only change over the post mix in the storeroom when they have *completely* run out,' said Maxine. 'There has been too much wastage as of late.'

Victor was texting on his phone. He seemed to have evolved into something of a rebel since his alleged encounter with Lizzy. Bree was never able to confirm the incident had taken place but she'd noticed a change in his demeanour. He was going out a lot and seemed less interested in work.

Kasey, despite being a casual employee, had turned up to the meeting with her brother Paul though it didn't seem like she wanted to be there at all. Warren had made himself almost invisible by standing beside the skill tester on the far side of the foyer. Nathan, Joel and Tristan were leaning against the back wall like some kind of teenage gang. Matt was missing, having been rostered in Projection that morning. The surprising gossip of the day was that Rita and Carl were now an item and were holding hands in full view of the staff. Apparently they'd been together since January but had kept their relationship under wraps. Both managers had arrived together, and their union did not appear to bother Maxine or Paul, who must have been given advanced notice. It was strange to see Carl and Rita smiling and doting on one another. Bree was used to their faces looking stern and disapproving. It was a pleasant change.

'The latest combo has been a good seller for us, but we need to use up the leftover boxes first please,' continued Maxine, 'before the new *Harry Potter* ones arrive...'

The Location Manager was standing in front of the Candy Bar in a teal-coloured suit, toying with her signature pearl necklace. Bree couldn't help but wonder what Maxine's casual clothes looked like, and what it must have been like for Liam having her as a mother. She was so commanding that Bree thought she must have been strict. Perhaps she was a driven career woman that wasn't around much. Maxine continued to project her voice to the gathered group.

'Some of you might be aware that since Andy's recent resignation we've had a Trainer position open up.'

A silence fell over the cinema employees. By now they had all heard about Andy and the missing three thousand dollars, although the actual amount that was taken seemed to vary depending on who you spoke to. Interviews for his replacement had been conducted and although they had decided against appointing a new Head Trainer they still needed someone to fill the void created by his departure.

'It's my pleasure to formally announce that Shannon has been promoted to the position of Staff Trainer,' said Maxine. 'Congratulations Shannon.'

A small applause bounced around the foyer. Bree thought it was a good decision. Shannon seemed like the kind of person that would be a positive influence on a new staff member. She had been nothing but nice to Bree, especially during the accusations of theft against her.

'Also,' continued Maxine, 'we've had a position open up in Projection. George has decided to leave us and has given notice.'

Bree spun to look at Mallory. This appeared to be a surprise to them both.

'My son Liam, who most of you already know, will be transferring here from Southern Cinemas to take over from George.'

This wasn't good news. Bree didn't trust Liam at all. Her intuition told her that his addition to the team spelled trouble for their future. Liam knew too much about their endeavours already.

When the staff meeting concluded, some of the employees decided to head into the food court and have breakfast. Nathan dragged his brother away in a playful headlock.

'I'm going to report you!' Joel yelled. Nathan released him momentarily before grabbing him for a second time, with additional force, the relationship between them blurring from brothers to co-workers and back again.

Mallory said she wasn't hungry and didn't want to tag along for breakfast. While Bree and Mallory spoke they were interrupted by Tristan, seemingly on an urgent mission.

'Hi Mallory,' he said.

'Morning.'

'Hey... do you want to go out sometime? Like... we could watch a m-movie or something?' stammered Tristan, clearly nervous.

'With you?'

'Yeah... with me... I thought maybe... since George...'

'No,' seethed Mallory.

'Oh…'

'Leave me alone, okay?'

'Okay… sorry to… yeah…'

Tristan wandered back towards Warren who was waiting at Candy Bar. Warren consoled his friend, which made Bree feel for them. It would have taken some courage to ask out Mallory, with her prickly exterior.

'Did you hear that? He was asking me out.'

'Yeah I heard. Hey… are you alright?' asked Bree as the rest of the group dispersed.

'I'm fine.'

'That's crappy news about Liam coming back.'

'I guess.'

'And are you going to tell me what happened with George? Why is he leaving all of a sudden?'

Mallory lowered her hood and kicked absent-mindedly at some stale popcorn that had been missed by the cleaners overnight.

'We kind of broke up.'

'When did this happen?' Bree's eyes were wide with shock. George was a nice guy and she wished Mallory would have confided in her earlier. She hated hearing about George's departure from Maxine during a staff meeting. Bree didn't want to be blindsided. She disliked surprises in general since her parents' break up.

'He wanted to get serious… like *married and babies* serious,' stated Mallory.

'He doesn't seem like the settling down type to me,' returned Bree. George had been romantically linked to multiple female employees, according to the Central Cinemas gossip pipeline.

'I didn't think so either. When I told him I didn't want those things we had a fight. I said I didn't want to see him anymore and then he must have quit.' Mallory started shaking her head. 'If he thinks *this* is going to change my mind he doesn't know me at all.'

'Are you okay?'

'I'll be fine. George was fun but I was just passing the time with him, I guess.'

Mallory was discarding him like a rogue hair that had attached itself to her jumper. It was so clinical.

After insisting she was fine Mallory drove herself home while Bree travelled upstairs to see Matt. Just like Carl and Rita, the two had been seeing each other in secret for a few weeks and the sneaking around made it even more fun. Nobody knew they were dating except for Mallory who, true to form, was excellent at keeping things to herself.

The Projection room door was propped open with a small cardboard box that had once housed light bulbs. Matt spotted her when she was halfway down the Projection room tunnel. He dropped what he was doing and made a beeline for Bree.

'How was the meeting?' he asked as he kissed her hello.

'Ugh. Boring. Maxine went on and on about procedures forever. I don't know why they insist on having these meetings at eight in the morning.'

'Yeah it's a dumb time to make everyone come in, but it's either early in the morning or super late at night. Maxine hates staying up late. That's why she's almost always on day shifts.'

'On a Saturday too. Some people were at work last night,' protested Bree.

'They say the meetings are mandatory but people still skip them.'

'Like you?' she said, kissing Matt again.

'Yeah… but I have to *work*.'

'Lucky you,' said Bree.

Matt sat at the desk in the middle of the room.

'Would you like some breakfast?' he asked gesturing to the cereal bar. 'I've added some new varieties.'

'No thanks. I'm not really hungry. Did you know Mallory and George broke up?'

'Did they?' Matt seemed genuinely surprised.

'George wanted to get married to her apparently… so she broke it off.'

'That doesn't sound right,' said Matt, furrowing his brow.

'Why? What did you hear?'

'Just some gossip…' Matt toyed with a spike of his brown hair.

'Are you going to tell me?' asked Bree, trying to pry the information from him.

'Well… take this with a grain of salt because I don't know this for sure. I heard that Carl came up to get some light bulbs for Candy Bar and saw Mallory and George in a… *compromising* position.'

It wasn't uncommon for managers to visit the Projection room. Maintenance around the complex was always performed by a manager or a projectionist and all of the necessary tools and bulbs were kept near the door of the Projection room. Bree knew Mallory well enough to know instantly that this rumour was most likely true. She'd often spoken about spending time alone with George up there.

'Wow,' was all she could manage to say.

'She didn't tell you about it? I heard it happened a few weeks ago.'

'Well, why didn't *you* tell me then?' There was something feral in Bree's words. She felt defensive of her friend and frustrated with the situation. Bree was also suddenly nervous about someone walking in and finding her there. Thinking about Mallory's reactions that morning, with this new information in mind, made things even worse for Bree. She'd been oblivious to her best friend's heartbreak, even though Mallory herself would never refer to her relationship with George in those words. Mallory wouldn't willingly admit weakness.

'Sorry,' she said quickly realising her tone towards Matt had been severe.

'It's okay,' he said reassuringly.

'So, did they ask George to quit? Like they did with Andy when he stole the money? Or did George quit on his own?' asked Bree.

'Nobody really knows what happened with Andy... don't just assume that's the truth. George gets to stay while they hire and train Liam's replacement at Southern and then he's done. That reads like he's leaving on good terms to me.'

'You haven't spoken to George about it?'

'Not yet,' said Matt.

'Did Mallory get in any trouble?' asked Bree.

'No idea. If she did she's doing a good job of hiding it. George got in *more* trouble because he's the projectionist. He's supposed to be responsible and he invited her in...'

'You invited *me* in today...'

'Yeah.'

'I don't want to get you in trouble...'

'Then don't.'

Matt stood up indicating he had work to do. Bree took the hint and, giving him a quick kiss goodbye, headed for the door. *No more rendezvous in Projection* she thought to herself. It was a shame. She had been enjoying sneaking up there to be alone with him.

That Monday Bree was working in the Box Office with Kasey, who had been called in to do a shift. It wasn't busy at all and the two chatted happily between ticket sales.

'Paul's a pussycat once you get to know him. He keeps rostering me on Box Office which is good,' said Kasey. 'Very brotherly of him.'

'Oh, I like Box Office the most,' said Bree in agreement. 'It's the easiest.'

'I know! I hate Floor, unless I get to be on Point tearing tickets.'

'Totally.' Bree nodded.

'I was on Point the other day when this big scary biker came in and thrust a ticket in my face. I told him the cinema was just being cleaned and asked him to wait to the side,' said Kasey, recalling the event.

'Did he wait?'

'No. He swore at me and walked right past!'

'What did you do?'

'What *could* I do! He was *huge*!' Kasey continued, enjoying the expression on her colleagues face. 'I think he gave Victor a fright too! He wasn't expecting anyone to walk in while he was cleaning, let alone a biker.'

The two laughed together. Bree liked Kasey much more than her brother Paul. If she didn't know them personally she wouldn't have guessed they were siblings at all. While they had matching blue eyes, Kasey's easy-going nature seemed in opposition to Paul's over-organised world. Kasey paused the story when the Box Office phone rang.

'Bree speaking.'

There was a short pause before the person on the other end spoke.

'You used your real name,' came the reply.

Mallory.

'How are you?' Bree had texted Mallory multiple times without a reply. She'd been curious about how her friend was handling the break up.

'You should use an alias… like I taught you.'

'I'll remember for next time. I asked how you were.'

'I'm fine. It's sort of crumby. George has been calling me late at night. I don't want to get back together though.'

'He wants to get back together?'

'Something like that.'

Bree resisted the urge to ask what had really transpired between them. The additional information from Matt had made her question things. *Was she in some trouble that she wasn't divulging?* Bree reasoned that if Mallory wanted her to know what had happened then she would reveal it in her own time. Pressing Mallory for information hadn't been fruitful in the past.

'Who are you on with?' asked Mallory.

'Kasey.'

'Why are there even two of you on? It's Monday morning. People aren't going to the movies on a Monday morning.'

'I know. It's dead.'

Bree tried to speak in generalisations so that Kasey didn't catch on to what they were talking about, but using her name had piqued her interest. When the patron she'd been serving walked away Kasey had nothing to do but eavesdrop.

'Let's hang out again soon. I have to get out of my head a bit,' said Mallory.

'I'd like that. Hey, listen I should go too.'

'Ok. Bye.'

Bree hung up the phone.

'Who was that?' Kasey asked.

'My Dad… he's probably going to pick me up later.'

Kasey seemed satisfied with the explanation and went on her break.

Bree took her phone out of her pocket and texted her mother. She wondered whether her promise of *always being there* was still true.

Hi Mum. How are you?

Not bad! Nice to hear from you. How are you Bree?

A fast response, as if she'd been expecting the text. Bree considered the question. She was feeling concerned for Mallory and nervous about Liam's return but she couldn't tell her mother that. Carol had no idea who either of those people were and would certainly have follow up questions. She decided that Mallory's problems weren't for her mother to know and Bree resolved that she could worry about Liam when he manifested himself.

Fine. How is Adrian?

This time it took a while before Carol replied to Bree. She'd thought about the night she'd seen them together. The smile on her mother's face had told the story.

We are having some problems. I am hopeful we can work through them.

They're having problems? Bree thought to herself. *What problems?* She wanted to know what was going on with Adrian but sensed it was unfair to expect her mother to say more, especially when she had withheld things herself.

Hope things settle down. Talk to you later.

Love you Bree.

She didn't respond. Bree had not been able to tell her mother that she loved her since that fateful night. She wondered whether Carol had noticed.

During that half hour of isolation Bree noticed a man in a black trench coat standing in the foyer. He was staring directly at her. When their eyes met the man quickly looked away. Bree watched him at different intervals and once more found herself on the end of the man's stare. She did not recognise him, as he was at least twice her age. He wore a purple scarf that was so long it was almost dragging on the tiled floor below. He scanned from the Box Office to the Candy Bar, which was manned by Victor and Joel. It appeared to Bree as if he was casing the place for some future criminal enterprise. *Had she just been watching too many movies? Or spending too much time concocting schemes with Mallory?* The man removed a notepad from his coat pocket and wrote something down inside. He glanced back at Bree and she looked away nervously.

Was she being watched?

CHAPTER TWENTY

Bree couldn't stop smiling when she looked at her phone. The message from Matt made her so happy.

Let's be boyfriend and girlfriend.

Bree hadn't dated anyone officially before. There had only been Ryan before Matt, and that had been disappointing to say the least. Here was a chance to start something real. Her mind wandered to the future as she imagined anniversaries and travel. Everything was perfect. Bree was falling in love with this guy and wanted to shout it from the fifth level of the mall.

Can I tell people that we're dating?

She waited anxiously for his reply.

Unless I tell them first xxx

Bree clutched her phone to her breast and gave out an involuntary squeal of delight. She suggested they go on a date and Matt happily agreed.

How about we go and see some comedy? There is a show this weekend.

I'd love to. Looking forward to it!

With the date on the horizon, her Candy Bar shift with Victor was going extremely slowly. Shannon was making choc tops and her Whitney Houston power anthems were creeping into the front of house. Victor closed the adjoining door so that patrons wouldn't hear her loud singing. She was so much noisier than the gentle music playing in the foyer.

'Our new staff trainer has a nice set of lungs on her,' said Victor with a grin.

'She's so happy when she gets called in to make choc tops. Maybe she owned an ice cream shop in a past life,' replied Bree with a shrug.

Victor and Bree played a few rounds of the Central Cinema Olympics using words like *spontaneous*, *refreshing* and *rigorous*. Victor was far superior at the game because Bree couldn't deliver her lines with a straight face, which meant she never got the sale required to attain the imaginary gold medal.

'Maybe it's a good thing that I keep laughing,' she said when the customers disappeared around the corner to their cinemas. 'I'm going to see some local comedians later. This is like a warm up.'

'Great. I *love* comedy. Where is it?'

Bree could tell that Victor was attempting to score an invitation as usual. Normally she wouldn't have minded letting him tag along but tonight was a special night. The moment afforded Bree the opportunity to tell someone the secret that she had been holding onto. Gossip had to start somewhere and she decided Victor was as good a person as any to share her news with.

'I'm actually going with Matt.'

'Matt from Projection?' he asked.

'Yeah. It's kind of a date,' she beamed. 'We're dating.'

'That's exciting. Wow.'

Victor only had nice things to say about Matt. They both agreed that he was the best projectionist and that he always played decent music.

'I requested a song once and he found it for me,' said Victor. '*Ain't No Mountain High Enough*. I was in the mood for a big song... kind of like Shannon is right now!'

In the back of house the song changed and they could hear Aretha Franklin being yelled from the walk in freezer. Victor headed through the door to remind Shannon where she was.

When her shift was over Bree had to carry her till out the back way to get to the manager's office. Shannon, whose face was now decorated with several accidental swipes of chocolate, stopped her as she started to climb the metal staircase. She turned off the radio to talk to Bree.

'Did I overhear you say you were going out with Matt tonight?' she asked in a suspicious tone. Shannon turned off the radio.

'Yeah.'

'Do you think that's a good idea? To mix business and pleasure like that?'

Shannon made a short case about not 'pooping where you eat' and then referenced a former employee of Central Cinemas that she'd been romantically involved with.

'His name was Cameron and he was tall and cute. He played basketball, but not professionally or anything. So anyway, we went out a few times and you know... it was fun because we'd be making out in the staff room or wherever and for a while it was like... a *secret*. But then people found out.'

'What happened?' asked Bree.

'Nothing really. We didn't care if people knew.'

'Did it end badly?' Bree wanted to ascend the stairs and be done with this potential lecture. She had waited all day to see Matt and Shannon was prolonging things unnecessarily.

'It sure did. After we watched a movie one night we were kissing in his car up on the third level car park and I realised I'd left my bag in my locker. So, I went to get it and by the time I got back to the car he was *pleasuring* himself.'

Bree let silence flood the room behind Candy Bar. She wanted to walk away more than ever but Shannon seemed to be demanding a response from her.

'Um... I'm not sure that your story really relates to what's happening with me and Matt...'

'Of course it does! Because I told that story to someone here at work after we broke up and they told *other* people. Even though I asked them not to! This place can be toxic for relationships. People still bring Cameron up to me even though it was years ago.'

'That sucks.'

'I'm just saying you should watch your back. Be careful who you trust. This place loves to twist the truth until it's something else entirely.'

'Okay... thanks for the heads up Shannon. I'd better go count my till now,' said Bree as she politely excused herself.

'If I were you Bree I wouldn't say *anything*. People can't repeat stories that they don't know.'

After Shannon's rant Bree balanced her till and left the complex through the usual fire exit near Point. She was surprised to see two familiar faces congregating near the bins, each with a lit cigarette in hand. It was Liam and Mallory. Bree was taken aback at the pairing, whose only common interests must have been smoking and black hair dye.

'Oh, hey Mallory. What are you doing here?'

Mallory placed her cigarette into her mouth, freeing her hand to unzip her oversized jacket. She revealed her orange work shirt.

'How's it going Bree?' asked Liam with a smirk.

'Fine.' Bree still wasn't used to his dark hair, which looked freshly re-dyed.

Mallory shifted her stance from one leg to the other. 'What are you doing tonight?'

Bree wanted to tell Mallory about Matt and their itinerary but she didn't want to say anything in front of Liam. He seemed to deal in information, understanding that knowledge equated power better than those around him. Bree was more than happy to keep things from Liam. Her recent conversation with Shannon had spooked her and suddenly she was concerned about revealing any details at all.

'Not much,' replied Bree.

'Let's talk soon, yeah?' said Mallory nonchalantly.

'Okay cool.'

Bree excused herself and headed off to meet her new boyfriend. It was beyond exciting.

The comedy club was a café during the day, which made it an odd space to arrange an audience. Matt had selected seats off to the side of the makeshift stage.

'If you sit in the comedian's eye-line then they'll make fun of you,' he said knowingly.

'Really?'

'Trust me. Lots of comedians use the audience for some early laughs. It's called crowd work.'

Matt ordered them two glasses of soft drink, which arrived promptly with tall clear straws. Bree wasn't legally allowed to drink yet and she appreciated that even though Matt could, he had chosen not to.

'So, I have a bit of a surprise,' he said after a particularly long sip of lemonade.

'What is it?'

'I'm actually going to do some comedy here tonight.'

'Oh wow! I was *wondering* if you were but I didn't want to ask. Matt, that's so exciting. How are you feeling?'

'Kind of nervous. It's been a while… and *you're* here now… but I wanted you to see me in action.'

'You'll be great. I'm so excited.' Bree gave Matt a kiss.

'Just promise if I bomb you won't dump me?'

'That's the funniest thing I've heard all night,' said Bree with a grin.

One after another the comedians took to the stage. Each seemed to make a point of referencing how small the venue was or make a joke about the terrible service from the café staff. Matt had been right to avoid the seats at the front of the room as the young couple who occupied them were set upon regularly throughout the evening. When it was Matt's turn he crept around to the back of the stage. The MC, looking like an overweight Ben Stiller who'd never been out in the light of day, introduced him to the crowd with a flourish.

'You might not be familiar with this next comedian since he's kind of new to the game. But he's going to get up on stage and show us his balls… sorry… show us that he's *got* balls… don't *actually* show us your balls… or we'll have a lawsuit on our hands… please welcome my buddy Matt-itude!'

Bree surprised herself with the volume of her cheering. Some of the other patrons made her feel a little self-conscious when they turned around and stared. Matt took the stage with a small hop and shook the hand of the MC, who whispered something in his ear before taking a seat in the front row. Matt gave the crowd a thankful wave, smiled at Bree and waited for the surges of clapping to dissipate.

'Wow... thank you so much,' he began. 'I think your applause might be a bit *premature*.'

Then Matt pointed at the MC in front of him.

'*THIS* guy knows what I'm talking about!'

The crowd erupted in laughter. They had been waiting for an opportunity to laugh at the man who had been speaking, on and off, throughout the night and introducing the comedians. The MC had been one of the key conspirators making fun of the couple at the front. The fact that Matt was now making jokes at his expense was welcomed by the entire audience. Bree noticed that the young couple were laughing the loudest of all.

'No, no... I'm only kidding. I've seen this man in action and it went for a *reeeeallllly* long time.'

The crowd chuckled.

'*THIS* guy knows what I'm talking about,' added Matt as he pointed to the gentleman next to the MC. Once again the crowd, including Bree, burst into laughter.

'Now how would I know that?' Matt paused while the audience laughed. 'I'm going to leave that to your imagination folks...'

It was in that moment of bliss that Bree noticed the zipper on Matt's pants was down. He stretched his leg slightly and the rest of the crowd noticed it too. As the audience observed the flash of bright red underwear they began laughing at him. Finally, one of the men at the back of the room called out, letting Matt in on the joke.

'Your fly's undone!' he yelled, cupping his hands around his mouth to amplify his cries.

'What's that?' asked Matt as he strained to hear.

Bree's stomach tightened. Things had started so well but now she was anxious for her boyfriend. She sunk into her chair.

'Your *zipper* is undone!' several people shouted over the top of one another.

Matt put his hands on his hips and leaned forward to inspect his groin. His zipper was indeed open and his underpants were visible to the crowd. He straightened up again and without doing up his fly Matt put the microphone to his lips.

'You guys... my eyes are up *here*!' he said as he indicated towards his pupils. The crowd started laughing again, impressed with how confidently and expertly he had avoided certain humiliation. Matt turned his back to the audience and started to do up his fly with one hand while keeping the microphone at his mouth with the other.

'Now while I'm facing this way, please resist the urge to look at my butt...'

Bree, and the forty or so other audience members *all* looked at his rear. Nobody could help themselves. Matt grinned, knowing he had orchestrated the joke and now had the audience in the palm of his hand. He wiggled his butt and they laughed in unison.

'You were amazing. *So* funny!'

'Thanks Bree. I'm glad you liked it.'

'I *loved* it! You were really great,' said Bree.

'Thanks.'

'I was so nervous when I saw that your fly was down.'

'That was always part of the show.'

'Has it been down all night?' she asked. 'I hadn't noticed.'

Matt shook his head. 'No, I unzipped it right before I went on. The MC spotted it and that's what he was whispering in my ear just before I started.'

'Oh wow. It all seemed so… *natural.* I wouldn't have guessed. You're *sneaky,* aren't you?'

She gave him a playful shove.

'Yeah… I do a bit of physical humour to lighten the mood. You have to give people permission to laugh at things.'

Bree absorbed this information.

'But how did you know they would point it out to you?' she asked.

'Someone *always* points it out.'

'Really?'

'There is always one heckler in any crowd who thinks he's a comedian. Or he thinks he's funnier than the person on stage anyway. That joke has worked every time I've tried it.'

'You're so brave. I could never do anything like that,' confessed Bree as they walked out of the venue together. 'I don't know how you get up there in front of a crowd and make them laugh.'

'So, you laughed? You admit it then?' asked Matt with a knowing smile. It was clearly important to him, and luckily Bree didn't have to lie about how much fun she was having.

'Yeah I laughed a lot,' she said as she gave him a hug.

Several people recognised Matt from his set and said hello. One guy even wanted to get a picture with him. It was like being on a date with a minor celebrity.

'You just have to embrace the chaos, you know?'

'What do you mean?' asked Bree.

'Well... if nobody is laughing then you just say something like *whoa tough crowd.* Then, knowing that they are indeed being a tough crowd, they'll laugh about it. It's like addressing the elephant in the room,' said Matt. 'You have to lean into whatever's happening, you know?'

'Embrace the chaos. I like that.'

CHAPTER TWENTY-ONE

'Are you being serious?'

Mallory tied her black hair into a small ponytail and nodded. It was short all year round, but Bree noticed that Mallory never looked like she'd just had a haircut.

'I'm totally serious Bree, I told you I wanted to get out of my head a bit. This is what's working for me right now.'

'Can't you just smoke weed or something?'

'I haven't stopped smoking.'

'But... you *can't*...' stammered Bree. 'You just can't.'

'Relax. It's no big deal.'

'But it's *Liam*.'

'Yeah. There's something about him.'

'There's something about *Liam*?' Bree was dumbfounded. It felt like their shared view on Liam White was the first thing she and Mallory had agreed on. It had been the foundation on which their friendship had been built. Mallory had been so certain that Liam was a tool. *What had changed?* Bree had a million questions, but she started with the most obvious one.

'So, are you two *dating* each other now?'

'Sort of. We haven't really labelled it. It's casual. I don't really want to *date* anyone so soon after George but we're hanging out and having fun.'

'Wow.' The staff room seemed to spin around her. *How did this happen?* Bree wanted to scream. Liam and Mallory were 'sort of' together.

'It's good.'

'Seriously?'

'Yeah, it's fun,' said Mallory. 'And that's what I need right now.'

'It's fun? I don't believe it...'

'Well, do you want the details?'

'No!'

Bree had been spending all of her free time with Matt. In her absence Mallory had sparked something up with Liam. *Was it her fault that her best friend had taken up with the boss' son?* Her first instinct still felt right about Liam. He was a tool who wasn't to be trusted. Bree didn't like this development.

'There's something else too,' said Mallory as she sat down next to Bree on the worn sofa.

'What?'

Mallory lowered her voice even though there were no staff in the change rooms who might overhear. They'd been chatting for most of Mallory's break without interruption.

'I was talking to Liam the other night about our little piracy attempt...'

'You mean the one that I didn't think was a good idea *from the start*...' interrupted Bree, emphasising her dislike for the plot.

'Uhuh, yeah... *that*. So, I was telling him how we'd run out of batteries and how we'd really just done it as a laugh.'

'Hilarious,' stated Bree.

'I was trying to show him we weren't *really* pirating the film and like... downplaying it...'

A sound in the distance, possibly down the hall behind the Candy Bar, made Mallory stop talking. It was only a momentary pause before she continued whispering to Bree.

'Liam has some connections. He wants to try and do it for real with a proper camera… and a full battery. Obviously.'

'No way.' Bree couldn't believe what she was hearing.

'He does. He's serious about it.'

'What? He was the one telling *us* it was stealing in the first place! Remember what he said? It was like stealing a cake from a bakery. You're not buying this, are you? Liam is probably setting you up. He's sneaky… and manipulative,' said Bree.

Mallory ignored her and continued.

'Well he thinks we could sell it to someone he knows. It's more money than the guy I was thinking of selling it to last time. Liam knows a lot of people.'

'Mallory, do you hear yourself? This is getting out of control.'

'I told him I'd think about it.'

'It's a bad idea,' said Bree.

'That's kind of what I like about it though. You know… I thought you and I were going to run my scams together but lately you've been shacked up with Matt.'

The swelling guilt inside Bree doubled in size.

'I'm sorry. I know I haven't been around as much. It's just that it's so new…'

'It's fine… I get it… Matt is one of the good ones,' replied Mallory in a forced tone, as if it pained her to admit she approved of him in the slightest.

'Thanks for saying that.'

'The thing is… Liam can help me. We're using *each other*. He's been introducing me to some of the managers that he knows in the mall. We've already lined up some new trades. Having Liam on our side makes everything easier.'

'So, you're using each other? That's what you're calling it?'

'Yeah.'

'I thought you didn't want to label it.'

'Well it's not *official* or anything,' replied Mallory, rolling her eyes.

'And what does he get from you?' asked Bree. Her friend had always told her the intimate details of her relationship with George, but with Liam she'd been deliberately coy.

Mallory raised one eyebrow.

'Touché Bree. I have to get back to work.'

July had brought with it an unexpected cold snap and Bree had to shed an unusually large amount of winter clothing before starting each shift. She hated the cold. It made everything seem worse, especially in Canberra. She was heading into the office to collect a two-way when she heard yelling on the other side of the door. Bree hesitated outside next to the pigeonholes and tried to work out what was going on. Did she dare enter the room? She had no idea what she might be interrupting but it sounded serious. Bree could only hear Maxine's voice, and she was obviously telling off a second party. The accused was silently accepting their fate, which made it impossible to tell who had attracted her ire. Bree went next door into the Box Office, hoping they might know what was going on. Manning the Box Office was Daniella, Liam's controversial date from Southern Cinemas.

'Hi,' Bree managed, while standing dumbstruck in the doorway.

'Hi. I'm Daniella.'

'I'm Bree.'

'Oh... yeah... I think I remember you.' There was a slight recognition on Daniella's face, but she wasn't overly embarrassed.

'Yeah we've met. What are you doing here?' asked Bree.

'I've transferred over. It's my first day.'

'Who's training you?'

'Liam. He's just in the office at the moment. But I know what I'm doing. I've worked Box Office heaps of times and it's the same setup as Southern.'

Liam was in the office. Bree wondered if Maxine was shouting at her own son right now. She had to know.

Leaving Daniella in the Box Office she punched the combination lock and headed towards the commotion. Maxine was in the Location Manager's office to the right. Seated alone in the back office, where the safe and computers were situated was Liam. He gave Bree a smile and appeared to be in good spirits.

'Hi Bree,' he said casually.

When she took a step inside and positioned herself at the two-way charging station, Bree peered into Maxine's office. It was Paul, not Liam, who was in trouble. He was sitting in the chair with his head slumped down. *What on Earth had Paul done?* Maxine noticed her lurking and closed the door without a word. Bree picked up the nearest two-way and crept past in the direction of Liam.

'What's going on? Why is Maxine shouting at Paul?' she asked in a hushed tone.

'I knew she was being too loud,' replied Liam with a chuckle. 'The walls are too thin here.'

Bree was thankful that Liam wasn't in trouble. He and Mallory were linked together now, whether she liked it or not. Bree was still concerned that her friend had received a warning for her Projection room tryst with George, even though she hadn't told Bree anything about it yet. Two warnings could be too many for management. Maxine clearly didn't tolerate bad behaviour. Nobody wanted to wind up in her office with the door closed. It was all the more reason to stay off

Maxine's radar. Bree couldn't explain to her friend why she wanted her to be careful without revealing how much she knew about the incident with George. Mallory was being reckless again and for whatever reason Bree was the one harbouring all the guilt for her actions. Liam had spoken of his mother's 'zero tolerance' policy. The last thing Bree wanted was for Mallory to get caught and end up in the firing line. Whatever Paul was guilty of seemed serious.

'Did he do something wrong?' she asked.

'Yeah. I noticed Paul was amending the roster and I tried to work out why. It turns out he's been calling staff and cancelling their shifts. Then he'd give their cancelled shifts to his sister Kasey.'

'That's not fair.'

'It's not fair to anyone. Kasey needs the money apparently. But she's older and it costs Central more every time we call her in. He's been doing it for ages and it all adds up. I simply... *highlighted* it for Mum.'

'Why would Paul do that?' Bree couldn't understand. He'd seemed like the picture of professionalism. Paul wanted to be the Location Manager one day. If *he* was corrupt, and Andy was corrupt, then anyone else could be too.

Liam seemed delighted with the way things were unfolding. He reclined in his chair and gave Bree a shrug of indifference. He was looking out for his own interests. Perhaps Liam and Mallory were more similar that she'd first thought.

'I heard Nathan was going to be the new projectionist.'

'No chance. It's bound to be Victor.'

'They'd never let him! I think that new girl Daniella was hired for it. She came over from Southern Cinemas just for the job.'

Paul was reprimanded without obvious ramifications. He remained a part of the management team but there was a noticeable shift in Maxine. In the aftermath of the scandal she seemed to favour her son over all others. Rita and Carl fell into line without discussion. Nobody dared go up against Liam for fear he would challenge them in the same manner he had with Paul. Maxine listened to her son's suggestions exclusively and he seemed to occupy the unofficial title of second in command. Daniella's recent transfer had been Liam's idea as well. The only people that knew about her history with the Location Manager's son were Bree and Mallory, and neither dared spread the gossip around. Gossip now seemed like a dangerous weapon to wield.

Matt and Bree were approaching their two-month anniversary. To celebrate he'd decided to test screen the romantic film *Before Sunset*. Bree had loved the first film *Before Sunrise* and was desperate to see the sequel.

'Will you stay up late and watch it with me?' he'd asked the night before.

'Oh, I'd love to.'

They had never test screened a film together despite Matt's claims that he did so regularly. The last time they had intended to watch one they had become side-tracked and engaged in alternate activities instead. Ultimately it was just another excuse to spend some time together, which they both wanted. On the night of the screening Matt finished his shift and met up with Bree in the staff room. The complex had been checked for loose patrons and the doors were now locked.

'There's something I've wanted to show you for a while,' said Bree.

'What's that?'

'Come with me.'

Bree led Matt back up the ramp towards the Projection room.

'Don't get upset Bree, but I've been up here before.'

She walked him through the first door before taking a sharp left and guiding Matt up to the restricted air conditioning room.

'The air con room?' asked Matt as they climbed the concrete steps.

'Yeah.'

'What's up there?'

'A great view.'

They journeyed through the vent-filled space and out onto the roof of the mall. Bree wedged a brick in the door to ensure they weren't locked out and together they made their way to the small concrete ledge. It was dark but the view was still spectacular, the lights of Canberra's northern residents stretching out before them.

'Wow. I didn't know this was even here. This was way too easy to get to. None of those doors were even locked!' commented Matt.

'It's nice up here, isn't it?'

'It's gorgeous. How did you know this was here?'

'I was… exploring… and I found it.'

'You're full of surprises, aren't you?' laughed Matt.

Bree had often thought about the way Mallory had leaned over this edge. She wanted Matt to help her erase that memory by replacing it with a new one, in the same way he had helped her to forget about Ryan.

'Kiss me, would you?' she asked.

'It would be my pleasure.' Matt gave Bree a tender kiss. 'We're still going to watch a movie, right? This isn't like last time…'

'A movie would be nice,' replied Bree.

'I just have to return my two-way and then we can kick the film off.'

'Sounds good,' she said with a glowing smile.

'Meet me in the foyer?'

'Ok.'

They walked back through the doors and descended the stairs.

Bree stood in the foyer waiting for Matt. She thought about how familiar and comfortable this workplace had become for her. While her life, and the Hotel Management course, was on hold she'd really enjoyed making the people at Central Cinemas into a surrogate family. Her father had been actively looking for work and revealed he was quite close to a new security position. Bree was hoping for the best. He'd been a little bit too *parental* with her lately. She suspected his increasingly overprotective nature was due to boredom and knew a job would give him some purpose. He'd also started lecturing her on boys, correctly assuming that Bree might be seeing one.

'At your age guys only want one thing Bree,' he'd warned.

'I'm seventeen… I *know*…'

'I know you do. And you're a beautiful girl. Almost eighteen really. I just want to make sure nothing happens to you.'

He'd started comparing her to her mother. Bree had to bite her tongue whenever he told her that they had the same hair, or the same smile. Bree hoped that in time he'd be able to relax his grip on her life and realise that she was old enough to take care of herself. If he couldn't accept her as an adult, then she'd never be able to see the world with Mallory… or Matt… depending on how things went. Her boyfriend had expressed a desire to travel with Bree, which had complicated things in her mind. The future was looking increasingly uncertain.

Bree was suddenly on high alert when Matt walked out of the office with Liam.

'Liam's keen to check out the film too. So… he's going to stay and watch the test screening.'

'Oh?'

Their mutual disappointment was palpable. Bree remembered that test screenings were at the discretion of management and knew they would have no choice but to let him tag along.

'A lot of people wouldn't think I'd be interested in this kind of movie,' Liam said waving his hands slightly, 'but I'm actually a big fan of love stories. I've been hanging out for it.'

Matt wandered upstairs to set the projector up while Liam escorted Bree towards Cinema Five. The test screenings were always conducted in Cinema Five or Six to take advantage of the stadium seating and higher quality sound. It suddenly felt like a long walk down the tunnel for Bree.

'Mallory speaks very highly of you. Did you know that?' asked Liam as he walked a half-step behind her, his voice projecting out ahead.

'I'd expect her to.'

'Has she said anything about me?'

'About *you*?' Bree was insulted that Liam thought she'd betray Mallory's trust by revealing anything at all.

'Yeah… what does she say about me?' he asked again.

'Nothing really.'

As they rounded the corner into the Cinema, Liam took Bree by the arm and spun her around to face him. He pressed his torso towards her, pinning her slender frame between his body and the wall of stadium seating. They were in a blind spot. No cameras could see them. Before Bree knew it, Liam was leaning in for a kiss.

'What are you *doing*?' she shouted, pressing him away from her as forcefully as she could. He was more solid than he looked and barely moved.

'I thought you wanted this?'

'No!'

Bree tried to get away from him, to break his grip. Liam held her in place dominantly.

'Hey,' he said in a low tone, 'sorry… maybe Mallory didn't tell you, but she and I are in a kind of… *casual* thing. I'm still free to date other people.'

'I'm with Matt,' she said quickly.

Liam screwed up his face as though this was impossible to comprehend. He released Bree and she stepped away from him. They scaled the stairs to occupy their seats. Bree spotted Matt peering down at them from the porthole, concern flashing across his face. *How much had he seen?* Bree wondered. *That could have looked really bad.* They sat in silence waiting for Matt to start the film. Liam, seemingly unable to let it go, spoke again.

'I'm going to be the boss here one day soon. My mother will be on her way to Sydney and I'll be the one she leaves in charge. Mark my words.'

Bree thought of Paul, who everyone had assumed would be her successor, and the way Liam had dismantled him so expertly. Even though she and Liam had been hired at the same time it was clear he had been evolving, sinking his influential talons into everything around him. Of course Liam's goal was to become the Location Manager. He'd been eyeing his mother's job from day one.

'Whatever schemes you have planned for the future, I hope you leave Mallory out of them,' she said. Bree hated that her friend was so indelibly linked to this man.

'She's even more committed than I am,' replied Liam without turning to face her. 'Do you even know her at all?'

Matt joined them in the cinema, taking his seat next to Bree on the far side of Liam, who had wisely left a space between them. The trio spent a tense eighty minutes together and despite the romantic nature of the film Bree feared that her boyfriend was going to break up with her. She couldn't tell if Matt was upset as they all faced the screen. When it was over Liam excused himself. He confessed that he'd abandoned his work in favour of the screening and would be working back late to complete it now.

'I already called the alarm company and warned them we'd be doing this. I didn't want them waking my mother. She wouldn't have appreciated that.'

Bree remembered that Maxine had been described as a morning person. When Liam disappeared she and Matt were left alone in the foyer with a strange tension between them.

'Come over to the games for a minute. Let's talk,' said Matt.

The two stepped over to the corner of the foyer where there were several stand-alone pinball machines and video games. Bree put a dollar in the skill tester and failed to collect a small purple giraffe.

'What's going on?' Matt asked as she put another dollar in. 'You've been in a weird mood tonight.'

'It's nothing. Did you like the movie?' she replied, failing once again to pick up the stuffed toy.

'It was ok. I liked the first one better. Did something happen with Liam? Did he say something to you?'

'Yeah... but it's a little embarrassing.'

'But we don't keep things from each other Bree. I know all about Ryan,' said Matt.

'I know.'

'What happened?' he asked again, taking her by the hand.

'Before I tell you… I just want you to know that I didn't ask for this. I don't want you to think that I'm enjoying the attention or anything.'

'What did he do?' asked Matt in a measured voice.

'He tried to *kiss* me before the movie started.'

'And… you kissed him back?'

'No! I would never…' she objected.

Matt hugged Bree tightly in his arms.

'Don't worry about Liam. Everyone is walking on eggshells around him, but he can't just do whatever he wants because he's the boss' kid.'

'He's been acting like he owns the place,' replied Bree.

'But he doesn't. And if he ever tries to touch you again please tell me, okay?'

'I will.'

'There will always be people like Ryan and Liam in every workplace,' said Matt. 'But we don't have to work here forever you know.'

'I know,' she replied.

Matt paused for a moment.

'So, he didn't actually kiss you?' he asked again.

'He tried, but I told him I was with you.'

'Good. I mean it. Please tell me if he ever tries anything again. I don't care who his mother is. I'll deck him. I'm not afraid of that guy.'

Matt was being so considerate. She was glad he wasn't upset about Liam's behaviour towards her. Bree was so happy that the attempted kiss hadn't jeopardised things between them.

'I love you Bree,' he said.

'I love you too.'

They kissed passionately by the blue neon light of the skill tester.

'Now do you want that giraffe or not?' he asked with a grin.

'Are you going to win it for me with all your skills?'

'So, you admit I have *some* skills?'

'You got me, didn't you?'

Matt turned off the machine and tipped it gently onto its side. He then raised one end and spilled all of the stuffed animals towards the prize door.

'Have you done this before?' asked Bree.

'Would you believe this is my first time?' he replied as casually as he could with the weight of the skill tester in his hands.

When the desired toy was sitting in position Matt lifted the skill tester so that it was the right way up. The giraffe, and several other stuffed toys were now waiting to be collected from the prize door.

'You know that's not the way these machines were intended to be played,' she stated with a smile.

'Well... sometimes you have to bend the rules just a bit to get what you want,' said Matt and he gave her another kiss.

'Thank you. I love it,' beamed Bree.

'Let's leave the other stuffed toys behind the prize door. Some lucky kids will get a surprise tomorrow.'

'Good idea.'

Bree noticed just beyond Matt's head that a security camera was pointed directly at them.

'Matt... the camera.'

He looked up into the lens and gave a playful wave.

'What about it?' he asked. 'Are you worried about me *besmirching* your good name?'

'I told you nobody says that anymore…'

'I'm bringing it back,' he replied.

'It's just recorded us tipping over a skill tester and stealing a toy. We're going to get in trouble. What if Liam is watching…' she trailed off. Bree was nervous. She didn't want to give Liam any additional ammunition and she'd just implicated herself in a theft.

'It's fine. Don't worry! Most of the security cameras in the complex are fakes. They are plastic knock offs that have only been put up to deter people. Central Cinemas is cheap like that. You can tell when you look at them up close, but yeah… it's hard to see from here. That cord is just going into a hole in the wall. There's nobody watching you.'

'How do you know they're fake?' asked Bree.

'I installed them.'

CHAPTER TWENTY-TWO

'Did you hear about Mallory and Liam?'

'What about them?'

'I heard they came out of the disabled toilet together.'

'What were they doing in there?'

'What do YOU think?'

The gossip that surrounded Mallory and Liam was now relentless. Neither of them seemed to care. Everyone suspected but nobody dared ask. It was much more fun for the staff to speculate.

As the end of the year approached Central Cinemas needed to take on more staff. Warren's parents had forced him to resign because he was falling behind in his studies. Even with additional tutelage from Tristan he'd been unable to pass maths. Maxine refused his resignation letter and told him that when he'd caught up, or the school year was over, he'd be welcomed back. The turnover at Central Cinemas was high and it seemed like new people started every other month. The reality was that people had become less available and less willing to work. Bree was polite to the new faces but none of them seemed to care for a friendship beyond the proximity of the workplace. It was difficult to make friends with people you saw only during work hours. All of that changed when Maxine hired Dan.

It was the perfect job for Dan, who seemed utterly *obsessed* with movies. He had a broad smile whenever he was reciting obscure film trivia or discussing the Academy Award winners, which he had seemingly memorised.

'1994 was a very contentious year!' stated Dan. '*The Shawshank Redemption* was robbed I tell you. Not a single Academy Award, and *seven* nominations!'

Bree thought he looked like an extremely happy version of Colin Firth but dressed like he was stuck in the 80's. The most unexplainable thing about Dan was that he refused to leave the cinema complex. He'd arrive early and chat to the staff before he started work. When his shift concluded he'd stay and talk to the night staff. On a regular basis he'd stick around and watch a film, or even *two*, long after his shift had ended. He was always around and impossible to ignore. His loitering became known colloquially as *Doing a Dan*. Bree liked his energy and he immediately became friends with everyone simply because he was around. Nobody could gossip about Dan because he was always there. It was a tactic Bree had never considered before. He was so jovial and pleasant that nobody had a bad word to say about him anyway.

Dan was hanging out at Point one Friday night as Bree and Matt were heading into a movie. Victor greeted them, as he was the one *actually* being paid to be there that night, but a nearby Dan stopped them for a chat too.

'*The Village*! You'll like that one. I saw it on opening day,' he said. 'Do you scare easily?'

Bree pulled a face, but Matt gave her a reassuring look.

'It's not going to be *that* scary,' offered Matt. 'If it is we can just leave.'

'Ugh. Now I'm nervous!' replied Bree.

'It will be great. You'll love it,' added Dan. 'See you after maybe.'

During the trailers Bree noticed a familiar face. The man with the purple scarf was sitting in the same row as them but further to the right. *What was he doing here?*

Still confused about his motives Bree had now seen him several times floating around the complex, always with the same purple scarf and notebook. She observed the man, who seemed disinterested in the images on the screen. He was looking at the audience, one face at a time, as if he were searching for someone in particular. When he saw Bree there was a strange moment of recognition. Instead of lingering he went on examining the faces around her. Bree had no idea what he was up to. He took the same notebook out of his coat pocket and wrote something down. *Could he be some kind of private investigator?* Bree became concerned that the man in the purple scarf was there specifically for *her*. *Had he been watching her movements? Did her mother hire him?* Bree thought back to the night of the stocktake with Mallory. *Had someone from the store been following her for that long?* Bree's head was spinning.

'You look worried. The movie hasn't even started yet.'

'Could we go?' pleaded Bree.

Matt was confused but could see she was serious.

'Uh... yeah. Okay. Let's go.'

Dan apologised for frightening her as the couple made their way out of the complex and meandered into the food court.

'Did you want to have dinner or something instead?' asked Matt, who was still not sure what precisely had startled Bree.

'Yeah. Let's do that.'

The couple sat down with a plate of pasta to share. The food court was reasonable busy, packed with its usual collection of angsty teenagers and posers with nowhere better to go.

'Are you okay? You looked like something spooked you back there in the cinema.'

'I'm fine Matt. I've just got a lot on my mind and I guess I wasn't really in the mood for a movie after all.'

'That's cool. We can watch *The Village* another day. When you're in the mood,' reasoned Matt.

This response seemed to annoy Bree. 'I mean... just because we get free movie tickets doesn't mean we *always* have to go to the movies. We probably spend enough time there as it is,' she said angrily.

Bree wasn't sure where the outburst had come from, but it was something she must have been holding onto for a while. They did seem to spend all of their free time surrounded by the watchful eyes of their colleagues. Bree didn't want to have her relationship with Matt scrutinised. She didn't want to be gossiped about. Bree needed more nights like the one they'd had at the comedy club. More memories like the kiss they'd shared five stories above the ground. Bree craved more 'movie moments' and less 'moments at the movies.'

'I understand. We are both there a lot. No sense in *Doing a Dan* all the time,' said Matt with a chuckle.

Bree's phone rang and for the first time in a long time she hoped it was her mother. They hadn't texted for a while and Bree had been thinking about suggesting they meet up. She'd been wondering how things were going with Adrian. But the call was from her father and she declined, returning her attention to Matt.

'Sorry... it's just that I've been feeling like I'm in kind of a bubble. Since my Dad stopped working full-time I feel like I can't stop picking up shifts. We need the money... it's fine. But then if I hang out with you I'm there all day. And I hardly ever see Mallory anymore. I don't know what she's been up to lately.'

Bree wasn't sure she wanted to know what Mallory had been doing in her spare time. She was afraid of the things she'd been hearing around the complex. Their colleagues had been speculating about what had been going on between Mallory and Liam behind the office doors at night.

'She's right in there... and that safe is wide open. It's unseemly,' said Shannon to Bree one afternoon.

Even Tristan, who at one stage had wanted to go on a date with Mallory, had changed his tune. 'She's trouble. I think I dodged a bullet,' he said, happily changing the narrative away from his rejection.

Bree couldn't control the flow of information amongst the staff but she could remove herself from it. The less time she and Matt spent around this toxic commentary the better.

'It's okay. We can go and do other things. We'll make it work.'

Bree gave Matt a kiss, but they were soon interrupted.

'Ahem.'

Bree was shocked to find the source of the sound was her own father, standing over them. Henry was dressed in the uniform of a mall security guard. He had a white dress shirt embroidered with the emblem of a security company. He wore black slacks and shiny shoes and looked very put together. The cherry on top of the cake was her father's new haircut. It was shaved evenly down to his scalp, embracing the direction his hairline was leading. He placed his hands on his hips triumphantly as he waited for Bree to react.

'Dad?' Bree was in shock. This was not the way she'd anticipated introducing Matt to her father.

'Hi honey.'

'You're a security guard?' she said, still collecting her thoughts. 'You got the job?'

'Yep. This is my second day. I was going to come in and surprise you at work, but it looks like you've surprised me!' he said, motioning towards Matt. Bree blushed as her boyfriend took the opportunity to introduce himself.

'I'm Matt. It's great to finally meet you. Congratulations on the new job. That's great.'

'Thanks Matt. Likewise. I'm Henry.'

The two men shook hands cordially while Bree composed herself.

'That's really great Dad. I'm so proud of you.' She stood and gave her father a hug.

'So… you're dating my Bree?'

'Um… yeah. I'm trying to… but… uh… security guards keep coming over and making sure I'm not *bothering* her.'

'Ha! What are you some kind of comedian?' he asked, squinting at Matt.

'Something like that,' he said throwing a knowing glance to Bree, who had been watching the exchange with trepidation.

'You're alright… I like you. Matt was it?' he asked.

'Yes sir.'

'Alright… try and tone down the displays of public affection for me please. I'm not used to all that.'

'Will do sir.'

'Maybe I'll see you again sometime,' said Henry with a nod.

'Thank you. I like you too… I mean… um… I like your daughter… very much.'

'Good. Well, I can't be seen mucking around and hugging people. I've got to get back to work. That feels good to say. I'll see you at home Bree,' said Henry as he straightened his thin black tie.

'Bye Dad.'

'Nice to meet you,' added Matt.

Her father gave a polite wave and strolled away from the food court, glowing with pride. After his departure Matt turned to Bree and the two laughed at the awkwardness that had unfolded.

'Promise me you won't turn this moment into a comedy bit?' pleaded Bree.

'I don't know babe! When you date a comedian you kind of have to assume everything will wind up in the routine.'

'What have I gotten myself into?'

Bree playfully hit him in the shoulder, and they shared another kiss.

'That's kind of great, huh? Your Dad working at the mall?'

'Yeah I suppose so. Maybe we can carpool now,' replied Bree.

'What I mean is, maybe now you can get back on track with your Hotel Management course.'

'Oh… yeah. For sure.'

Postponing her studies had completely slipped her mind. She didn't know if Hotel Management was even the plan anymore. Bree had a lot to think about.

There was a memo on the corkboard in the staff room when Bree started work the next day. It had been written by Liam White and was titled *Congratulations!* It announced that management, after an exhaustive interview process, had decided to promote from within to fill the vacancy in Projection. *Please join me in welcoming Mallory to the team! She commences her training this week.*

Bree was more confused than anything. Nathan, who was in the staff room washing a plate, saw Bree reading the memo.

'How *exhaustive* do you think the search was?' he asked, before laughing out loud. 'This place is a joke. A freakin' joke.'

This is how I find out Mallory was promoted? Bree thought to herself.

She had renewed cause to worry about the state of her friendship with Mallory, and the intensity at which her friend's 'casual' relationship with Liam was growing. It was time to bridge the gap.

CHAPTER TWENTY-THREE

'I feel like we haven't talked like this in ages,' said Bree as she took a sip of her strawberry milkshake.

Mallory stirred the hot chocolate in front of her and casually dropped the two accompanying marshmallows into the hot liquid.

'Yeah. I guess we've both been kind of busy,' said Mallory.

'I wanted to say congratulations on the promotion. You deserve it.'

'A lot of people have been saying the opposite you know.'

'They have?' Bree had heard things, but she was surprised that they were getting back to Mallory.

'They think I'm jumping the queue by not serving any time as a staff trainer first. Some people are pretty annoyed about it, I guess,' said Mallory as she nudged a pink marshmallow around on the surface of her drink.

'Well, at least you won't have to work with them anymore. But if I hear anything like that, I'll let you know,' offered Bree. *From now on* she promised herself.

'How's it going with Matt?'

'Good. It's going really well.' Bree knew she was beaming and tried to downplay her level of happiness for Mallory's benefit. She didn't want to seem like she was bragging. 'Something happened yesterday actually. Matt got a call from this comedian that had seen him perform.'

'Matt does stand-up comedy?'

'Yeah. He's pretty good too,' replied Bree, realising yet again how detached she'd been from her friend.

'Fair enough,' said Mallory, who seemed nonplussed.

'So, he's been invited to open for him on a tour. It's a big break apparently, but he won't make much money. He says it's more about the exposure.'

'Is he quitting Central?' asked Mallory.

'Oh no… nothing like that. He's just going to be on the road for a while. He'll be back.'

'Fair enough.'

'How are things with Liam?'

'Yeah… fine…'

Mallory seemed reluctant to tell Bree about her personal life, and she didn't want to force anything out of her. The mysteries surrounding Mallory were building up though. It was more work than Bree was used to. She thought about Kasey and how easily the two of them had bonded working together. *Why can't it be that easy with Mallory? Why doesn't she just tell me what she's thinking?* Eventually Bree asked about the transition to Projection, which was a topic Mallory was happy to elaborate on.

'It's been alright. Training has been with Liam and this technician called Norman who is like seventy years old. They bring him in twice a year to service all of the projector parts. He's the only one who knows how to do it all properly because he built them all when Central Cinemas first opened. But he's really expensive because he insists they fly him in and put him up in a hotel.'

'Wow.'

'He's pretty sexist and he thinks I can't do it. He told me that men make better projectionists.'

'That's rude,' said Bree.

'Yeah, I want to become really good at it just to spite him.'

The two continued to chat about work and soon, to her surprise, Mallory was confiding a new scam to Bree.

'*Another* one? Haven't we moved past this?' asked Bree with uncertainty.

'I think you have to look at them as enterprising opportunities. But… no… *I* haven't moved past this. Maybe you have…'

Bree sensed a divide growing between them. If she couldn't support Mallory in these sneaky endeavours, or at the very least listen to her talk about them, then why was she here? Bree tried to keep an open mind.

'What's your latest idea?' she asked. 'I'm listening.'

'I've been looking at the posters that we store in the Projection room. There's no system and they just sit around up there after the films are finished.'

'So?'

Mallory always revealed her plans to Bree so slowly, and her delivery of a scheme became all the more captivating for it.

'The comic book shop in the mall sells movie posters and I've been talking to one of the managers about buying up our old stock.'

'But the posters belong to the cinema, right?'

'I thought so too at first,' said Mallory, 'but it turns out that all promotional materials actually belong to the film distributor. We send back the film prints when we're done, and we're supposed to send back the posters too, but nobody does. And if Maxine or anyone ever asked about them, we could say that we sent them back. They'd never check.'

'I guess so,' said Bree. It wasn't the worst idea, but it did involve a layer of stealth. Mallory would still need to transport the posters from the Projection room to the comic book shop without getting caught.

'Remember when you were doing poster shifts?' she asked Bree.

'Yeah.'

'Did anyone supervise you?'

'Well, Matt helped me once.'

'But did you have to tell anyone what posters you used and which ones you changed?'

'No.'

'There was no poster log? You didn't have to sign them out?'

'No.'

'Because nobody cares Bree! They are just bits of paper to most people. But if I collect the vinyl ones and the paper ones that are in the best condition, I can sell them.'

Mallory had wild eyes, like no one Bree had ever known. Today they were surrounded by yellow and black eye shadow, giving her the appearance of a tiger.

'You're always thinking about this stuff, aren't you?'

'Always. I've started taking the best posters out of Projection and hiding them. Did you know that there are storage spaces at the front of each of the cinemas? Below the screens?'

'No... I didn't know that. Why do *you* know that?' asked Bree.

'Because I've spent time looking.'

'But Mallory, taking the posters is stealing. Just because they belong to the distributor and not to Central... at some point we have to draw the line.'

'They're just posters Bree.'

'Right, so how much can they really be worth?'

'It all adds up...'

'Aren't you worried about getting in trouble? Or getting caught by Maxine?'

'Not really.' Mallory oozed confidence. Bree couldn't see any cracks in her exterior. Mallory was as sure as ever that she was going to get away with this.

'Why do you tell me *any* of this? I mean… I'm obviously not going to tell anyone but why do you feel the need to share these plans with me? You don't need me for this,' asked Bree, suddenly irritated.

Mallory contemplated for a moment before answering. 'Well, it's like… if I don't tell someone then the story dies with me, you know? What's the point in doing anything so *cool* if nobody knows I did it?'

'But if you get another… if you get *any* warnings they'll demote you out of Projection, won't they?'

'Can I trust you with a secret Bree?'

'Of course. You know you can.'

'I'm not going to stay in Projection.'

This was the last thing Bree expected to hear. She'd only just been promoted, and Mallory had ruffled a lot of feathers by accepting the role.

'What are you talking about? Why not?'

'It's not for me. I'm just going to learn how to do it and then tell Maxine I don't like it. Then I'll offer to do the occasional casual shift up there. When it suits me.'

'Really? That's *it*? You'll just say you don't *like* it?'

'I told you that I had bigger plans than becoming a staff trainer or a manager or some *lowly* projectionist.'

'So, what do you want?'

'I don't want to *settle*,' explained Mallory.

They finished their drinks and walked aimlessly through the mall. Bree wondered if Mallory thought *she* was settling. She had fallen into a loving relationship with Matt, who was one of those *lowly* projectionists she'd described. He'd now met her father, and everything seemed on track. *But on track to become what?* It had crossed her mind that she might not take up her Hotel Management course after all and instead attempt to move up through the ranks at Central Cinemas. It was hard to hear Mallory being so dismissive of the opportunities that she was being given, now that Bree herself was interested in them. She had been delaying telling her new life plan to her father, as Bree knew he wouldn't be happy to hear it. Matt was actively encouraging her to apply for other jobs too, citing her happiness as the most important thing. Bree wasn't sure what she wanted anymore and talking to Mallory hadn't helped things.

'Oh, I have something for you as well,' said Mallory.

'What?'

'Mallory took a large zip-locked bag of gold and silver keys out of her purse and pushed it towards Bree. Some of them looked quite old.

'I don't understand...' This was an odd gift and without context she wasn't sure how to react to the bag or its contents.

'I found these keys in the Projection room while I was training. I'm betting one of them opens our mystery door.'

'Well, we're not doing anything now. Let's go try them out.'

They walked past a sunglasses store on their way back up to the cinema complex and Bree noticed Andy working at the counter. *He was still in Canberra? Still in the mall?* Bree had heard rumours that he'd skipped town, but there he was, helping a woman try on several pairs of sunglasses. Andy looked up, detected her, and then immediately looked away as if the sight of Bree had stirred up a bad memory. If Andy had been guilty of stealing three thousand dollars it hadn't stopped him from getting another job within the mall. Bree couldn't tell Mallory that she'd seen him. She didn't want to escalate the situation and cause a scene, as Mallory was exactly the kind of person that would confront him about the theft for her own amusement. However, she did wonder how Andy got away with his crime and, more importantly, how he'd seemingly escaped any real punishment at all.

'So, Liam and I did a test screening together last night and recorded a copy of the film *Catwoman*. He brought in a camera with heaps of space and the battery lasted the whole time.'

'As easy as that?' asked Bree.

'I was surprised too.'

Mallory was sitting on the concrete steps with a pile of keys on either side of her. To her left were the ones they had not yet tried, while on her right sat a growing pile that had failed to open the mystery door. Mallory had set a black lighter and a box of cigarettes down on the step between her legs.

'Great. So, what now?'

'Well that was just a dry run. Next time we might try it with a few more people. Some potential *investors* in the project. You're welcome to come if you like.'

'I don't know. Liam probably wouldn't want me there.'

'You should give him a chance. He's not as bad as you think.'

Bree thought back to his aggressive advance. First Ryan and now Liam. *What was it about her that made men think they could be so bold?* At least if anything happened, she could tell Matt.

'Think about it,' said Mallory as she handed Bree another key.

They spent thirty minutes trying one key after another, but none of them unlocked the door. When they backtracked through the Projection room Bree noticed that Matt had been adding to the flyer wall. It made her smile.

CHAPTER TWENTY-FOUR

'Old Lou passed away last night. Heart attack apparently.'

'Oh man... I just saw him a couple of weeks ago...'

'Maybe he heard the news about Mallory's promotion!'

'Ha ha!'

At the beginning of October 2004 Warren started working again. Apparently his parents were satisfied that he was on top of his studies and Maxine was happy to offer him regular shifts. He seemed to have missed the place and was talking more than ever. Warren was also especially happy to see Tristan, and Bree had seen them hug at changeover. It was nice to know that some friendships at Central Cinemas were still strong.

Bree was enjoying working with Daniella and Warren more than she'd expected. Daniella was trying to get to know Warren by asking him more and more random questions.

'Say there were two boulders being suspended in the air. Underneath one of the boulders is your mother and underneath the other is your father. You only have time to save one... who do you save?' asked Daniella.

'My mother,' replied Warren.

'Ah, so you're a Mamma's boy, are you?' teased Daniella.

'No... it's not that.'

'Then why wouldn't you save your father?'

'Because... he'd survive. At least he'd have a better chance. He's a bodybuilder.'

Bree wondered why she hadn't tried to get to know Warren before. She'd assumed that he didn't want to talk and so she'd left him alone. Bree was learning from Daniella's interactions with him that the opposite was true. Warren was just shy. Daniella went down the stairs to clean the women's toilets.

'What do you want to do next session Warren?' asked Bree. 'Clean cinemas or take Point?'

'I'll check the men's toilets and then I'll clean cinemas,' he replied decisively.

'You got it.'

'Thanks Bree.'

Warren smiled. He was finally creeping out of his shell. A short time later, while Bree was leaning against Point, she heard a shaky voice over the two-way.

'Warren to Bree.'

'Bree speaking.'

'Can you come to the foyer please?'

Bree was the only person left working on Floor and couldn't really abandon her post at Point. She asked Warren to elaborate.

'There is a woman in the foyer and... um...'

'What's going on Warren?' demanded Bree.

'There's a woman here and I think she's having a *baby*.'

Without hesitation Bree hopped down the stairs two at a time. She ran into the foyer and clocked Warren and a heavily pregnant woman cowering on one of the yellow seats near the games area. She was face down, dress hiked up above her knees, and breathing intensely.

'Ma'am? Are you alright?' asked Bree as she approached.

'The baby's… *coming…*' she said between laboured breaths.

Bree turned to Warren.

'Tell Paul. Get him out here.'

By virtue of the fact that they were using two-ways everyone that was within earshot was already aware of the situation in the foyer. Shannon, who was covering Candy Bar, wandered out from her register and hovered like a spectator. Daniella emerged from the women's toilets and raced over. Moments later Paul also burst forth from the office and announced that he had called security for aid.

'Is she alright?' Shannon called out from a safe distance, as if the woman was carrying an infectious disease and not a baby.

The woman, whose eyes had been closed for several minutes, seemed to be in some kind of trance. She didn't respond to their questions and nobody wanted to touch her except for Daniella. She whipped around to the pregnant woman's side and held her hand.

'Everything's going to be okay,' said Daniella in a calm voice.

The woman exhaled a deep breath.

'Are you here by yourself?' continued Daniella.

'Y-yes,' she spluttered.

'What's your name?'

'Claudia.'

'And is this your first baby Claudia?'

'No… *third.*'

'Fantastic,' said Daniella in her most soothing voice. 'Do you know what you're having?'

'A boy.'

Bree's father was the first security guard on the scene. Henry raced into the foyer and assessed the situation.

'Miss, can you tell me how far along you are?' he asked in a booming voice, deeply in contrast to the one Daniella had been using.

Claudia confirmed that she was thirty-nine weeks, just one week shy of her due date. Shannon and Warren had wandered away and were back behind the Candy Bar now, leaving Henry, Paul, Daniella and Bree to deal with the impending birth.

'What was she doing going to the movies?' asked Paul as he clutched his tie. He was sweating and making no attempts to hide his clear panic from his staff.

'It's a hot one today. My guess is she was here for the air conditioning,' returned Henry.

'Can you move at all?' asked Daniella, who was positioned on the carpet beside her. The woman had been clutching her hand the whole time.

'No,' said Claudia, as she started to wail.

'I'm getting a wheelchair,' announced Paul and he took off out the front doors. He seemed thrilled to have something to do.

'I think Claudia is going to have the baby right here,' said Henry to his daughter.

'Are you sure?' asked Bree.

'Yeah… it's her third baby and it's not unusual to have it early.'

'What do we do?'

'She's getting ready to push,' replied Henry. 'I've got a hunch we won't be moving her.'

He rang through to the security desk and explained the situation, asking them to call for an ambulance as soon as possible. He then commanded Bree to give the woman some privacy by dragging over several tall cardboard standees and hiding her from view, in case a session ended before the baby arrived. Bree did as instructed, creating a hidden area with a *Shaun of the Dead* and a *Collateral* standee. She asked Shannon and Warren to keep an eye on Candy Bar and Floor and called up to Projection to let them know that they might not check slides, trailers or features for a while.

'The baby's coming *OUT*,' called Daniella, who had become Claudia's default support person, though she'd never volunteered for the role. Bree steeled herself and changed angles so she could see what was happening. Sure enough Daniella's cries had been correct. The baby was crowning, pressing against the fabric of Claudia's underwear. Henry repositioned himself as the catcher.

'Claudia… you're doing great,' said Henry, 'Let's work together now. It won't be long. Just try to keep breathing, okay?'

The pregnant woman couldn't talk but nodded her approval at Henry and Daniella. Claudia wasn't going anywhere. Bree wondered where Paul had disappeared to and hoped that the paramedics would be there soon. The movie characters on the standees were facing inwards, Tom Cruise and Simon Pegg watching over the woman, creating a surreal nativity scene. Bree momentarily considered that this story would have certainly ended up in one of Matt's routines, were he present. Her father kept speaking in a low but steady tone.

'Miss, I'm sorry to do this but I need to remove your underwear so we can help to get that baby out, is that alright?'

Claudia changed her position, by raising one leg and then the other. Henry was able to help her out of her underwear in two proficient movements. Bree spotted some *Intencity* employees, who were stopping in to use the toilets, peering over with curiosity.

'Do you have a ticket?' Shannon asked one, waving them away. 'You need a valid ticket to use our bathrooms. They're for paying customers!' The aggressive stance worked, and they departed.

The cardboard standees proved sufficient in shielding any wandering eyes and after a short labour the woman gave birth right there in the foyer. Shannon gave a loud cheer when she heard the baby crying. Henry wrapped the infant in his security shirt. The paramedics arrived and checked the woman and the newborn boy until they were satisfied that both were in good shape. Paul reappeared nearly fifteen minutes after the birth and confessed that he had been suffering from a panic attack near the escalators. He'd had to stay away on purpose. Claudia thanked Henry and Daniella for their help and Bree for the standees.

'My husband is going to be very surprised. He's taken our other kids swimming and they were going to pick me up after the film. Thank goodness we put the baby seat in the car!'

Daniella and Bree looked at each other happily. Both were relieved that it was all over.

'They don't pay me enough to do this!' grumbled Daniella.

'Yeah... this one wasn't in the job description, that's for sure,' agreed Bree.

The girls found themselves cleaning up a range of liquids that had been created during the incident.

'I think that all this mess might have improved the carpet,' Bree said with a chuckle. Daniella started laughing.

'You don't like the carpet?' asked Maxine, appearing suddenly behind them like a ninja. *How long had she been standing there?*

'Oh hi...'

'I'll have you know that this particular carpet is one of a kind. It was commissioned especially for this Cinema complex,' she added.

'Okay,' said Bree quickly.

'I actually met the designer once... lovely chap.'

Maxine had come in on her day off and was doing an interview with the local paper about the birth. Standing beside her and answering questions was Henry who, under the circumstances, was being portrayed as a hero.

'We had a great result today and a lot of that is because of this man,' said Maxine indicating toward Henry, who was now wearing only a white singlet. His muscular arms were folded in front of him. 'The security guards in this mall really go above and beyond the call of duty.'

Bree was glad her Dad could enjoy a moment of well-deserved praise. *The Canberra Times* reporter insisted on taking multiple photos of Henry and Maxine for the article. There was even discussion that Prime News wanted to feature the story. On her break Bree called Mallory to tell her about the foyer birth, but she didn't answer the phone. She tried her mother, who also didn't reply. Bree then called Matt and got him straight away.

At the conclusion of such a strange shift Bree had the urge to change out of her orange shirt. Even though it had survived the ordeal without attracting a single stain it *felt* dirty. Standing in her bra Bree heard footsteps clomping up the stairs towards her and she quickly threw a black t-shirt on. The change room doors never felt secure enough for her. A timid hand knocked twice.

'Who is it?'

'It's Daniella.'

Bree opened the door and saw Daniella for the first time as a dishevelled teenage girl. After the unexpected birth Bree wondered whether she regretted coming over to work at this complex after all.

'Are you alright?' she asked Daniella.

'Yeah I'll be fine. I used to live on a farm, so I've actually been present for a few births now. I'm glad your Dad was there though. I've never been involved in a human one.'

Bree smiled.

'It's funny actually,' continued Daniella, 'I'm studying to be a Midwife.'

'Really?'

'Yeah. It's just been theoretical up until now... but after today I guess I have a story to tell in class.'

'You did really well. I was impressed,' said Bree. 'From the looks of things you'll be an excellent Midwife. You were so calm.'

'Thanks. So, I'm supposed to grab you before you leave. Maxine wanted to talk to you about today. She's in her office.'

'Ok sure.'

Bree clutched her orange shirt with both hands and wandered downstairs into the office. Paul was nowhere to be seen but Maxine beckoned her to come in.

'Well... that was quite an event, wasn't it?' she said with a smile. Bree knew right away that the meeting was informal. Maxine, while dressed in her usual management garb, was missing her trademark necklace and seemed more relaxed than usual.

'It certainly was memorable,' agreed Bree.

Maxine nodded enthusiastically.

'I have been instructed by Head Office to offer you counselling in the wake of this... unique situation,' said Maxine. 'How are you feeling about things Bree?'

'Oh, I'm okay. I didn't really *see* anything, you know? Nothing that has traumatised me, anyway! I wasn't really at the... *business* end of things like Daniella was.' Bree had only glanced at the event, too afraid to stare for long.

'I heard your father telling the reporter from *The Canberra Times* all about your birth. He sounded like he was pretty involved in that one too.'

Bree knew the tale well. Apparently on the way to the hospital her mother made him pull over and she'd been born right by the side of the road. Her father had called the hospital and they'd talked him through what to do.

'He's told me the story many times,' she replied. 'It's a family favourite.'

'You and your mother must be very proud of him,' said Maxine.

'Oh… my mother's… not… they're not together anymore.'

'Well, I'm sorry to hear that,' Maxine said, although the smile never left her face.

'So Carl and Rita found a bag of burnt garbage under their car the other night.'

'Yeah, I heard. Apparently Rita's car stinks now.'

'I wonder who did it?'

'Probably Andy. I'll bet he's pissed off about getting fired.'

Maxine took two weeks off and during that time Liam became acting Location Manager. There had been no directive from Maxine to treat him as the boss but where there was once a void, Liam filled it. The first thing he did was move into his mother's office. Nobody said anything to him directly and so he continued to abuse his power.

'Liam's got Mallory in the Location Manager's office.'

'Again?'

'They've closed the door.'

'Do they have to do that here? This is a workplace!'

Mallory and Liam seemed to be having private and secretive conversations every time Bree saw them together. They'd take multiple smoke breaks per shift and when she was on Point, Bree could hear them laughing. They were like fire and gasoline, combining to create something much more volatile. Their union wasn't the strengthening of a romantic relationship either. Bree felt sure that they were up to something more sinister.

Her suspicions were confirmed when she caught up with Mallory alone.

'He's a *really* bad influence on me Bree,' Mallory said with a wicked grin. 'Do you remember the scam where I used the complaints system to get free movie passes sent to me in the mail?'

'Of course.'

Bree remembered it fondly because it was a turning point in their friendship and the moment Mallory seemed to realise she was a trustworthy ally. She had also been heavily involved in writing the false complaint letters, although she hadn't participated in months.

'Well Liam just wrote off a massive pile of movie passes all at once! He just put down *Air conditioning failed* and took them. He's way wilder than I am. He's intercepting poster tubes and deliveries before anyone even sees what we have.' Mallory was wearing red eye shadow that made her look like a devil.

Bree wasn't sure how to proceed. She thought about slipping away and calling Matt but remembered the incident with Ryan and how swiftly he'd acted on her behalf. *Who would Matt report this behaviour to anyway?* Maxine was away and Liam was her son. *Would she even believe an accusation against him?* Bree decided not to involve Matt just in case there were repercussions. He was at home practicing his routine for his comedy tour, which was due to commence soon. Instead of burdening him, Bree decided she would try to deal with Mallory on her own.

'Is this making you happy?' she asked as earnestly as she could.

'Are *you* happy Bree?'

'This isn't about me... and you don't even know what's going on with me Mallory because we never talk anymore.'

'I don't know what's going on with you anymore because you're always off with Matt. When I was with George I still made time for you. We were still friends.'

'It was different with George. You didn't...' she trailed off.

'I didn't *what?*' demanded Mallory.

'You didn't love him.'

'How would you know?'

'Because if he'd asked you to marry him, like you claim he did, then you would've said yes!'

'Like I *claim* he did? What's that supposed to mean?'

'You tell me.'

A calm fell over Mallory's face. Bree hadn't mentioned George since the break-up and was suddenly afraid she'd said too much.

'I told you I don't want to get stuck in Canberra,' said Mallory in a measured voice.

'Well, if you ask me this business with Liam is going to get you fired. And that scares me because I worry we'll never see each other again.'

'Don't be stupid. I'm not going to get fired.'

'If you keep going like this it's going to be worse than that. You're my friend and I don't want anything bad to happen to you. Please.'

'Nothing bad will happen.'

'How can you be so sure?' asked Bree.

'Because you'll be there with me. *If* I can still trust you.' Mallory posed it as a challenging statement and waited, lips pursed and one eyebrow raised, for Bree to speak.

'Of course you can. You can always trust me.'

Bree listened as Mallory told her about a secret gathering that was happening tonight in one of the cinemas. Liam had organised a screening of *Anchorman: The Legend of Ron Burgundy* that had arrived early for an approaching movie marathon. The plan was to screen the print as a demonstration for some men that wanted to bootleg the film. The men were paying a premium for the privilege of an advanced copy.

'And you're just going to tag along?' asked Bree.

'Yeah. I think it will be fun.'

Mallory's defensive attitude was making Bree annoyed.

'What if it goes wrong?'

'It won't.'

'Mallory...'

'Come with me Bree. It'll be like old times. I could use your help...'

'Fine...' Bree felt like her moral barometer was broken. She'd reluctantly agreed to accompany Mallory to the screening that night, bending to her will. 'But when is it going to be enough?' asked Bree.

'You choose how involved you want to be,' stated Mallory. 'I want more than food court dinners, don't you?'

'I guess.'

'Everything will work out just fine.'

It was difficult to argue with Mallory. She'd been right about everything so far.

That night Bree waited anxiously while Mallory finished her marijuana cigarette. They were outside the fire exits, next to the large garbage bins where they had met all those months ago. Bree suddenly felt her age. Worrying about her father, and her mother and now Mallory, had altered her. It had been a year unlike any other. Mallory was dressed up like she was going clubbing, with a short dark skirt and a tight fitted top. Her make-up seemed excessive to Bree. Whereas Mallory would normally just use eyeliner, tonight she'd added lipstick and blush into the mix. Mallory usually looked composed, like Angelina Jolie in *Tomb Raider*. With her overdone look Bree thought she more closely resembled a promotional model, the kind that might walk a sign that said *Round Three* around a boxing ring.

'You don't want to smoke with me anymore?' Mallory asked as she brushed some loose ash from her skirt.

'Not tonight.'

Bree's phone rang. *Matt.* She declined the call and Mallory nodded in approval.

'Matt?'

'He knows I'm hanging out with you,' replied Bree.

'Good to know you have your priorities in check. Remember what we're doing this for Bree, when we have enough money we can leave this place and be anyone we want. This is a stepping stone.'

'Is this just about money to you?'

'Of course not. But money makes everything easier.'

The two girls wandered back into the cinema complex and waited in the foyer. It was almost one in the morning now and their guests were expected at any time. Liam strode out from the office and gave Mallory a kiss on the cheek. He wore a shiny gold blazer on top of his regular work clothes. It looked gaudy and over the top to Bree. If Mallory was dressed up like a ring girl, Liam was the boxing promoter.

'Are you two ready?' he asked.

Mallory nodded. Bree crossed her arms. She was glad she hadn't overdressed and felt right at home in black slacks and a plain black top.

'Are you *cool* Bree? If you're not feeling this then tell me and I'll put you in a taxi,' he said, burrowing his gaze into her in the same way his mother often had.

'I'm fine Liam.'

There was a loud knock at the back door. Bree's stomach tightened. Liam greeted each of the two men in cheap brown suits with a handshake.

'Let's get this party started,' said the first, a thin-faced gentleman with sideburns, who introduced himself as Jeff. He opened a suitcase and revealed several medium-sized glass bottles of rum. Jeff handed one to his partner, who Bree heard Liam address as Ray, before offering them to the girls. Ray was carrying an impressive looking camera that was attached to the top of a tripod. There was nothing subtle about it. Malloy took a swig of alcohol without hesitation. Bree took her own bottle with a forced smile and held it by her side.

'Are you two ladies staying for the screening?' Ray asked.

'Yeah. Hope that's cool,' replied Mallory, on Bree's behalf.

'The more the merrier,' said Jeff. He was staring at Bree as he drank, and sizing her up, which made her feel uneasy.

Jeff and Ray. They look like a couple of forgettable movie goons.

'Are you two on MySpace?' asked Jeff.

'Mallory, can you escort our new friends to Cinema Six?' interrupted Liam before Bree or Mallory had a chance to answer.

'Sure.'

'You guys can set up the camera wherever you'd like,' Liam added. 'Mallory will get you sorted.'

'Thanks bro,' replied Jeff, and he gave Liam a fist-bump.

'Bree, you hang back for a moment.'

Mallory led the men up the stairs and down the tunnel towards the cinema. When they were out of sight Liam gripped his fingers around Bree's wrist in a firm and deliberate way.

'Hey!' His tone had changed to menacing now. Liam was seething at her. 'Listen to me, you will *not* mess this up for us, alright?'

'You're hurting me,' Bree said as she tried to free her hand.

'This is happening, with or without you. We're going to make a tidy sum of money pirating this movie. Mallory said you were cool. Are you *cool*, Bree?'

'Yes.'

'You don't seem very cool to me!'

'I am...' Bree was cowering as she spoke.

'You didn't say anything to Maxine about me, did you?'

'No.'

'Good, because if you want to keep working at Central Cinemas when I become the Location Manager you need to learn to do as you're told. You need to *behave* Bree.'

'Liam, let me go.' Bree was still holding the glass rum bottle in her free hand. She didn't want to drop it, in case it shattered on the tile below, meaning she couldn't use that hand to break out of his grip. Just as she was debating whether to hit him with the bottle, Liam released her and straightened his gold jacket.

'These are good guys. I want to make a good impression on them, alright?'

'Fine.' They hadn't seemed like good guys to her.

'Now go to the cinema and wait for me while I start the movie. And lighten up, okay?'

'Okay.'

Liam shocked her again when he gave Bree a solid smack on the rear. He walked around the Candy Bar, bound for the Projection room. A horribly familiar feeling of shame flooded through her at the violating act. Bree was numb.

In the cinema the men had chosen an appropriate position for the camera and were making their final checks. Mallory was waiting alone at the bottom of the steps for Bree when she walked in.

'What did Liam want?'

'Nothing.' Bree hid her wrist behind her back, just in case his rough hands had left their mark.

'*Nothing?*' asked Mallory, seeming more than a little perturbed.

'What? What do you want from me Mallory?'

She'd had enough. Bree knew Mallory was cosy with Liam, and thought it was affecting her judgement. Even though she wanted to tell her friend that her new beau had just physically assaulted her she wasn't sure how Mallory would react. The two stood in tense silence for a moment before Bree, remembering she was still holding it, opened her own bottle of rum and took a drink. It burned her throat, but she winced and took another slug. *I can be reckless too,* she thought to herself as she swallowed the liquid. Mallory was completely unfazed with her actions, which only made Bree angrier.

'How much are these two paying you, huh?' she demanded.

'A grand.'

'You're doing this for a thousand dollars?'

'Well, Liam gets half.'

'That's *it*? You could go to jail for five hundred dollars. You're not thinking clearly.'

'We're being careful Bree. And it's five hundred dollars every time we do this for them.'

'So, you're going to keep pirating movies? Who's even buying them?'

'You're like a broken record Bree. Leave it alone, okay?'

'No, you're being an idiot.' Bree took a third swig of rum. 'Don't you remember when Andy took three grand? You said that wasn't your style. What's changed, huh? Why are you risking everything now?'

Mallory noticed Liam in the Projection room and then, as if remembering something, turned to Bree.

'Why didn't you tell me that Liam made a move on you?' asked Mallory, seemingly out of the blue.

'I did! I told you he hit on me the first time we ever spoke.'

Mallory shook her head. 'No, not that time. Why didn't you tell me he tried to kiss you that night when you and Matt test screened a movie?'

'I did… didn't I?'

'No.'

Bree realised that she'd told Matt, but had never discussed it with Mallory. *How long had this been weighing on her friend's mind?*

'It was nothing. Nothing happened,' said Bree.

'Why don't I believe you Bree?'

'Is this what it comes down to? We're not friends anymore because *Liam* is coming between us?'

'We're not friends anymore because you're in love with Matt. You're planning the future with him in mind and I don't seem to fit into your little life anymore.'

'So? Is that a reason to *hate* me? You have to know that if you *ever* really needed me, I would drop everything to be with you. You're my best friend Mallory. That's why I'm here right now… tonight. For you.'

Mallory ran her tongue across her top teeth.

'I just figured you'd outgrown me,' she said.

'I haven't outgrown you. But don't you want me to be happy too?'

'I guess I do,' said Mallory softly.

'Look, I know you've been hurt in the past. I have too. You want to know what *I've* been going through? My mother cheated on my Dad with some guy from her work. Now she's living with him and that's why we moved to the Walker Court Apartments. My ex-boyfriend Ryan assaulted me. I've got my own issues Mallory. I've been trying so hard to let you in.'

Bree decided it was best to leave out the recent incident with Liam. This wasn't the time to mention it.

'That's messed up. Why didn't you say anything earlier?' asked Mallory.

'I guess I've been trying to pretend things never happened. I haven't wanted to admit that my Mum broke up my family. It hurts too much.'

'I mean... the real reason I've been mad at you is because... you've kind of become like family to me. And it feels like you're pulling away,' said Mallory.

'We're in this together. I'm not going to leave you,' replied Bree.

Mallory gave Bree a hug.

'Thanks,' said Mallory.

'Anytime.'

Bree led Mallory by the hand and they occupied two seats near Jeff and Ray. Liam, who had setup a timer to trigger the projector, walked in and sat down just as the lights were dimming. Jeff took out a remote control and hit record on the camera. As they sat in the dark waiting for the film to start Bree suddenly felt very light-headed. She had tasted alcohol frequently during the year, at various parties with Mallory, and knew its effect on her well. This sensation was not from the rum. She'd never felt like this before.

'I think there was something in my drink,' she whispered to Mallory.

It was the last thing Bree managed to say before she blacked out.

CHAPTER TWENTY-SIX

Bree woke up in her own bedroom with a rotten headache. She was still wearing the same clothes as the night before but couldn't recall how she'd gotten back to her bed. Her mouth tasted of vomit. Asleep on the floor, facing away from her, was Mallory. She'd grabbed one of the spare pillows from the bed but without a blanket she'd curled up into the foetal position for warmth during the night.

'Mallory?' she called out with a croaky voice.

Mallory stirred and as she turned to face the bed Bree saw that beneath her unkempt dark hair Mallory was sporting a black eye.

'Oh my God! Are you okay? What happened?'

Mallory touched her bruised eye and recoiled slightly from the pain.

'This is Liam's handiwork.'

'He *hit* you?'

'Yeah. But don't worry I hit him right back,' said Mallory a little too proudly.

Bree tried to focus on the events of the previous evening but the last thing she could recall was blacking out in her seat.

'I... passed out I think. I can't remember anything,' said Bree.

Mallory nodded a confirmation.

'Jeff, that tool from last night, put something in your rum. Do you remember him?'

'Yeah.'

'He'd been given some drugs and he wasn't sure what they were. He tested them on you. Like a guinea pig. None of us knew he was doing that by the way.'

'Oh God.' Bree's head was spinning. She may have sat up too quickly. 'Why did Liam punch you?'

Mallory changed position on the floor. 'Well, you were slipping in and out of consciousness and making a bunch of noise while Liam and his mates were trying to pirate the movie.'

'Was I?' Bree hoped she didn't say anything too embarrassing. At a primary school camp once she had told one of her classmates to stick her tongue in a pinecone. She'd been talking in her sleep at the time and they'd mocked her for it the next day.

'Yeah you were pretty sloppy. And I'd realised you were under the influence of something. So, I kicked off with Jeff… calling him names and stuff. Liam came to his defence, saying what a great guy he was. I was livid!'

'I don't remember *any* of this,' said Bree shaking her head.

'So, Liam told me I had to be quiet while they were trying to bootleg the movie and I started screaming at him. That's when he hit me.'

'Oh Mallory. I'm so sorry,' said Bree.

'That's nothing. You missed a lot more last night.'

Mallory explained that she'd witnessed Bree in her altered state calling her mother for help.

'I called my mother? On the phone?'

'You sure did,' replied Mallory.

'And what did she do?'

'She called your Dad.'

Mallory explained that Henry had been sleeping next to Maxine White at the time, having been on their third date that evening. Carol's panicked phone call had woken them both up.

'Sorry… Maxine's been dating… *my* Dad?'

'Yeah. It's hilarious. Three dates Bree! You know what that means! They met when that baby was born in the foyer. I'm so glad I got to tell you that.' Mallory smiled but then winced again. Her bruised eye was still very fresh.

'Then what happened?' asked Bree.

'Well you'd told your mother where you were. Your Mum told your Dad, and then he woke up Maxine.'

Mallory explained that Maxine had contacted the alarm company and been informed that the alarm was never set. They'd received a call from the 'acting' Location Manager Liam White letting them know that it would not be turned on that night due to overnight maintenance.

'He referred to himself as the acting Location Manager?'

'Sure did. You should have seen the look on Liam's face when the lights came on and Maxine and your Dad walked in at like two in the morning.'

Bree could imagine it. She'd seen Liam caught like a deer in the headlights when he was loitering in the cinema with Daniella. Bree couldn't get past the fact that her father had started dating again, or who he'd moved on with.

'So... Maxine was sleeping at *my* place? Here? With *my* Dad?' Bree struggled out loud with this revelation.

'Yeah. You should probably keep your voice down. They might be in the next room. They seemed pretty cosy actually. If you play your cards right maybe Maxine will be your new Mum,' laughed Mallory.

'Don't say that...'

'And that would make Liam your stepbrother!' mocked Mallory.

'Stop it! So, what happened next?'

'Well Maxine exploded. I've never seen her get so angry. She walked straight up to the camera and unclipped it from the tripod. Then she started filming Liam, Jeff and Ray and saying, *these men are criminals* and *they are attempting to pirate a film*, and the guys were trying to cover their faces and stuff. Jeff and Ray tried to run off, and your Dad could only tackle one of them, so he tackled Jeff to the ground.'

Bree wondered if her father and her boss were awake in the next room. While she was thankful for their interference, it was a strange new situation where her home-life and work-life were colliding. It was odd to wake up with Mallory too. The whole world was off balance.

'So, I used my phone and called the police. Ray escaped but your Dad held Jeff in some kind of wrestling hold until they arrived. He was shouting and kicking. When the police came they arrested Liam and Jeff. Maxine gave the police the tape as evidence.'

'She handed over her own son?'

'Yeah. But she fired him first! It was *wild*.'

'I can't believe it.'

'Liam had some kind of criminal past. He was on probation!' exclaimed Mallory.

'Are you serious?'

'Yeah! He'd been released under his mother's care, and while she'd been trying to keep an eye on him and hoping for the best, last night was the final straw.'

'I can't believe it.' The amount that Bree couldn't remember was staggering.

'Your Dad said it would be fine if I stayed here under the circumstances. I hope you don't mind.'

'Of course not.'

'Good,' replied Mallory with a half-smile, so as not to irritate her eye further.

'Oh... I was supposed to be there to help you,' said Bree as she sat up straighter. 'I feel awful. I'm so sorry Liam hit you.'

'That wasn't your fault! You were right about everything and I should have listened to you. In the end I told Liam to stop. I said I didn't want to be a part of it anymore.'

'What did Maxine say to you about it?'

'She heard me say that on the tape and she decided not to fire me, even though I didn't report Liam right away.' In hindsight Mallory appeared to regret the whole enterprise.

'So, are you done now?'

'I'm done.'

'No more scams?' asked Bree.

'No more scams. I promise,' stated Mallory.

In the kitchen Bree found her father and Maxine sitting at the table with a selection of food in front of them. Henry got up and gave Bree a hug.

'I'm so glad you're awake. How do you feel?'

'A little groggy... but I'll be okay.'

'Can we get you something to eat?' asked Maxine, her voice soft and caring. She was dressed in sweatpants and an oversized t-shirt. Bree recognised them from her father's closet.

'No, I don't think I could stomach anything just yet.'

Maxine recounted the events of the morning and told Bree that the police might want a statement in the next few days.

'Don't worry though, they probably just want to confirm some facts.'

'I'm really sorry that all of this even happened. I know we shouldn't have been there,' said Bree.

'It's okay,' replied Maxine. 'You made a mistake, but Liam was ultimately responsible for everything. He betrayed me and took advantage of the business in my absence. It's actually not the first time he's tried something like this. He's displayed some very aggressive tactics to move up the ladder at a couple of other jobs before arriving at Central. I was hoping he would have known better this time around.'

'I'm sorry too,' said Mallory, joining them in the room. 'This all got out of hand.'

'Forget it. It's over now. I hope the police can apprehend the other man involved and we can close this whole dark chapter,' said Maxine with a nod.

'By the way… this isn't exactly how I pictured telling you this… but I'm dating your boss,' said Henry with a cheeky grin.

'Shhh…' said Maxine, trying to cover his mouth playfully.

Bree could tell that Maxine didn't have all of the facts. She was looking at this event as a one-time thing. She didn't seem aware of Liam and Mallory's other activities, such as stealing and trading the complimentary passes or the possible theft of posters. Maxine wouldn't have known that Mallory was equally guilty in this endeavour. She probably didn't know about her relationship with Liam either. Bree kept quiet about everything that had transpired for her friend's sake as well as her own. She might not have been involved anymore, but Bree hands were dirty too.

'It's over now, and everyone's safe. That's the most important thing,' said Henry as he placed a hand on Bree's shoulder. 'I'm just glad that you had the presence of mind to call your Mum. You're a good kid.'

Bree gave a smile. She didn't feel like she'd done the right thing, but she wanted the ordeal to be over. With Liam gone things could go back to normal.

'I've got to call Mum and tell her I'm okay,' she said, heading back to her room.

Mallory went to take a shower, which allowed Bree a moment alone. Carol picked up on the first ring, desperation in her voice.

'Bree? Honey, are you okay?'

'I'm fine. Did Dad tell you what happened?'

'Yes… but I'm so glad you called.'

'I'm glad you answered.'

'Oh, Bree… what were you *thinking*?' asked her mother.

'I guess I wasn't thinking. I was trying to help a friend.'

'You need to be more careful from now on.'

'Mum?'

'Yeah?'

'I need you in my life again. I want to be able to talk to you about my day, and any problems I might be having. I want us to be close again.'

'I'd really like that.'

'I love you Mum,' said Bree, tears now welling in her eyes.

'I love you too. You're the most important person in the world to your father and me. You know no matter what we're going through, we'll always love you.'

'Dad's started dating again,' Bree blurted out.

'Yeah… I know.'

'It's weird.'

'We'll have to get used to it. I think after last night your father and I will have to mend some fences. We both want to be in your life, and that means we need to be adult about things. I promise that we'll try to get along from now on,' her mother said. It was a sincere and beautiful sentiment.

'That would be nice.'

Bree heard Mallory turn off the shower. She wiped her eyes and took a breath.

'I'm going to call you soon, and we can get together, okay?'

'Okay, thank you Bree. You have no idea how much this means to me. And I'm so glad you're alright.'

Standing at the Central Cinemas podium tearing tickets felt bizarre to Bree after the events of the week before. Mallory had taken some time off at Maxine's insistence, in order to let her eye heal. The swelling had gone down, and it had reached the point that it could now easily be hidden by make-up. Maxine didn't want the incident to become yet another source of gossip for the staff of Central Cinemas. Mallory was due to return tomorrow, having declined the projectionist position entirely. Maxine was extremely supportive of the decision and borrowed one of the projectionists from Southern Cinemas to temporarily cover. He was a skateboarder named Evan that everyone seemed to like. He would bring his board into work and roll up and down the Projection room while he checked the machines. He reminded everyone of Keanu Reeves.

Bree watched the orange-shirted employees buzz around her, oblivious to the real reason for Liam's departure. Maxine had sworn the girls to secrecy and Bree hadn't even let Matt in on the truth. He was preparing to embark on his comedy tour and she didn't want him to be distracted.

A hastily written memo about Liam leaving had appeared on the cork noticeboard. It claimed he was going to pursue a career in music, which strangely nobody questioned despite his complete lack of interest in music during his tenure at Central. Maxine had all of the combination door locks in the complex changed right away, just in case he decided to come back.

'Bree?'

A familiar voice woke her from her daydreaming. It was Lizzy, and she had a huge grin on her face. Holding her hand was Dan, who it appeared was her date for the evening.

'Hi. I didn't know you guys knew each other,' replied Bree taking their tickets.

'We actually met at a party a few weeks ago,' said Lizzy.

'Isn't she beautiful? She *finally* agreed to come out to a movie with me,' chimed in Dan.

'Well, I don't really like coming back here. There's too many memories,' shrugged Lizzy.

'It's nice to see you either way. *The Notebook* is in Cinema Seven tonight… I think you know the way.'

With a flourish of her hands Bree waved them through. Lizzy looked so content and comfortable with Dan. Bree could tell he was completely smitten too. She watched them walk down the tunnel hand in hand and straight towards Victor. He spotted Lizzy, put down his broom and dustpan and gave her a hug. There appeared to be no bad blood between them. When Victor returned to Point Bree decided she would ask him about that party and what may, or may not, have happened between them on that fateful night.

'Nothing. I didn't hook up with Lizzy. Who told you *that?*' he asked, a little bemused.

'There was a rumour after that party that the two of you had been alone together in a toilet.'

'Oh yeah. We talked in the bathroom that night. Mostly Lizzy just told me about George and how much she used to like him. There was some kind of love triangle between Lizzy, George and Mallory that she was worrying about.'

'So, you two never…'

'No. I'm getting married, remember?' Victor looked offended at the idea that he'd done anything indecent with Lizzy.

'I'm sorry Victor. I should have just asked you about it when I first heard the rumour… instead of just believing it blindly.'

'It's alright. You and Mallory are close, and I couldn't really betray my friendship with Lizzy to talk to you about any of it. We've stayed in touch through text messages since she left Central. I actually had a hand in setting her and Dan up.'

'That's great. They seem pretty happy with each other.'

It turned out that Victor was just playing matchmaker all along. It was refreshing to hear that he only wanted good things for Lizzy, and it was great to see how happy Dan was making her.

'Did I tell you I spoke with Andy the other day?' announced Victor.

'You did?' Bree couldn't believe it.

'Yeah… I wanted to talk to you about it because I know you were affected by his theft.'

'Yeah… they took me over to the Police Station,' replied Bree.

'If I tell you what I know, can you keep it to yourself?' asked Victor.

'Of course I can.'

'Matt and Mallory… nobody really needs to know about this.'

'You have my word.'

'Andy *did* steal the money. He took it from the safe two weeks in a row. I think he'd been taking money here and there for a lot longer than that.'

'Why? What was he thinking?'

'Andy had a gambling problem. He was going to the Casino most nights after work and spending everything. He stole money from his mother too. When it all came out they suspected it was him. Maxine confronted him about it in her office and he told her everything.'

'Oh.'

'He agreed to pay back the money and Maxine paid for him to undergo treatment… some kind of gambling program. He's been seeing someone regularly about it. It really took over his life for a while there.'

'That's awful.'

'So, he's been attending meetings and he's turned things around. Andy's doing much better now.'

'Well that's good news. I can't believe it.' Bree wondered whether he'd taken the fifty dollars from her till. It was safe to assume he probably had. His actions sounded desperate. 'He was fighting this inner battle and we all just assumed he got away with something.'

'Not everything is always how it appears on the surface,' said Victor.

CHAPTER TWENTY-SEVEN

Maxine's loyalty to her corporate bosses over her son was soon rewarded with a promotion to the Sydney Head Office. It was bittersweet for Bree as she was just starting to get used to the idea of her father dating her boss. The move would result in Henry and Maxine trying long distance, with the promise of many visits back and forth. Bree could see that her father was falling for Maxine and knew that this outcome was better than the alternative. She hadn't enjoyed seeing her Dad without a girlfriend or a job. Keeping both would be preferable.

'So, who will be taking over for you at Central?' Bree asked Maxine when she was visiting the Walker Court Apartment one weekend. She'd ditched the familiar pearl necklace and had started wearing floral dresses since starting a relationship with Bree's father. While Maxine had probably always owned the dresses, Bree wasn't accustomed to them yet.

'I'll be recommending Paul. He's got the experience, but there will be a formal interview process for the position of Location Manager.'

'I'll be sad to see you go. I think you might be the best boss I've ever had,' said Bree.

'It's lucky that I'm dating your Dad then. I'll be around if you need to vent in the future,' replied Maxine with a nod.

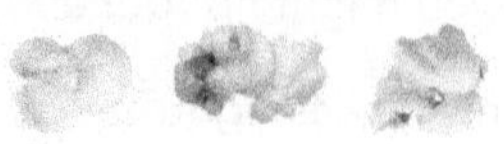

'So, have you heard Liam's band?'

'Is he in a band now?'

'Yeah. That's why he left. Cos his band is blowing up.'

'I'll have to look out for them!'

'Do you see that guy over there?' Bree asked from behind the Box Office glass. She pointed into the foyer towards the leather seats.

'There are a lot of guys in the foyer. Which one do you mean?' Daniella squinted at the sea of faces as they moved before her. Bree had seen the man while she was serving customers and was surprised that he had remained seated in the foyer for the last ten minutes.

'The guy with the purple scarf. He's sitting on the chair where the lady gave birth.' The seat was now synonymous with the event.

'Oh yeah I see him. What about him?'

'Did you serve him?'

'Yeah I think so. He just bought a single ticket,' stated Daniella.

Bree watched as the man took out his notebook and, while scoping out the Candy Bar, began to write something down.

'I don't know who he is, but I have such a bad feeling about him. I've seen him come in before and he always does this. He takes notes. What is he up to?'

'Why don't you go and ask him? Point blank,' enquired Daniella. She was a very point blank kind of person. Bree decided that she would take her advice.

'Will you be okay to serve without me?'

'I'll be fine. Go on, you might not get another chance like this.'

Bree knew that Daniella was right. It was a quiet Thursday and he was sitting by himself. Daniella could handle the stray patrons as they arrived for their tickets. Bree circled out of the Box Office and into the foyer. She marched across the ugly carpet and stopped directly in front of the man.

'What are you doing? Why are you taking notes?' she asked, mid-stride.

'Excuse me?' His voice was squeaky and he became immediately nervous.

'Show me your notepad,' demanded Bree.

'Uh... no... I can't do that.'

'Then I'm going to call mall security and they can escort you from the premises.' Bree unclipped a two-way from her belt as a threatening gesture. In truth, mall security guards like her father were on an entirely different frequency to the cinema staff, but her bluff was effective.

'No, no... please... you don't have to do that. I'll show you.'

The man revealed a series of complicated notes, scratchings and numbers that Bree couldn't decipher.

'What does this mean? Why are you always writing things down?'

'I have to take note of how many patrons there are in my sessions. And I write down the films and their classifications.'

'Why? Do you have OCD or something?' asked an increasingly curious Bree.

'No, it's not like that. I'm a mystery customer. I'm paid to check in on the staff and make sure everyone is doing the right thing.'

'Oh...'

Suddenly it made so much sense. His observational manner and his fastidious note taking. He was trying to remain inconspicuous but Bree had noticed him on multiple occasions. 'I'm sorry. I thought you were spying on us or something.'

'Well, I suppose I kind of am,' the man replied. 'Please, you mustn't tell anyone about me. If people know I'm a mystery shopper then they'll act differently.'

'I won't say anything.'

'Thank you.'

Bree left the man alone to his work.

'What did he say?' asked Daniella when Bree returned to the Box Office.

'He's writing poetry,' lied Bree.

'What a weirdo.'

At the dinner table her father was in a very talkative mood. He was so chatty that he'd barely touched his sausages and beans.

'So, Maxine's settling in well. She told me she has her own office with a door but it's in the middle of a corridor, so she doesn't have a window.'

'Oh well. I'm sure she can put up a poster or something.'

'I'll suggest that! Anyway… how was your day Bree?'

'Pretty uneventful.'

'Didn't the air conditioning fail?' asked her father. He was often in the loop with mall-related events, due to the nature of his job.

'Yeah. We had a few old ladies complain but it was nothing major.'

'I heard that the air conditioning guy made an interesting discovery up on Level Five.'

Level Five was one storey above Projection and a site that Bree knew well. She used to think of it as the place where Mallory had balanced on that concrete ledge as a kind of trust exercise, but now she associated it with Matt, as the secret place they went to make out sometimes.

'Oh yeah? What was up there?' she asked, trying to sound nonchalant.

'Apparently there were five or six marijuana plants growing in the sunlight. Nobody's sure how long they've been up there but someone's been watering them,' he said, pointing his fork at Bree.

'That's crazy.'

She hadn't seen any plants up there before, although she would have been focussing on Matt at the time.

'Yeah. They were placed in direct sunlight too. The police have them now.' Henry took a big bite of his sausage and chewed with his mouth slightly open. 'Oh,' he said before realising his mouth was quite full. He finished chewing, while Bree waited patiently, and then continued. 'Do you know a boy named Ryan… something? He used to work at Central Cinemas.'

Ryan.

The name sent a shiver down her spine. Bree hadn't thought about him for some time. *Why is my father bringing his name up now?*

'Ryan Kellerman?'

'Yeah. That's it!'

'I know him,' she replied. *What an understatement.*

'One of the security guards caught him hanging out in the car park after dark last week.'

'Okay…' she implored him to continue, afraid of the next piece of information he would reveal.

Henry put down his fork and folded his hands in front of him.

'My buddy followed him for a while because he was acting suspiciously. So, he's watching him… trying to suss him out… and this Ryan guy goes down to the docks, where all of the stores in the mall bring their garbage.'

'I know it. We take our bins there too,' said Bree.

'Okay yeah, and he goes down and picks up a bag of garbage. Your standard black plastic bag, right? And he takes it back up to the car park and wedges it underneath this white car and then he lights it on fire! It was so reckless and stupid. The whole car could have exploded right there. So, the guard on duty kicks the bag out from underneath the car and stomps on it. Ryan tried to run but my buddy caught him.'

'Someone did that to Mallory's car one night.'

'Yeah? You never told me that. We've had a couple of burning garbage incidents. Ryan's got a restraining order against him now. He has to stay away from the mall. And he'll be in court sometime soon about it.'

'Wow… well he wasn't a very good employee when I knew him,' added Bree, minimising his impact on her life again.

'You'll let me know if you see him lurking around, won't you?'

'I will.'

'Have you heard from Matt? How's the material coming along?' asked her father.

'He's putting the finishing touches on it. He's pretty happy with it I think. Matt's got one more shift tomorrow in Projection and then he's leaving for the tour,' reported Bree.

'Good. He's going to have a great time.'

'And I've been talking to Mum.'

'Me too…'

'We're going to get together this weekend,' announced Bree.

'That sounds good.'

'It's been too long.'

Bree was wiping the glass freezer doors at the Candy Bar when two women approached her. They were middle-aged and both had confused looks on their faces.

'Excuse me, I'm sorry to interrupt your cleaning,' said one.

'Oh, it's no problem,' replied Bree with a smile. Cleaning was the last thing she wanted to do and she was more than happy to stop.

'We were just looking at our tickets and we wanted to ask what these letters meant?'

Bree looked at their tickets and explained that the letters at the bottom reflected the specific coupon they had used at the Box Office.

'But we *didn't* use a coupon.'

'There's obviously been some kind of mistake. Who served you?'

'The girl on the end, with the short black hair.'

Mallory.

'Thanks for letting me know,' said Bree, 'I'll follow it up.'

As the women walked away to enjoy *Bridget Jones: The Edge of Reason* Bree felt overwhelmed with this new information. She knew the code from her Box Office training.

BOGOF.

Buy One Get One Free.

It meant a two for one coupon had been used by the customer. Except on this occasion it hadn't.

The scam that Mallory was running became immediately clear to Bree. When she'd processed the sale at the Box Office, Mallory had the option to input the code for the coupon. The computer would print two tickets, as the customer requested, but they'd only be charged for one in the system. They were paying the amount *they* expected, and they were being handed the correct change so they were none the wiser to the scam. Mallory only had to put half the money in the till, provided she also threw in a two for one coupon, while the other half of the money was hers for the taking.

Bree asked Kasey, who was making a casual appearance, to watch Candy Bar while she went over to investigate. She entered the Box Office via the back door and startled Mallory, who was all by herself.

'Oh, it's you. I'm about to go on my break, are you sitting in for me?'

Bree spotted a stack of unused two for one coupons placed near Mallory's keyboard. It was enough to confirm her suspicions of a scam in progress. Before she could say anything else Paul opened the office door.

'I was going to sit in for Mallory. Unless you wanted to?' offered Paul, who didn't seem too enthusiastic about serving patrons.

'No,' Bree replied quickly, 'I have to get back to Candy Bar shortly. I was just checking in.'

Mallory stood up and pressed past Bree on her way up to the staff room. Bree followed half a step behind. She didn't want to make a scene in front of Paul, just in case her suspicions were somehow incorrect. Bree stalked Mallory up the stairs. She checked the men's change room was empty, without knocking, and then stood in front of the female change room door. She knew they were about to have a confrontation, and that terrified her. Bree took a deep breath. Mallory had thrown her black hoodie on over the top of her orange shirt before she'd opened the door.

'What are you doing?' asked Bree, arms folded.

'Having a break. What are *you* doing?' she replied.

'Are you doing some kind of two for one scam?'

'What are you talking about Bree?' Mallory's eyes remained vacant. She wasn't giving anything away.

'A woman came up to the Candy Bar and showed me her ticket. It said she used a coupon.'

'Then she used a coupon. I can't remember every customer I serve in Box,' replied Mallory.

'She *didn't* use a coupon. That's why she came up to me. She asked me what it meant.'

'So what?'

'So, she told me you served her Mallory. I saw the stack of coupons in front of you in Box. I'm willing to bet that if I ask Paul to do a drawer-pull on you right now, you'll have more money in that till than you're supposed to.'

Mallory fell silent.

'Now tell me the truth.'

'Okay… you got me.'

'Mallory! What are you *doing*? You promised me that you were done with these scams,' seethed Bree. She was furious.

'Well, I guess I'm not.' Mallory was trying to remain collected, but it was clear to Bree that there had been a power shift between them.

'How long have you been doing this?'

'Years.'

Bree did a rough version of the maths involved in her head. Each pair of adult patrons she substituted a coupon for were paying twenty-four dollars for their two tickets. Mallory had been keeping half of that. If she ran the scam eight times a night, she was taking home almost a hundred extra dollars from the cinema. Mallory was *always* swapping herself into Box Office shifts. If she'd been doing this undetected for years, there was no telling how much money she'd stolen. Bree asked her outright.

'How much have you taken?'

'A lot.'

'How *much*?'

'A LOT Bree. I've lost track, okay?' replied Mallory. 'Honestly... I just keep going.'

'Mallory... I can't... I have to say something. You can't just take whatever you want like this.'

'You *have* to say something? Not really though...' Mallory was asking for yet another free pass.

'Yes. This is the last straw.' Bree was done with this deception. Mallory had enjoyed things her way for long enough.

'I thought I knew you Bree. I thought we were friends.'

This wasn't a friendship. Mallory had suggestive sold Bree on the *idea* of friendship. This was Mallory using her and only looking out for herself. She couldn't let this behaviour slide anymore. At the end of the day Mallory had made a promise and broken it.

'I guess we were both wrong about that.'

Suddenly Mallory shoved Bree out of the way and ran out of the staff room. Instead of making tracks towards the foyer, and certain escape, she turned sharply to the right and ran up the ramp for the Projection room door.

Bree made chase and hurried towards her as Mallory punched in the combination. She flung the door open and ran through. Bree didn't know the new code as it had been changed when Liam had been fired. She almost never went into Projection anymore, instead favouring the air conditioning room as the place to rendezvous with Matt. Bree had to prevent the door from swinging closed. She almost fell over in her attempt to catch it but was successful in stopping it before it clicked shut. Bree wished she'd had the foresight to bring a two-way. If she had then catching Mallory would have been as simple as calling Matt, who was in Projection winding spools of film at the desk.

'Matt!' Bree shouted out. Her voice was hard to hear against the clicking of film running through projectors and the noise from the radio next to his ear. Mallory turned around as she ran. Her years of smoking cigarettes had taken an unexpected toll on her ability to flee and she doubled over near the flyer wall at the far end of the room. Matt, now curious at the interruption, had turned off the radio and stood up from his workbench. Bree crept towards Mallory as she took in big gulps of air.

'What's going on?' asked Matt.

'I'll explain later,' said Bree. 'Mallory... don't make me chase you anymore...'

Mallory exhaled and took out a blue cigarette lighter.

'I've got to stop smoking,' she said with a smirk.

As she was standing there Mallory's expression changed. The mask that she'd been wearing throughout her time at Central Cinemas had finally fallen away. Bree had discovered her true identity and she no longer needed to hide everything that she was capable of. Bree knew now that her friend had always had one foot out the door. She'd been biding her time in Canberra while she ran the two for one scam, as well as goodness knows how many others. Mallory would do whatever she needed to in order to survive, all the while looking out for number one.

'What's going on between you two?' asked Matt. They both ignored him, and he looked more confused than ever.

The realisation that this was the end of her friendship with Bree seemed to wash over Mallory and she started to cry. As tears rolled down her cheeks the rest of her face remained still and unmoving, refusing to acknowledge them.

'We had fun, didn't we?' Mallory asked in a friendly way, as if somehow she thought she could still talk her way out of trouble. Matt was cautiously standing behind Bree, still unsure of what exactly was unfolding before him.

'Yeah. But this isn't fun anymore. It's time to grow up,' stated Bree.

Mallory nodded, accepting the news, then stretched out her arm and sparked the blue lighter against the flyer wall. The flames spread quickly from one flyer to the next, racing towards the ceiling. The wall was ablaze before Matt or Bree could react.

'Shit!' said Matt.

'Mallory,' cried Bree, 'what are you *doing!*'

The cigarette lighter was dropped as Mallory ran towards the door at the far end of the tunnel. Matt leapt past the desk and grabbed a medium-sized fire extinguisher from the wall. Bree stepped back and was frozen for a moment. It was a surreal sight to see. The laminate on the cinema flyers must have been more flammable than they'd previously thought. Matt's flyer wall had been a fire hazard all along. The bright flames danced upwards, smoke billowing towards the detectors as the wall of cinematic propaganda was burned beyond recognition. The sprinklers were set off, firing thick mists of water from above and shocking them into action.

'I'll deal with this, you follow Mallory,' directed Matt over the sound of the fire alarm, which had ignited the air around them.

Bree ran, liquid splashing down ahead of her from all angles. She could see the downpour impacting several of the film prints, warping them as they tried to hold their shape on their journey through the rollers. Bree pushed open the Projection room door at the far end of the corridor and, taking the steps two at a time, was soon one floor below at the mystery door.

It was open.

Bree looked into the small room beyond the doorway, which was only about four-square metres in size. Mallory was kneeling down in the centre of the space.

'Mallory?'

'The door was open,' she replied, without looking up.

There was a strange silence between them as this mystery door, that had driven them mad for almost a year, was finally accessible. Bree knelt down next to Mallory and examined the oversized black storage container in front of them. It was one of three identical containers that filled the room. Bree slid open one of the long drawers on the side. Staring up at them were promotional Christmas posters. Bree had seen them before, on display throughout the mall during the festive season.

The door was most likely open right now because someone was putting these posters up around the mall in the lead up to Christmas. Mallory slid open another drawer to reveal a pile of blueprints. The room was just a cupboard for the employees of the mall.

'I can't believe it,' said Mallory. The dull reality was hitting her now. 'It's full of garbage.'

'Sometimes things aren't what you want them to be.'

Mallory wiped her eyes and stood up. Her make-up had suffered, and she now had mascara on her cheeks. Bree remained on her knees but turned to face her friend.

'You can't run forever Mallory.'

'And now I've ruined things… I have to.'

She watched Mallory dart towards the outer door and crash out into the sunlight. Bree knew she would be behind the wheel of her Cortina in a matter of minutes. Beyond that she had no idea where Mallory would go. It wasn't her job to watch out for her anymore. Bree had to say goodbye.

She headed back upstairs to find the flyer wall was still smouldering. Smoke had ensconced the room and Matt had been joined by three firemen, who were assessing the scene.

'You're really going to need to tell me what that was all about,' he said, when Bree approached.

'Mallory's gone.'

'She won't get far. I gave mall security a description of her. They've probably tracked her down already.'

Bree knew Matt was wrong. Mallory was far too smart for that.

CHAPTER TWENTY-NINE

'I'm sorry that I only have time for a coffee. I have to be at work in about an hour.'

'Do you drink *coffee* now Bree?'

'I guess my tastes have been changing.'

Carol was wearing a dress that Bree had seen several times before, as if for the past twelve months she'd been frozen and unable to alter her appearance. Perhaps the year had moved more slowly for Carol than her daughter had imagined. Bree had always been told that they looked alike by strangers, and more recently by her father, but she never saw the resemblance until now.

'Thank you for inviting me for coffee,' her mother said.

'No problem.'

'If I'm allowed to ask… what's been going on with you? Since the last time we caught up, I mean.'

Bree let out a sigh. 'It's been a crazy time.'

'I'm sure. I'm just trying to keep up with you,' her mother said with a soft smile. 'Anything you want to talk about?'

'I guess… I lost a friend recently… and it's made me take stock of my life a little bit more.'

'I'm sorry to hear that honey…'

'She's not *dead*… I just mean we're not friends anymore.'

'This is Mallory we're talking about?'

'Yeah.'

'Sometimes when you lose a close friend it can feel just as bad as if they were dead. I know I felt that way when I lost you.'

The two had slipped into their old routine with an ease that Bree found comforting. She had wanted to have an open and honest conversation with her mother for some time now. This felt like as good a time as any.

'Mum?'

'Yeah?'

'Why did you do it?'

Carol shifted in her seat.

'I wish I could say it was just one thing. I know now that I shouldn't have let it happen the way they did. I'm so sorry. I didn't mean for you to get caught up in all of that.'

'It's not about me. At first I was mad,' said Bree, 'I thought you were doing this to me. But really you did this to Dad.'

'I know, and I don't think he's ready to forgive me yet.'

'I don't think he is either. Dad was a wreck when you left. I've had to watch him struggle. You don't do that to the people you love.'

'I'll be honest with you Bree, I fell out of love with Henry... with your father... so long ago. We were both in this loveless marriage... waiting around...'

'For something better to come along?' snapped Bree.

'It just happened. I swear I thought Adrian and I... would... well, I guess I was wrong.'

Carol was fighting to get the words out. She started telling Bree that after the affair with Adrian she had left Henry and moved in with her lover.

'I know Mum... I know that part.'

'Sorry... of course you do. I forgot that your father probably told you some things... from his point of view anyway.'

Carol went on to say that the relationship had apparently been snowballing at work for months and although it seemed out of the blue to Bree, she'd agonised over the decision to end her marriage for a lot longer.

'In the end I made a mistake.'

'Yes, you did,' agreed Bree.

'I need you to know that even though things are over with Adrian and I… and I'm trying to be civil with your father… it's still difficult,' she said with sadness in her eyes.

'I know.'

'I'm glad he's found some happiness. He deserves someone to be good to him.' Carol's words were positive, but her tone remained unenthusiastic. Perhaps she was still surprised that Henry had found love with another. Maxine seemed to be making him really happy, even via long distance, which made Bree wonder if everything hadn't happened for a reason. Her mother had been cast out, alone and avoided like some kind of leper. Bree had felt sorry for her, absolutely, but more than anything she wanted her back in her life, in any capacity. She'd missed her mother and knew that she'd suffered enough for her misstep. Bree wanted to repair the damage that the affair had caused. She wanted both her parents around again.

'I wish I'd handled things better,' said Carol suddenly.

'So do I,' replied Bree. 'But it's done now.'

'I'm sorry I haven't been there for you. I don't want to lose what we had.'

'Either do I, Mum. Things haven't been the same without you. I haven't been myself.'

The drinks were delivered to the table and for both women a weight seemed to lift from their shoulders. When the waitress walked away Carol picked up her coffee and raised it towards her daughter.

'Happy Birthday Bree,' her mother said with a smile. 'You're an adult now.'

'I don't feel any different,' she said.

'You're probably wiser,' her mother offered.

'Maybe we both are.' Bree reached into her bag and placed a small gift-wrapped box onto the table. 'I brought you something.'

'You're not supposed to do that! It's *your* birthday!'

'It's just something small,' said Bree.

'What is it?' asked Carol.

Bree removed the paper to reveal her mother's favourite ocean blue mug, the one she used to have her morning cup of tea in.

'I thought you should have it back.'

'Thanks Bree. That's perfect. I hope we can do this again soon. If that's alright with you honey.'

'Of course.'

Annabelle seemed like a nice girl but no matter how pleasant she was Bree knew that she could never replace Mallory. It would have been true of whomever they'd hired to fill her shoes. Annabelle was fresh and innocent, with no idea about the recent events at Central Cinemas. She looked like a young Lisa Kudrow, with her hair pinned back in a tidy ponytail. Annabelle had been hired with a cluster of assorted newcomers that Paul had brought in. They had all attended the Christmas party, even though most of them hadn't officially worked a shift yet. They were still strangers to Bree, and she was a little annoyed at being forced to train Annabelle in Box Office, due to a lack of staff trainers on station.

'So, what do you say if someone comes up and complains to you?' Annabelle asked. She was clearly frightened at the prospect of being yelled at. She had told Bree that this was her first real job.

'Don't worry, you're usually safe behind the glass in Box Office or on the other side of the bench in Candy Bar. If you need someone to talk to an irate customer, you can just summon a manager. They're never far away from a two-way.'

Bree's phone vibrated in her pocket and she checked it between ticket sales. Matt was sending her pictures from the road. His travels were almost over and he'd be returning to Canberra tomorrow. Bree couldn't wait to see him again. She was happy he was finally doing his *something*, and getting paid for it. The reviews had been kind enough to highlight Matt's work, which was more than what he'd bargained for. As a result he'd started to get some other offers and was building a small fan base online. Bree was proud of him. She had made him a gift for their six-month anniversary while he'd been away. She'd compiled the images of the flyer wall that she'd taken with her camera before it burnt down and had them blown up into an impressive framed collage. Matt was going to love it.

Bree messaged Kasey during the lull between customers. They were planning on going to a gig that weekend with Shannon. The trio had become fast friends in the wake of Mallory's departure, much to Bree's delight.

Can Matt spare you for a night? joked Kasey via text.

He'll have to! Is Shannon coming? asked Bree.

Yeah. If she can bring Pierre. I told her that was fine.

Shannon and Pierre had been a surprise coupling, bonding over their mutual appreciation of bear claws and action films.

'Um... I don't think we're supposed to have our phones on us while we're at work,' said Annabelle timidly.

Her goody-too-shoes nature felt all too familiar. Bree wondered if she'd been this irritating to Lizzy when she'd first started at Central Cinemas.

Warren pushed the scissor lift out into the middle of the foyer accompanied by Dan. Between the two of them they'd redesigned the vast space. Dan had taken over doing poster shifts on Wednesday nights and everyone agreed that his obsessive film knowledge made him the perfect person to do it. He would place promotional materials in positions where he felt they would get the most traction. Action films near the men's toilet. Art house films near the yellow seats. Nobody had ever put that much thought into it before. The walls were completely covered and when Paul sent some pictures to the distributers, they sent Dan a double pass to an interstate premiere as a thank you for his dedication. He was planning on taking Lizzy, who had started working at Central again. Dan had stopped hanging around after work since getting together with her. Warren whistled as he secured the metal legs of the scissor lift and plugged it in. Following a promotion to Projection he'd made a point of attending to all of the lights in the foyer. Warren was quite the handyman.

After a burst of customers Annabelle indicated that she needed more change.

'Phone the office then. You shouldn't announce things like that on the two-way.'

She did as she was told and within a minute Victor opened the Box Office door.

'Did you need change too Bree?' he asked.

'Not for me.'

Victor asked Annabelle how she was 'travelling' and then raved about Bree, stating that she was simply the best employee to learn from. Victor had been an excellent salesman behind the Candy Bar but had really come into his own as a member of the management team. He'd also become something of a confidant to Bree in the wake of the Mallory saga. After the fire in the Projection room Paul had changed all the combination locks again and fitted every entrance with working security cameras. Bree thought Mallory would have considered the move the ultimate compliment.

In the days after Mallory's disappearance Bree had served Dex at the Candy Bar while she'd filled in for a meal break. He'd waved Bree to the side, away from prying eyes for a secret chat.

'Hey, it was Bree, wasn't it?' asked Dex, clearly reading her badge.

'Yeah.'

'Um… since you're friends with Mallory I was wondering if you would know where I could get some pot? She hasn't been answering her phone,' he whispered behind his hand.

'I can't help you,' she'd replied.

'Well… tell her to give me a call. If she even *wants* to see me.'

'We're not really friends anymore.'

Dex asking for drugs, that he would usually have sourced from Mallory, confirmed Bree's suspicion that the plants found on Level Five were hers. She didn't know whether selling marijuana had been a new enterprise for Mallory, but it had clearly stopped when she had skipped town.

The police had questioned Bree at length about their friendship and the various cons that Mallory had been running without detection. She'd still been seventeen at the time and she'd asked her mother to accompany her to the official interview. The process had been eye-opening for Carol, who now realised the scope of what her daughter had been dealing with that year.

When the authorities had travelled to Mallory's residence, a place that Bree had been to dozens of times, it was deserted. The house had been leased to two guys that, when they could be located, confessed they had lived there years ago. Mallory had moved in with them briefly and then, they thought she'd taken over the lease. Evidently, Mallory never submitted any paperwork to put the residence in her name and had happily kept paying the bills unofficially. The real estate agency didn't have her details on file at all, and hadn't inspected the property in years. Among the items that she'd left behind was the phone that Mallory had found at Central Cinemas. She'd never handed it into lost property. It was loaded with the names and numbers of employees that worked at the mall. After talking to the contacts the Police determined that Mallory had been hoping to set up a series of sly trade deals with managers and staff across more than sixty stores. She'd promised Bree that she'd stop but she never had. Most were in touch with her until the day she'd fled.

The only clue as to her whereabouts was her blue Ford Cortina, which had been found by the police, unlocked in the domestic airport terminal. Bree no longer felt any malice towards Mallory. She knew that the memory of this phantom friend would stay with her forever, even if they never saw each other again. Bree was learning to embrace the chaos, and learn from her experiences, as well as her mistakes.

'So, are you… like… working here full time?' asked Annabelle.

'No. I was full time for a while but I'm actually starting a Hotel Management course. I'm going to CIT at the beginning of next year.'

'That's exciting.'

'Yeah. I'm looking forward to it,' said Bree with a smile. She finally felt like her life had a solid direction again.

Annabelle looked timid when the phone rang, so Bree intercepted it to save her from potential embarrassment.

'Hello Bree speaking.'

On the phone was a male patron that wanted to complain about the lacklustre service that he and his wife had been given at the Box Office. He felt that the employee had been rude to him and that she'd been dismissive when he'd asked for information on certain films.

They'd complained previously over the phone but they'd never heard back.

'And do you remember the name of the employee who served you sir?' asked Bree.

'Her name was Mallory,' replied the man.

'Well I'm sorry that happened to you. It won't happen again. You'll be pleased to know that Mallory no longer works for Central Cinemas.'

Bree apologised again and when the man seemed satisfied that he had been heard he hung up the phone.

'Who's Mallory?' asked Annabelle.

Bree had learned a lot that year, including that the people around her craved gossip. But she'd also learned that people can't repeat stories that they don't know.

'Nobody.'

<u>**About the Author.**</u>

David Farrell lives in Melbourne with his wife and children.

He has Directed two independent feature films:
The Last Resort & *The Young and The Wrestlers.*

His stories *The Last Resort, The Glove, Twelve, Dropping the Belt,*
Twelve More and *Portals* are all available now on Amazon.
Most of his titles can also be purchased as audiobooks.

His children's story *You Can't Get Rid of Me That Easily*
is also available now.

You can contact him @DaveFarrell1 on Twitter
Or see what he's working on at www.PodMeIfYouCan.com